Zetta's Mark

Also by Sandra P. Aldrich

The Zetta Series

Zetta's Dream (Book 1)

Zetta's Coal Camp Recipes (Book 2)

Nonfiction

Heart Hugs for Single Moms

Honey, Hang in There!

One Hundred One Upward Glances

Bless Your Socks Off

Will I Ever Be Whole Again?

From One Single Mother to Another

Men Read Newspapers, Not Minds

ZETTA'S MARK
An Appalachian Widow's Victorious Journey

SANDRA PICKLESIMER ALDRICH

• BOLD WORDS •
COLORADO SPRINGS

Copyright © 2019 by Sandra Picklesimer Aldrich

Published by Bold Words, Inc.
P.O. Box 51351
Colorado Springs, CO 80949-1351

All rights reserved. No part of this publication may be reproduced in any form, stored in any retrieval system, posted on any website, or transmitted in any form or by any means—digital, electronic, scanning, photocopying, recording, or otherwise—without written permission from the publisher and/or author, except for brief quotations in printed reviews and articles.

NOTE: While the faint basis of this story is the 1923 Eastern Kentucky environment of some of the author's relatives, the characters, dialogue and actual details are the creation of the author. Thus, any resemblance to persons living or dead is purely coincidental. The names chosen are common to that area, and do not reflect the activities of anyone currently alive who may share that name.

Cover cabin photo copyright © by Sandra P. Aldrich, 1994

Cover design by Miller Media Soltions
www.millermediasolutions.com

Edited by Cheri Gillard www.cherigillard.com

Library of Congress CIB data has been requested.

Scripture is from the *King James Version*.

Printed in the United States of America
ISBN-13: 9781694833587

Dedication

To Connie Garcia, who keeps me organized.

To Luke Hulen and Noah Hulen, who keep me smiling.

Chapter 1

Zetta knew someone was behind the oak tree.
She tried to sound nonchalant as she scattered cracked corn to the chickens.
"Here, greedy girls," she said. "Better enjoy this. Now that spring's here, you can fend for yourselves."
She shook out her apron and turned toward the tree.
Might as well get this over with, she thought as she pushed her dark hair from her face.
"Jesse Allen, you best quit skulking around."
She shivered at the muffled sound of retreating footsteps.
"Go ahead and run off! You ain't scaring me!"
Who am I trying to kid? she thought as she turned toward the cabin.
If Asa was here, Jesse wouldn't dare pull a stunt like that.
She took a deep breath. Oh, Asa. If only you was still here. If only you hadn't worked coal. If only you had listened when I told you about my bad dreams. If only....
Zetta opened the door into the kitchen quietly, hoping she wouldn't awaken the children. But three-year-old Rachel already was in the front room, staring at the picture of Jesus near the door. Her rag doll dangled from her hand.
The child turned as her mother approached.

"Poppy's not with Jesus!"

Not again, Zetta thought. She pulled the child close.

"Poppy *is* with Jesus, honey. We just can't see him. Now let's get you some breakfast."

As Zetta took Rachel's hand, two-year-old Micah came from the bedroom. His bare feet made soft slapping sounds against the wood.

"There's my sweet boy. Did you use the chamber pot?"

As Micah nodded, Zetta smiled. "Come here with Sister so I can wash y'all's hands."

Both children thrust out their hands as Zetta pulled the kettle from the back of the wood-burning stove and poured warm water over the washcloth.

"After y'all eat, and I feed your little brother, we're gonna make applesauce cake. Your Uncle Luttrell likes that."

Rachel smiled. "Miz Clarie comin'?"

"No. Miz Clarie lives in the coal camp. But when I write her next, I'll tell her we still miss her. Now you and Brother—"

Before Zetta could finish her sentence, a woman's voice called from the porch.

"Hello in the cabin."

Sally!

"Come on in!"

"Can't! My hands are full."

Zetta hurried to the door and smiled at her autumn-haired neighbor, one hand clutching a filled apron, the other holding a skillet of cornbread.

"Lands, Sally. What are you up to so early?"

"Here. Take the skillet. Wait 'til you see the poke I brung. First of the season."

In the kitchen, Sally opened her apron and dumped short green stalks on the table.

"Jim found these back of the barn. Made me fry up a mess right then. Whoever heard of eating poke and cornbread for breakfast? But the stalks are good and tender."

"Fresh poke! Luttrell's turn is tonight," Zetta said. "He'll be tickled. Thank you."

Sally smiled. "I was hoping Luttrell would be the one here. Jim wants to talk to him about the men pitching in to get your plowing done."

Zetta took a jagged breath. "Asa always liked plowing. And this year he was gonna enjoy it even more since the land was gonna be ours." She sank into the nearest chair, determined not to cry in front of the children.

Sally put her hand on the young mother's shoulder. "There's no way in the world I meant to make you feel bad. Like I told you that night y'all brung Asa back, I can name plenty others I'd druther we bury. One of 'em is Jim's worthless brother-in-law."

Zetta tilted her head toward the children, causing Sally to sigh.

"I shouldna said that. So you planning on being at Sarah's quilting tomorrow?"

"Might as well. Becky won't be happy to see me," Zetta said. "But she'll be even less happy if I don't show up. I just hope Mable Collins won't come."

"There'll be food, so Mable will be there."

Zetta stood to spoon gravy over biscuits for Rachel and Micah. "And the whole time she'll call my sweet babies 'poor little fatherless youngins' and say to me 'and you with three little ones not yet four years old.' Like I don't know that. But I shouldn't be badmouthing so. Her being the preacher's wife."

She held the plate of biscuits toward Sally.

"No, thanks," Sally said. "I'm still tight as a tick from eating so much poke this morning. But speaking of Mable, I heard tell she's gonna visit a sister in a few days. So if you decide you are up to church this Sunday, she won't be there."

"I know I shouldna stayed home these weeks," Zetta said. "But I couldn't face her after what she and Becky was saying about Asa and me deserving what happened. Them saying that with him laid out in the next room."

"I know. People can be so unthoughted. If Mable says anything mean tomorrow, I'll accidently stab her with my needle."

"Sally!"

"I said *accidently*. But don't worry. I have to be on my best behavior since my girl Abigail got invited to quilt, too. This is the first time she gets to sit at the frame, so she thinks she's all growed up now. Of course, Deborah's in a snit about not going. She thinks she has to do everything her big sister does."

"I'm glad Becky invited y'all. I was kindly afraid Paw wouldn't allow it since he still holds a grudge against your Jim."

"And maybe he remembers I held a grudge against him for marrying Becky so soon after your sweet mama died. But I realize now that men can't seem to get along by themselves."

Tears sprang into Zetta's eyes. "You and Mama was good friends, Sally. And now here you are a good friend to me."

Sally pulled a handkerchief from her apron pocket and swiped at her own eyes.

"She helped me bear little Mary's death when fever come on quick. I couldna made it otherwise. And then she was gone, too. I still remember you and Loren and Luttrell standing next to y'all's paw. And you holding y'all's baby brother, and you just a little girl yourself."

Sally blew her nose. "Well, I'm a sight now. I come over here all happy to give you a mess of poke, but then got us both crying."

Before she could say more, the baby wailed from the bedroom.

"Your sweet Isaac's hollering for his breakfast, so I best be going," Sally said. "We'll get you tomorrow morning. And this time I won't start us crying."

Zetta hugged her friend goodbye. "Oh, Sally. You're the

only one who *lets* me cry."

Then she opened her dress as she hurried to her hungry baby.

* * * * *

With all three children napping that afternoon, the cabin was quiet as Zetta pulled two perfectly browned applesauce cakes from the oven.

One for tonight and one for Sarah's quilting tomorrow, she thought.

A shout of "Hello in the cabin" interrupted her thoughts.

That sounds like Jesse Allen, Zetta thought. Oh, I hope not.

But he was the one standing in the front yard as Zetta opened the door.

"I told you before, you ain't welcome here, Jesse."

He pulled off his hat. "Now is that any way to greet a feller who's been gone for a while?" he said. "You could at least ask how I'm doing and where I been."

"I don't care how you're doing and I know where you've been. You was skulking around my chicken coop this morning."

Jesse frowned. "Wudn't me. Both times I visited, I come to the front of the cabin. Skulking ain't part of my plan!"

Zetta put her hands behind her back. If that wasn't him behind the tree, who was watching this morning? She squared her shoulders.

"I told you before I ain't interested in your plan, Jesse."

"And I told you before Asa's dead, but I'm not. And neither are you," he said. "But I'm a patient man. When a respectful amount of time has passed, I'll come calling proper like."

"You won't be welcome then, neither. Now, I'm done arguing with you."

Zetta stepped back and started to close the door.

"Wait! I got news about the trees around here! And that includes yours!"

Zetta huffed. "All right. What?"

"Even though you don't care where I been, I was over in Virginia helping a cousin cut his chestnut trees for burning," Jesse said. "There's some kind of bad disease over there, so folks are burning the trees to stop it. And I hear tell it's all over. In fact, your trees at the lane ain't showing leaves yet. And mine ain't neither."

"Burning trees? But chestnuts are all over these hills."

Jesse nodded. "Yes. And if we lose 'em, every one of us is in trouble. Make sure you tell whichever brother stays here tonight."

"How you know about them staying?"

"Zetta, there's not much I don't know when it comes to you."

And he walked away.

* * * * *

The cut poke stalks, covered in yellow cornmeal, sizzled as Zetta stirred them in the hot lard covering the bottom of her favorite cast-iron skillet.

Between stirs, she watched Micah in front of the fireplace as he bounced the dancing man on a stick against the floor then stacked his wooden blocks, knocked them down and restacked them. Rachel folded a tiny quilt around her rag doll and lined peach seed baskets on her toy stove.

Zetta smiled as she remembered Christmas morning when the children received the toys.

That was a happy day even if we was at the coal camp, she thought. We was all together, and the youngins was spoilt with all them play pretties. Oh, Asa. I wish I'd worn the red sweater then that you give me. What was the matter with me thinking it ain't a proper color for a decent woman?

She shook her head, determined to think of other things.

"Time to put your play pretties up for now," Zetta said.

"Your Uncle Luttrell will be here soon and ready to eat."

Her words were barely out of her mouth when both Loren and Luttrell opened the back door. Rachel smiled at the uncles, but Micah gave the blocks another whack before running to Loren, who promptly grabbed the child and turned him upside down.

"Loren! You're gonna drop my boy! He's getting too big for that."

"Nah, Sis. I got a good hold on him," Loren said. "Besides, you know I like shaking the vinegar out of him now and again."

Then over Micah's giggles, Loren continued. "You get both of us for supper, but I'm not staying the night. We come over to talk to Jim Reed about getting your plowing done. He was already pondering the same thing. We're thinking Tuesday. We'll tell some of the men at church Sunday, and that'll give you and the women Monday to cook."

Their brother Luttrell gestured toward the pail of milk he had set on the sideboard.

"Brownie's doing a good job keeping y'all in milk."

"That reminds me," Loren said. "You gotta be thinking about building up your livestock. The sows had piglets, so when they're ready, Paw's sending you two. Same to me and Sarah. And with us doing your plowing, you won't need that new team of mules Asa talked about."

Zetta nodded, but her thoughts were elsewhere. *Oh, Asa. You had so many plans for the farm. For our youngins. How could everything change in those awful minutes?*

She turned toward the stove. "Y'all wash up. Supper's ready. Sally brung over poke stalks and cornbread this morning. And along with the soup beans, I made applesauce cake for tonight and a second one for the quilting tomorrow."

Luttrell patted Zetta's shoulder as he reached for the kettle of hot water on the stove.

Zetta's eyes filled with tears. *He always knows what my heart's holding,* she thought.

Loren righted the giggling Micah and plopped him into his chair at the table.

"Hey, Sis. You mentioned the quilting," Loren said. "You should've seen Becky ordering around our little brothers today getting ready. She was making them sweep floors and tote chairs. Next thing you know, she'll have 'em cooking and doing washings and other women's work."

"You're sounding like Paw now," Zetta said as she set food on the table. "They have names. Hobie and Frankie. And it never hurt a man to know how to fix a meal or two. Comes in handy now and again."

"Well, not me," Loren said as he waited behind Luttrell for his turn at the wash pan.

"I'll take care of the barn and animals, and Sarah will take care of the house and the youngins when they come. And we see eye to eye on that."

Loren nudged his brother's arm. "And speaking of eyes, Jim's girl Abigail is a real beauty now that she's growed into hers," he said. "I was just a little feller, but I remember when she was born. She looked like a white frog with them big eyes. And tonight she was using them to look at you real sweet like. And you didn't even notice."

Zetta saw Luttrell's face flush. "Oh, I noticed," he said. "But she was a little girl when we left and was all growed by the time we brung Asa back. Her growing up takes getting used to."

"Well, you better get used to it fast or you're gonna be left in another man's dust," Loren said. "Just like you was at the camp when Clarence beat you out of that pretty teacher."

"No need to bring that up again."

"Now look, I'm not exactly partial to the Reeds," Loren said. "But I'm your big brother and trying to look out for you. And if you don't like Abigail, Sarah's cousin Naomi is visiting this week."

Zetta saw Luttrell shake his head as he sat down. She knew he was through talking.

"Loren, you ain't no more than ten months older than Luttrell," Zetta said as she helped Rachel into her chair. "I don't know if that counts as being a big brother. But one of you pray for the food. Then I got something I need to talk to y'all about."

Loren shrugged. "All right. We thank you, Lord, for this food and ask you to bless the hands that prepared it. Amen."

"Loren! You ain't even sitting down. And you didn't give us a chance to bow our heads!"

"You said you had something to talk to us about," Loren said as he pulled out a chair. "So I was just trying to hurry and let you have your say."

"And I was hoping you getting married in a few weeks would settle you down," Zetta said. "But I guess not. Anyway, somebody told me chestnut trees over in Virginia are being burned to stop a bad disease. And that our trees here are in danger, too."

"I've been wondering why our chestnuts ain't leafing out good," Loren said. "I noticed yours the day me and Sarah brung you and the youngins back to your farm. But who told you about the Virginia trees?"

Zetta shrugged. "That ain't important. I'm just wondering if you'd heard anything about a disease."

"And I'm wondering who you been talking to," Loren said. "You ain't left this farm since we come back. Not even for church."

"Well, I'm planning on church this Sunday."

"Zetta."

"All right. Jesse Allen stopped by and said he'd been over in Virginia helping a cousin cut his trees for burning," Zetta said. "They're trying to stop the disease from spreading."

"Jesse Allen? That no good—"

"Loren! Mind your mouth!"

"Did he come right up on the porch?"

"No. No. He stayed in the yard and hollered for me to come to the door," Zetta said. "And I told him he wudn't welcome."

"Good thing. You know Asa and me didn't agree on much, but neither one of us trusted Jesse as far as we could throw him. Same with Thorn, that so-called sheriff brother of his. You let me know if he shows up again. Now how about passing me that good looking poke?"

*****

Long after the children were in bed and Loren had left, Zetta and Luttrell sat by the fireplace. Luttrell stared at the embers while his sister leaned toward the kerosene lamp to mend one of Rachel's dresses.

"That child's growing so fast, I'm having to let her hems down," Zetta said.

Luttrell nodded. "Asa was right proud of all three of 'em," he said. "I'm sorry he's not here to see 'em grow. And I worry about you trying to run the farm without him."

Zetta tucked the needle into the hem of the little dress and slowly folded her hands over the material.

"I appreciate you and Loren taking turns being here these past weeks," she said. "I confess I been dreading him and Sarah getting married since he won't be around much. But I'm gonna be all right, and I don't want you worrying about me."

Luttrell turned to face her. "Still being the big sister and taking care of us, huh?"

Zetta smiled. "The three of us are so close together, I don't reckon I can claim that title. But I know I can't lean on others forever, not even y'all. In time, I'll get my bearings. But I'm glad you're here now."

Luttrell pushed the embers to the back of the fireplace. "Asa always said you was stronger than you give yourself credit for."

Zetta was grateful her brother wasn't looking at her as she swiped at sudden tears.

She stood and reached for the quilts stacked nearby. "I wish I had something better for you to sleep on than a pallet in front of the fire."

"Don't you worry about that," Luttrell said as he handed the lamp to her. "You just enjoy some good dreams."

Dreams. How I wish Asa had listened to mine, Zetta thought as she left the room.

* * * * *

In the bedroom, Zetta leaned over the crib where Isaac stirred, making little smacking sounds. In the small bed near the window, Rachel had one arm around Micah. Her rag doll was crumpled between them.

Zetta set the lamp on the dresser and turned down the wick. As her eyes adjusted to the room's darkness, she quietly stepped to the window and looked into the blackness near the chicken coop.

She rubbed her forehead, trying to sort her thoughts.

If Jesse wasn't the one hiding there this morning, who was? But what if he was lying? Loren won't be staying here much longer, and I can't let Luttrell be here all the time. What am I gonna do? Lord, you have to help me.

Finally, she sighed and turned toward her empty bed.

Chapter 2

Luttrell was folding the pallet quilts as Zetta entered the front room the next morning.

"I'm not staying for one of your good breakfasts," he said. "But before I go, I'll gather the eggs and take care of Brownie and put everything in the springhouse."

"I appreciate your help," Zetta said. "And I won't tell Loren what all you did. I don't want him accusing you of doing women's work."

Luttrell was solemn. "I know you got a big day ahead. You all right about going?"

Zetta shrugged. "Good as I'm gonna be, I guess. You know I ain't been back to Paw and Becky's since the funeral. But I can't stay away forever."

Just then, the call of "Hello in the cabin" came from the front porch.

"Sally! You and Abigail come on in!"

"Abigail?" Luttrell stammered. And he hurried out the back door.

* * * * *

As Sally and Abigail stepped into the front room, Isaac cried for his breakfast. At the same moment, Micah and Rachel, clutching her rag doll, ran in from the bedroom. When they saw the visitors, they hugged Zetta's legs.

Sally smiled. "This reminds me of long-ago mornings when all my youngins was little. I miss those days. Well, we are here to help. So let Abigail feed these two whilst you tend Isaac."

Abigail held out her hand to the toddlers as they continued to grip Zetta's legs.

"See this here basket?" she said quietly. "It's got egg gravy and biscuits for y'all's breakfast. And when you finish that, we might find some cookies in there."

Zetta smiled as both children hurried to the kitchen ahead of Abigail.

"She's got a sweet way with youngins," Zetta said as she and Sally stepped into the bedroom.

At the crib, Zetta cooed, "Oh, sweet boy," as she changed Isaac's diaper and then sat in the rocking chair near the window to feed him. As Zetta unbuttoned her dress, Isaac wiggled as though anticipating his breakfast.

"Now that beats all," Sally said. "That boy is just a couple months old, but he already knows what's coming."

As Zetta pulled the baby close, Sally turned to make up both beds.

"I'm guessing these clothes on the hook are what you want for Rachel and Micah today," she said. "And you're all pretty in your blue dress. I'm glad you ain't in widow's weeds. You gonna wear your red sweater, too?"

Zetta raised her head. "I figured I better not wear black, or Becky would accuse me of drawing attention to myself when this day is Sarah's. But how'd you know about the sweater?"

"I saw you wearing it a few mornings after your brothers set Asa's tombstone," Sally said. "I figured you and the youngins was headed to the cemetery. I started to holler at you and tell you how pretty the sweater looked with your black hair. But then I thought better of it and figured maybe you wanted to be by yourselves."

"Asa give me the sweater at Christmas," Zetta said. "But the morning you saw me was the first time I wore it. I'm sorry I never wore it for him."

As tears spilled out of Zetta's eyes, Sally pulled a handkerchief from her sleeve and handed it to the young mother.

"There I go again, making you cry," she said. "Maybe someday I'll watch my mouth."

Zetta shook her head. "You didn't make me cry. Every breath I take reminds me that Asa is under the ground. Oh, Sally. Am I ever gonna get over this?"

Sally eased onto the end of the bed and took Zetta's hand into hers.

"No, you will never *get over* this," she said. "But I've learned the hard way that we can get *through* it. When we love somebody, we're always gonna miss 'em when they die. But the time comes when we don't cry with every thought. We couldn't stand to go on if every day hurt as bad as the first ones."

At that moment, Abigail appeared in the doorway.

"I didn't mean to interrupt," she said. "But they're done eating, and I washed their faces and hands. What would you like me to dress them in?"

Both Zetta and Sally swiped at their eyes.

"The things here on the hook is theirs," Zetta said quietly.

As Abigail reached for the clothing, Sally took a deep breath.

"Well, time to change the subject, I reckon," Sally said. "What did you decide to cook for the quilting? Jim brung in more poke this morning, so I decided on that. And cornbread."

"I'm taking applesauce cake," Zetta said. "I made two yesterday since Luttrell was coming for supper last night."

Zetta glanced sideways at Abigail. "That's one of his favorite sweets."

Zetta was pleased to see Abigail blush.

* * * * *

Once everyone was settled in the wagon, Sally gently slapped the reins across the mules' shoulders. Zetta clutched quilt-wrapped Isaac as the wagon jerked forward, then looked toward the oak tree near the chicken coop.

No one was there.

Zetta looked at Rachel and Micah huddled close to Abigail in the back of the wagon.

"You both better be extra good today," she said. "You hear me?"

The children nodded.

"All right. Show me the play pretties y'all are taking."

Rachel hugged her rag doll while Micah held up the wooden dancing man.

"That's my good youngins."

As they passed the lane's chestnut trees, Zetta looked up at the bare branches.

"Sally, have you heard anything about a disease that's hitting chestnut trees?"

Sally nodded. "Yes, and it's got Jim plumb worried. Like everybody else's hogs, ours eat the nuts come fall. And the nuts we don't need for ourselves, Jim takes to Salyersville and sells to the man that comes in from Lexington."

"When Asa bought our farm, the old man told about his granddaddy planting the lane trees from saplings he dug out of the mountains," Zetta said. "I hear tell they're burning diseased trees over in Virginia. I'd hate to think we'd have to do that here."

Sally nodded. "I know. But like a lot of things, we'll have to wait and see what happens."

I reckon I've had enough of that already, Zetta thought as she pulled Isaac closer.

* * * * *

As Sally guided the wagon to the front of Becky's cabin, Hobie and Frankie jumped up from the steps. Twelve-year-old Hobie helped Zetta from the wagon then reached for Rachel and Micah as Abigail handed them down. Eleven-year-old Frankie held the mules' bridles.

"Me and Frankie will take care of the mules," Hobie said. "Ma's been waiting for y'all."

Rachel and Micah scampered up the steps. Zetta took a deep breath as she stared at the porch.

The last time I climbed up there was after we brung Asa back from the coal camp, she thought. I had to go in that cabin and see my sweet husband all laid out for a funeral.

Becky opened the door while Zetta was lost in sad memories.

"About time y'all got here."

Sally, with her basket on her arm, started up the steps. "Hidy, Becky. We appreciate being invited."

Sally gestured toward her daughter, who was holding Zetta's applesauce cake.

"This is Abigail's first time at a quilting, but she's a good hand with a needle."

Becky frowned. "Well, I was thinking more of her watching the youngins. But if they take a nap, I reckon she can sit at the frame for a while."

Zetta saw Abigail's shoulders slump at the news, but the young woman didn't respond. Then before either Sally or Zetta could say anything, Mable Collins stepped onto the porch.

My goodness, I forgot how big that woman is, Zetta thought. She started up the steps to greet her before Mable could swoop toward Rachel and Micah. But it was too late.

"Oh, these poor little fatherless babies. And you with three of 'em not yet four years old."

To Zetta's relief, Sally quickly stepped forward and pulled the cloth back from the dish inside her basket.

"I hope it's okay I brung fried poke and cornbread for our noon dinner."

Mable leaned toward the basket. "Poke's the best spring tonic in the world."

Then before Sally could stop her, Mable thrust her hand into the dish and pulled out a crisp breaded stalk.

Even as she chewed, she licked her fingers.

"Now that's mighty good," she said as she reached toward the basket again.

But Sally pulled the cloth over the dish. "I reckon we'll save the rest for later."

Becky opened the screen door. "Let's quit the lollygagging. We've got a quilt to finish."

As they stepped into the front room that was crowded with the quilting frame and women, Zetta glanced toward the left wall.

That's where Asa's coffin was, she thought. *How am I going to sit and quilt when I'm remembering him being in here?*

Loren's bride-to-be, Sarah, giggled as she grabbed Zetta in a quick hug and patted Rachel and Micah on their heads. But she merely nodded at Sally and Abigail.

You might better be kinder to Abigail, Zetta thought. *You never know but what she might be your future sister-in-law.*

Behind Sarah was her mother, Blanche. She smiled, but her hello was barely audible.

Zetta returned Blanche's smile but remembered how much Sarah's father had talked the night the men sat up with Asa's body before the funeral.

No wonder Sarah's mother is quiet, Zetta thought. *Between her husband and her daughter, she probably can't get a word in edgewise.*

Sarah pulled Zetta toward a young woman whose curly blonde hair refused to stay tucked into a proper bun.

"This here is my favorite cousin, Naomi," Sarah said. "And that's her mother, Aunt Agnes, standing over there. They're from near Rosefork."

Agnes wiggled her fingers in greeting.

"Naomi's the same age as Luttrell," Sarah continued. "Loren and me was talking. Wouldn't it be fun if they got together?"

Agnes huffed. "Luttrell's a good looking man, all right. But he ain't said a word to Naomi since we arrived. Just look at her. She can have any man she wants at home. What's he doing being so standoffish?"

"He's mighty bashful," Sarah said.

"I've learned even bashful man can be won over," Naomi said as she tossed her head.

Zetta heard Abigail take a tiny gasp, but she forced herself not to look at her. Instead, she turned to Becky.

"I'll get the youngins settled in the bedroom whilst you show Sally and Abigail where you want the food to go."

Mable stepped forward. "Here, I'll take everything to the kitchen."

As Mable took the baskets and headed toward the kitchen, Zetta saw her sneak another crispy piece of poke and lick her fingers again.

Good thing Sally didn't see that, Zetta thought as she headed toward the bedroom.

Abigail took Rachel's and Micah's hands and followed.

As Zetta eased the sleeping Isaac onto the bed and pulled pillows around him, she spoke quietly to Abigail.

"I wish Becky had told us you wouldn't be sitting at the frame," she said. "But you can take my place when I feed Isaac in a while."

Abigail continued holding␣Rachel's and Micah's hands. She didn't look up.

"I'm not sure I want to be at the frame when I ain't been invited proper like."

"Don't you give in like that," Zetta said. "I want you to go in there and show Becky and the other women you deserve to be there. And I don't want you paying no mind to that prideful Naomi."

Abigail raised her head then. "Thank you," she said softly. Then she smiled at her young charges. "Let's go sit over there so we don't wake your little brother," she said. "And I'm gonna tell you a story about a rag doll and a dancing man who fell in love."

* * * * *

When Zetta went back to the quilting room, she forced herself to study the frame instead of concentrating on the memory of Asa in a coffin in this very room.

The quilt was stretched between two long wooden strips that formed the frame. The squares of the quilt top were bright orange, yellow and pale blue as they formed the eight wide points of the morning star pattern on a white background. Zetta knew a layer of cotton batting was between the quilt top and the bottom layer of colored calico.

Eight chairs, four on each side, were beside the frame.

Sarah, her mother, aunt and cousin settled into chairs on the window side of the frame.

On the side nearest the kitchen, Sally and Becky positioned their straight-back chairs to make room for Mable's overflowing girth. An empty chair was to Sally's left.

Zetta eased herself into the empty chair, grateful Sally was next to her. She bent over the quilt pretending to admire the bright colors of the material.

As Sarah's aunt, Agnes, reached for a spool of white thread, she looked at Zetta.

"I hear tell you're a widow woman. Well, you are young. You'll find another man."

Becky nodded. "That's what I told her. After all, she ain't the only one who had her first man die and leave her with little youngins."

Outwardly, Zetta was calm. But her thoughts were racing.

I had to hear about your first man when Asa was laying in this very room, she thought. *And you was all the time talking about being left with three little boys. But you give them up quick enough when you married Paw and then had Frankie. Don't you dare compare yourself to me and my youngins!*

As though reading her thoughts, Sally put her hand under the frame and patted Zetta's knee. Then she smiled at Sarah.

"This morning star design sure is pretty, Sarah. What other quilts you done?"

Sarah giggled. "Mama helped me make a crazy quilt when I was eleven. Since then, we've done basket quilts and log cabin ones and grandmaw's flower gardens. We made a double wedding ring one when Loren started courting me. We was working on this here one all last winter. We was gonna have it done by the time the men come back from working coal the end of March. But then Asa up and died, and they come back early."

He didn't up and die, Zetta thought. He was killed by that awful machine, and Clarence not knowing how to run it after Jack got hurt. Lord, help me not look up. Help me not cry in front of these women.

Sally again patted Zetta's knee.

"Good for you for getting your hope chest all ready. And you are marrying into a good family. Not like the one my cousin from Breathitt County married into," Sally said. "Rose was a shy little thing, but the man she was marrying had three rowdy older brothers. The stunt they pulled on their wedding night beats all."

The women stared at Sally, as though waiting for details. But she appeared to be concentrating on pulling the right amount of thread from the spool.

"Tell us what they did," Sarah said.

Sally bit the thread off from its spool before speaking. "Well, first I need to tell you that the groom—his name was Cain—why on earth a mother would name a child Cain is beyond me. But anyway, Cain had been a rascal when his older brothers got married. He pulled pranks on every one of them."

She licked the end of the thread and aimed it toward the needle eye.

"What kind of pranks?" Sarah demanded.

Sally slowly pulled both threads until they were the same length.

"Oh, pranks like supposedly going to get the preacher when the first brother was getting married at the bride's house, but deliberately getting lost and not showing up with him 'til hours later."

Sarah gasped. "That's mean!"

Sally nodded. "Of course, when the next brother got married, Cain wasn't sent for the preacher. But that time, he unhitched the horses from the new couple's wagon and turned them loose. It took all night for the men to find the horses. That brother was fit to be tied, but their mother calmed him down, saying it was all in good fun. But what Cain did to his third brother was even worse."

Zetta bit her lip to keep from smiling as Sally leaned over the quilt area in front of her, seemingly trying to decide where to thrust the needle.

Bless you, sweet friend, for getting everyone's attention off me, Zetta thought.

"Worse than the other two things?" Sarah asked.

"Yes, indeed. That's when he kidnapped his third brother's bride right after the wedding," Sally said. "Swung her right up on his fancy horse—her screaming and him laughing like a crazy man. And he didn't bring her back 'til almost midnight. His brother took off after them, but he couldn't catch up. He was ready to knock Cain senseless when he brung the bride back, but their mother stepped in and said there was no harm done. She always babied Cain, what with him being the youngest. Her babying him was what spoilt him so bad. It's no wonder those three brothers were out to get him when he married Rose."

Sally slowly smoothed the material before her, then thrust the needle to the right of a yellow strip.

Before anyone spoke, Mable Collins, sitting on Sally's right, elbowed her.

"You are wearing us out with this long tale," Mable said. "Get to the point. What did those brothers do?"

Sally pulled the thread to the underside of the quilt, then poked the needle up a stitch-length before she spoke.

"Well, Cain figured his brothers were going to try to get back at him when he got married. So he took precautions. He got the preacher hisself that morning, had everything moved into their cabin the day before, hid his fine horse, and wrapped wire around Rose's wrist and attached it to his wrist to make sure nobody kidnapped her."

Sally paused, straightening the thread, before she continued.

"The wedding went off without a hitch. And everybody had a good time eating and talking. The three brothers were real nice, wishing the new couple well. They kindly slipped away then, but none of us noticed. Cain didn't seem to pay them no mind neither. I reckon he thought he was safe. Was he ever wrong!"

Sally picked up the spool of thread as though to hand it to Zetta. Instead she dropped it.

"Oh, I'm sorry," she said. As she leaned under the frame to retrieve the thread, she looked up at Zetta and winked. Zetta feigned a cough to keep from laughing.

Mable huffed. "What did they do?"

Sally handed the thread to Zetta then slowly settled in her chair again.

"Well, Cain and Rose got to their new home and hurriedly undressed to begin their wedding night. Sweet little Rose later told me she and Cain didn't sleep much—just enjoying being together like that. Everything would have been perfect, yes, sir, everything would have been perfect if only...."

As Sally paused and turned her needle as though untangling the thread.

Mable bellowed, "If only *what*?"

Sally sighed. "If only all three of Cain's brothers hadn't crawled out from under the bed the next morning!"

Every listener had sudden and different reactions: Sarah gasped, "Oh, poor Rose!" Sarah's mother slapped both hands over her mouth. Mable yelped, "Those sinners!" Becky shook her head. Agnes shouted, "I hope Cain beat those rascals to a pulp!" But Naomi smiled. "Good for them for getting back at him that way."

None of the women seemed to notice Zetta lean toward Sally and whisper, "Thank you."

Sally smiled as she gently nudged Zetta's shoulder with her own. "Believe it or not, that's a true story."

* * * * *

As the women hurled questions as to how Rose ever faced Cain's brothers again or what Cain's mother said that time, Isaac wailed from the bedroom. Zetta was glad to leave the frame.

Abigail was rocking Isaac as Zetta stepped into the room. Rachel stood close to Abigail while Micah bounced the wooden dancing man against the floor.

"He woke up a few minutes ago," Abigail said as she stood and handed the baby to Zetta.

"I let him suck on my finger, trying to keep him content so you could hear the end of Mama's story about Cousin Rose."

Zetta sat down and opened her dress to the eager baby. "That was quite a story all right. But I'm glad the women have something to talk about other than me. Are you ready to quilt?"

Abigail stroked Rachel's hair as the child leaned against her. "I've been pondering that. And I decided I'd druther not. No need to give them more to talk about later."

Zetta frowned. "Well, I understand that."

"I'll fill plates for Rachel and Micah in a little bit," Abigail said. "Then when they take their nap, I'll eat with y'all. I'll prove my worth when I clean up the kitchen after."

"We always say there's more than one way to skin a cat," Zetta said. "But I still feel bad about how you got treated. And I don't want you giving in easy like."

"But I'm not giving in if I'm doing what I know is best for me," Abigail said.

Zetta smiled at the young woman. "Now that's wisdom we all can use. So you go right ahead and do what you need to do."

And somehow Zetta knew she, too, would lean on that wisdom in the days ahead.

Chapter 3

The women finished the quilt just as Rachel and Micah awakened from their afternoon nap. Even though Zetta was grateful the gathering was over, she forced herself to keep a pleasant expression as she said goodbye to everyone. But as soon as she and the children were settled in Sally's wagon, she pulled Isaac close and let out a long sigh.

Sally nodded. "That was quite a day. And you were exactly right about what Mable would say to you."

"She always comes up with that," Zetta said. "But I appreciate you getting the attention off me with the story about Rose. Everybody still was talking about it when we was eating instead of telling me to get over my grief and just get another man."

She turned back to Abigail, who was sitting with her arms around Rachel and Micah.

"I appreciate you taking good care of the youngins today. And Becky was plumb pleased at how you cleaned up the kitchen whilst we finished the quilt."

Abigail smiled. "Mama always says we catch more flies with honey than we do with vinegar. So I decided on working instead of feeling sorry for myself."

"Well, Becky was pleased. And she's not a woman who pleases easy like."

Sally slowed the wagon as they approached the chestnut trees near Zetta's house.

"Every time I look at the branches, I keep hoping to see healthy leaves," Sally said. "But nothing yet. Same with our trees up the mountain. What will our bees do this summer if the trees don't bloom?"

Zetta nodded. "There's nothing sweeter than the chestnut honey from your hives."

"All these troubles lately make me feel even older than I am," Sally said as she gently slapped the reins. "But I reckon there ain't nothing to do but face it in good time. You want us to get you for church Sunday?"

"No. Luttrell will bring us since he's staying tomorrow night," Zetta said. "Loren's turn is tonight. But I don't expect him 'til late since he usually stays at Sarah's each evening."

"Well, holler if plans change," Sally said as she guided the wagon to Zetta's cabin. "And remember what I said about Mable visiting her sister. At least you won't have to face her."

* * * * *

Even though Zetta wasn't expecting Loren until long after dark, he opened the kitchen door as she placed buttered cornbread on the children's plates.

"You're just in time for supper," Zetta said. "But I figured you'd be a while at Sarah's."

Loren patted both children's heads then pulled the nearest chair out from the table.

"Nope. She was so busy talking girl stuff with Naomi she didn't care if I was around or not," he said. "She was showing everything she's got ready for when we set up housekeeping. To see all that, you'd think we was moving into a big fine house instead of her granddaddy's old cabin up the mountain for now."

Zetta set the bowl of soup beans in front to Loren. "We already prayed, so dig in. And remember, women like getting everything just so for their own home and for their own man."

Loren reached for the serving spoon. "Maybe. But all I need is a stove for her to cook on and a bed for us to sleep in. But her and Naomi was giggling over every little thing."

"Now you know good and well skillets and dishes need to go with the stove," Zetta said. "And the bed needs pillows and quilts."

"I reckon," Loren said. "But a man can stand only so much girl talk. And that Naomi sure can girl talk."

He nodded his thanks as Zetta poured his coffee. "Speaking of Naomi, since Luttrell listens to you better than to me, talk to him tomorrow. Naomi has her pick of fellers over in Rosefork, but she kindly took a shine to Luttrell, and he acted like she wudn't even there. Just like he did when the Reed girl smiled at him the other evening."

"You know Luttrell ain't a feller to be pushed into anything," Zetta said. "And for somebody who is getting married in just a few more weeks, you sure do spend a lot of time worrying about other folks' business."

Loren shrugged and reached for the cornbread.

*****

The next morning, Zetta milked Brownie and gathered the eggs while Loren lingered over a cup of coffee, and Rachel and Micah ate biscuits and gravy. She glanced toward the oak tree. No one was there.

If Jesse Allen wasn't hiding there before, maybe it was just somebody taking a shortcut home and didn't want to show himself, she thought. *I've got to stop being silly.*

As she pulled an egg from the last nest, she frowned. *There ain't as many eggs today as normal,* she thought. *And the hens ain't laying eggs in the broody boxes yet. I hope some varmint ain't been in here. Maybe Loren can check the back of the coop before he goes.*

But Loren was watching for her as she opened the kitchen door.

"I'll be heading out now," he said. "But later me and Luttrell will go over to the store and get cornmeal. We'll have Ben put it on the books for you 'til later. What else you reckon you gonna need for feeding the men Tuesday?"

"I could use flour," Zetta said. "And a couple ham hocks for the beans. We used up most of the meat at the camp. I appreciate y'all toting that for me."

"Glad to do it," Loren said. "Nothing worse than not having enough food for everybody doing the work."

And he was out the door.

Zetta watched him go. Then she poured a dipperful of water over the eggs to wash them before turning to Rachel and Micah.

"Did y'all eat enough?" she asked the toddlers as she put the eggs into a pan to boil.

Both children nodded.

"Good. Now let me wash your hands. We're gonna be extra busy the next few days what with cooking for the men who come to do the plowing. But today's a pretty day so what do you say to us having a little picnic?"

Rachel smiled. "Where Poppy is?"

Zetta sighed. "Sure. We'll walk up to the cemetery and eat there. But first we need to wash these dishes. Brother, you go play with your play pretties whilst Sister and me clean up here. But don't go making noise. I don't want Isaac waking up 'til he's good and ready."

* * * * *

After she and Rachel had washed the breakfast dishes and placed the boiled eggs in a bowl of spring water to cool, Zetta untied the apron from around the child's tiny waist.

"You was good help, Sister. Thank you."

"I'm a big girl, huh, Mama?"

Zetta kissed the top of the child's head, breathing in the sweetness.

"You are indeed. I'm right proud of you."

She watched Micah bouncing the toy dancing man in front of the fireplace, then turned back to Rachel.

"Sister, you stay with Brother whilst I run to the root cellar for apples. I'll be right back."

The root cellar was dug into the hillside at the left of the barn. Before Zetta tugged the heavy door open, she studied the path at the entrance to make sure no copperhead snakes were sunning themselves. The ground was clear. Inside the cellar, Zetta paused to allow her eyes to adjust to the darkness. Then as she lifted the covering from the basket, she frowned.

I was sure they was more in here last time, Zetta thought as she put several apples into her held-out apron. Maybe I'm wrong, she decided as she hurried back to the children.

Isaac was howling for his breakfast as Zetta opened the kitchen door.

*****

Zetta nursed Isaac in the bedroom while Micah stacked and restacked his blocks just outside the door. Rachel stood next to their mother and gently rubbed Isaac's head as he gulped the milk. When the baby's stomach was filled, Zetta gently kissed his forehead and eased him back into the crib. Then she stared at the bottom dresser drawer for several moments before opening it. The red sweater Asa had given her at Christmas lay near her nightgowns. She took a deep breath as she ran her hands over the material. At last she put the sweater on.

Rachel smiled. "I like when you wear that, Mama. You look pretty."

Zetta hugged her. "Let's get our vittles. I'll take the water. Can you tote the basket?"

Rachel nodded eagerly. "Uh-huh."

After Zetta put three boiled eggs, butter and jelly biscuits and sliced apples into her smallest basket for Rachel, and loosely wrapped a quilt around Isaac, the little family stepped onto the front porch. Zetta studied the entire yard as they descended the steps. They were alone.

As they passed the Reed's cabin, Sally was sweeping the porch. She smiled, raised her broom and rubbed her arm to show approval of the red sweater.

As Zetta waved back, she saw a tall figure on the hillside above the cabin.

That must be Jim gathering more polk, she thought as she waved to him.

But the man did not return her greeting. Instead, he darted behind the nearest tree.

That's strange, Zetta thought. Jim always waves. He must not have seen me.

But a prickly feeling crept up her neck.

* * * * *

As they started up the cemetery hill, Rachel tugged on Micah's hand. "Hurry, Brother!"

"Oh, Asa," Zetta whispered as she slowly followed the running children. At the grave, she put the quilt-wrapped Isaac on the ground.

"Sister, you and Brother sit here with little Isaac and eat," she said. "And when y'all are finished, I've got water for you."

She took a deep breath as she put her hand on top of the tombstone.

"Asa, someday, I'm gonna get a proper stone with your name spelled right instead of what the camp give," she whispered. "But right now I'm just trying to get my bearings."

She paused, fighting tears. "The grass is starting to show over you. I know you ain't really here, but this is all I've got to talk to. Well, I'm wearing the sweater again. Do you see that from heaven? Does what we do down here matter to you there?"

She watched Rachel hand Micah a jelly biscuit. "Asa, I wish you could see how the youngins are growing. Rachel tells me she's a big girl now that she can help in the kitchen. But she's just a little youngin who needs her Poppy. And the same with Micah and Isaac. How am I gonna teach them to be men all by myself? Oh, Asa. How we need you!"

Zetta swiped at sudden tears. "Well, it won't do for me to carry on in front of the youngins. So I'll tell you about Loren and Luttrell planning to tell the men at church tomorrow about plowing for me on Tuesday."

More tears ran down her cheeks. "I recollect how much you loved plowing—turning the dirt and getting it ready for the seeds. And this year you was gonna be plowing our own ground—and not what belonged to somebody else. But I paid off the four hundred dollars on the farm a couple weeks after we come home. Well, I sent Luttrell with the money since I couldn't bear going myself. You worked so hard digging coal, but them dollars took you away from us."

She rubbed her forehead. "I don't know how I'm gonna get along without you, Asa."

At that moment, Rachel hollered, "Mama, there's ants here!"

And Zetta swooped to move her children away from the ant hill.

* * * * *

That evening, just as Zetta tied on her apron, Luttrell opened the kitchen door.

"Hidy. I got the wagon and Jack put up in the barn. That old mule is gonna enjoy having a stall all to hisself and not having to worry about Zack eating his fodder. Them mules plow good together but can't stand each other if they ain't wearing the harness. And I'm starting to wonder if Jack's not getting too old for the fields."

He held up a burlap bag. "Anyway, here's your store goods," he said. "Ben threw in two extra ham hocks for Tuesday's plowing. He said June can run the store then. He'll be here."

At the sound of their uncle's voice, Rachel and Micah ran into the kitchen. Luttrell knelt to give both children a hug.

"I know y'all been good today," he said. "So look what I brung you."

He pulled two red and white peppermint sticks from his shirt pocket. "But you can't eat them 'til your mommy says so."

Both children quickly looked at their mother as Luttrell stood to empty the bag.

"Y'all each can have half a piece after supper, but only if you eat good," Zetta said.

Then she turned to her brother. "You're gonna spoil them youngins rotten."

Luttrell gave both children another hug. "Aw, Sis. That's the least I can do."

He reached back into his shirt pocket. "And I got something for you, too. Clarie wrote you a letter."

Zetta smiled. "Read it to me whilst I mix the cornbread. I been hankering to hear from her. That sweet woman made being at the camp bearable."

Luttrell sat down and pulled Rachel and Micah onto his lap and opened the envelope.

"'Dear Zetta,'" he began. "'I hope this letter finds you and your precious babies doing good. I still miss you and pray for you every day. And I think about the mornings when me and Dosha and Polly would be in your kitchen for coffee and sweets and good talking.'"

Zetta brushed tears away from her cheeks. "All I wanted to do every morning was get us out of there and back home," she said. "Well, I'm here now with the youngins, and you and Loren are here and safe, but nothing is right. And it ain't never gonna be again."

"I'd give anything in the world to undo what happened," Luttrell said. "All the time I think about how you tried to tell Asa something bad was ahead. But he was like most of us. Not wanting to hear what he didn't want to hear."

"I know," Zetta said. "Go on with the letter."

Luttrell cleared his throat. " 'I reckon mornings like that are a thing of the past now. Things are getting bad here at the camp. No work tomorrow signs are being posted more and more. Something is going on but we don't know what it is. And Mr. Gray don't give nobody news, not even Perton. But I feel right sorry for him. He walks around looking pitiful since his wife and girl Julie went to Lexington. He says they went for a visit, but that was a while ago. Nobody is saying nothing out loud, but we all figure Mrs. Gray and Julie won't be coming back.' "

Zetta held up her hand. "That girl, Julie, wore me out coming around all the time," she said. "And I recollect Clarie saying Mr. Gray was a big man in the mine since he was supervisor but was a little man in his own house."

Luttrell nodded. "The men was all the time talking about how his shoulders sagged the closer he got to home each evening."

He turned back to the letter. " 'Polly's birthing time is way down the road, but she's not doing good at all. Me and the other women take meals in, but I'm worried about her.' "

Luttrell looked up. "It don't help much that Perton's her man."

"I know," Zetta said. "I still cringe every time I think about him threatening to hit her when everybody was at our house for sweets. That poor woman. Well, go on with the letter."

He turned the page. " 'I expect you hear from Dosha. I smile every time I get a letter from her. And I thank the good Lord for leading them to the Hindman School.' "

Zetta set a cup of coffee in front of Luttrell. "That's good of Clarie to give the Lord credit, but she's the one who got her cousin over there to take Dosha on as a cook and give 'em a place to live whilst Jack's foot mended."

"I can't tell you how often I think how everything would've been different if only Jack had been driving the mantrip that day instead of Clarence," Luttrell said. "But I reckon life is full of *if onlys.*"

"Now there's the truth," Zetta said. "And we can start that list with *if only* our mother hadn't died so young."

Both Zetta and Luttrell were silent for several moments. Finally, Luttrell said, "Well, Clarie finishes the letter by saying she's sending more hugs and prayers across the miles."

Zetta took a deep breath. "I'd love one of her hugs right now. I couldn't wait to get out of that camp. Now I'd go back in a heartbeat if we could all be together like we was before."

She looked at her brother. "Why does life have to be so hard!"

Luttrell eased the children off his lap. "If I had the answer, I'd sure give it to you. I reckon that's a question we'll have to ask the Lord one of these days. But when we finally see him face to face, problems like that probably won't matter anymore."

"In my heart, I know you're right," Zetta said. "But I sure would like some answers now."

And she poured the cornbread batter into the skillet.

Chapter 4

By the time Zetta, Rachel and Micah entered the kitchen Sunday morning, Luttrell had milked Brownie, gathered the eggs, stoked the stove fire and made coffee.

"Lands! You already done a day's work," Zetta said. "And that's after toting all our bath water last night."

Luttrell lifted his coffee cup in greeting. "I heard you in there talking to the youngins about being good at church whilst you was feeding Isaac, so I figured I'd better help a little. But you notice I didn't make the biscuits. Nobody can make 'em like you do."

As Rachel and Micah rushed to hug their uncle, Zetta reached for her apron.

"You reckon Paw will be at church since the preacher is announcing Loren's wedding?"

"Your guess is as good as mine," Luttrell said. "About the only thing that gets him to church since Maw died is another funeral or somebody's wedding."

"Well, I reckon I can't say much since I ain't set foot in church neither since we been back from the camp," Zetta said.

"I know you're dreading today. You sleep okay last night?"

"No. I kept thinking about seeing folks I ain't seen since

Asa's funeral. And I guess one part of me is afraid they're gonna make over me and another part is afraid they won't. Finally, I got tired of worrying about church and thought about Clarie's letter and pondered how I'm gonna answer her when I write back."

Zetta dumped two handfuls of flour into a bowl then reached for the lard and milk.

"And thinking about writing the letter and giving it to Loren or you to mail got me to thinking," she said. "I can't be asking y'all to tote my mail and bring food goods from the store all the time. I need me a gentle mule to do my own toting."

Luttrell helped both children into their chairs. "You got Asa's wagon still in the barn. You okay with driving with these little ones?"

"No, I mean us riding the mule. I got this all figured out. I can bridle the mule and bring him around to the porch. From there, I'll put Rachel on his back, put Micah in front of her to hang onto the mule's mane and then give Isaac to Rachel to hold 'til I get on. Then I'll climb on behind them and off we'll go."

"What about a saddle?"

"Won't use one. I'll just use a quilt. When we was little, I used to ride that old white mule of Paw's bareback," Zetta said. "I reckon I can still do that."

"You can do anything you put your mind to," Luttrell said as he watched Zetta shape the biscuit dough into large rounds and place them in the greased skillet.

"What would you think about this?" he said at last. "I told you last night, I'm thinking Jack is getting too old for the field. And none of the men are gonna buy a mule that can't plow. How about I give him to you?"

"Jack's gentle all right," Zetta said. "But I can't let you just give him to me."

"You know good and well Paw won't have me keep him around if he's no use," Luttrell said. "You taking him would solve both our problems."

Zetta wiped her hands on her apron. "Well, that's something for me to think on."

Luttrell stood to refill his cup. "Look, I know you are easing toward not needing me and Loren around. If you take my old mule, I won't worry about you as much."

"Here you are watching out for me and making it sound like I'm doing you a favor," Zetta said.

But she smiled as she thrust the skillet into the oven.

* * * * *

As Luttrell guided the wagon in front of the little clapboard church, Zetta took a strengthening breath and clutched Isaac all the tighter. Several families already were there, unloading children from mule-drawn wagons and calling greetings to each other.

Lord, please help, Zetta silently prayed as Luttrell helped her and the baby down from the wagon before he reached for Rachel and Micah. As several women, including Sarah, her mother, aunt and cousin swarmed toward Zetta, Luttrell joined the men. The women's welcomes and comments about the children rolled together.

"Loren and me was hoping you'd come today," Sarah said.

"I told 'em you'd be here since Preacher Collins is announcing the wedding date," Sarah's mother said.

"Well, about time you decided to rejoin life," Becky said.

Zetta took a deep breath to keep from replying to her stepmother's comment.

"My, how your youngins have growed just since the funeral," someone said.

"They're growing like little weeds," another woman said.

Sarah's Aunt Agnes gestured toward the blue sky. "You brung pretty weather with you."

"And your good looking brother," Naomi said as she raised her voice toward the men.

You said that for Luttrell's benefit, Zetta thought. But you needn't bother.

"Ben told me he's helping the men plow on Tuesday," June said. "So I'm minding the store. But I'd druther be at your house. That's gonna be a fun day."

Zetta forced herself to nod at the comments even though she was sure Tuesday's plowing would not be fun. Just then Sally Reed was at her side.

"I'm sorry we didn't get here before you," Sally whispered as she touched Zetta's arm. "I know this first time back is hard. But you can do this. I do wish you was wearing your pretty sweater, though."

As Zetta turned to smile at Sally, she could see beyond her friend's shoulder. Loren was talking to the men near the wagons while Luttrell stood quietly by his side. Paw Davis was not with them. Suddenly two men on matching black stallions rode up to the group.

Zetta gasped. What's Jesse Allen and his brother doing here? she thought.

She quickly turned back to Sally, hoping Jesse hadn't seen her. As Zetta tried to calm her pounding heart, Mable Collins appeared.

"Oh, there you are with your poor little fatherless babies."

Zetta was too startled to respond, but Sally spoke. "You mentioned last week you was gonna be visiting your sister today."

"That was before Becky told me after the quilting about getting the men together for the plowing Tuesday," Mable said. "I knew I'd be needed to help with the cooking."

And the eating, Zetta thought.

Becky reached for Isaac. "Let me hold that child. Yes, me and Mable will be over bright and early tomorrow morning to help get everything ready."

Zetta again glanced toward the men as she reluctantly released Isaac. Loren was pointing his finger wildly at Jesse who stood with his chin thrust out.

Please, Lord. Don't let 'em get in a fight here.

"Did you hear me?" Becky asked. "I said me and Mable will be over first thing."

Zetta struggled for a reply as she looked at her stepmother. "I appreciate your offer, Becky. I truly do," she said. "But Sally and her girls will be helping me tomorrow with chopping cabbage and scrubbing the other vegetables I need to get ready early. I'll do the biggest part of cooking the meats the next morning."

As Becky frowned, Zetta hurriedly continued. "But I sure will appreciate y'all's help when the men eat noon dinner Tuesday."

"Well, all right," Becky said. But she didn't sound happy.

Sarah's mother, Blanche, leaned close. "I'm not supposed to tell you this yet, but the women are gonna plant your garden whilst the men plant the corn and tobacca after they plow."

"Oh! I wudn't expecting that," Zetta managed. "But I sure do appreciate y'all's help."

As the other women nodded and smiled, Blanche spoke again. "Well, it could have been any one of us needing help. It just happened to be you this time."

Zetta fought a sob as she reached to take Isaac from Becky. *But why did it have to be me so soon?* she thought.

* * * * *

As a deacon rang the church bell, craggy-faced Preacher Collins stood by the weathered front door to nod a welcome to each woman and shake the men's hands as they entered.

Oh, Asa. How I wish you was here, Zetta thought. But she pushed aside her longing as she held Isaac in one arm and with the other steered Rachel and Micah toward an empty bench at the back. Sally gestured for her family to sit in their usual spot while she slid next to Micah, forcing Becky to sit in front of them.

Zetta took a deep breath as Preacher Collins strode to the front of the room then turned his solemn gaze upon her.

"I'm glad y'all are here today. And I want to give a special welcome to Sister Zetta Berghoffer for joining us."

Zetta felt her face flush. Please don't ask me to say anything, she thought. But Mable Collins interrupted those worries.

"And welcome her three little fatherless babies, too," she hollered. "We gotta keep them all in our prayers. Yes, Jesus."

I'm more than a little tired of her always saying that, Zetta thought.

"Yes, we're glad she's here with her sweet youngins," Preacher Collins said. "And there's them that would be here if they could, like Brother Jeems suffering so with them leg ulcers. But too many folks think they don't need to be with us."

Preacher Collins raised his voice with each following sentence. "Yes, they go on in their prideful ways, bound and determined they don't need the Lord. But one of these days, they will have to face an Almighty God who won't give a hoot about their excuses. And they will have to face up to the pride that sent them to an eternity of torment in that great lake of fire."

As he shouted "lake of fire," Preacher Collins slammed his fist against the wooden pulpit, causing Zetta to gasp and clutch Isaac tighter as he jerked in his sleep. In the same moment, Rachel burst into tears and Micah thrust his head onto his mother's lap.

While Zetta and Sally tried to calm the children, Becky cried out, "Yes. Oh, yes. That fire is waiting!"

That's Paw he's talking about, Zetta thought as she frowned at the back of Becky's head. You ought to be crying out for his soul, not shouting praises.

Preacher Collins continued with a softer tone. "Yes, even as we see their prideful ways, we need to keep encouraging them to get right with God before it's too late. Now let's worship the Lord with song. Somebody want to start us in a hymn?"

A voice from the back launched into "Amazing Grace." As the others joined in, Zetta bit her lip. Oh, Lord, that was one of Asa's favorite songs. He'd nod as he sang. And he certainly wasn't the wretch the song talked about. He was a good man who loved you and loved his family. Why'd he have to die?

As the song ended, Preacher Collins held up his hand. "That's all the singing we're gonna do today since we've got a busy time ahead. So if you brung your Bible, I want you to turn to Psalm 106:15 as we continue looking at some of the truths King David set forth."

Preacher Collins waited as the few people with Bibles opened them to the appropriate verse. Then he read, "'And he gave them their request and gave leanness into their soul.'"

"When David wrote this, he was talking about the Israelites forgetting all God had done for them to take them out of slavery in Egypt," Preacher Collins said. "And I reckon he was remembering how they wanted to be like other countries, so they demanded God give them a king."

He brought his fist down on the pulpit and shouted, "That's right. They demanded God give them what they wanted. And they brung trouble on their own heads."

As Preacher Collins shouted louder, Rachel and Micah pressed harder against their mother. Without a word, Sally gently took the still sleeping baby onto her own lap so Zetta could put both arms around the toddlers.

Zetta closed her eyes. *Lord, Preacher Howard never yelled when he opened your word,* she silently prayed. *He cared about the miners and their families and tried to encourage them. I never thought I'd miss him like this, but I do. Bless him wherever he is now.*

She hugged Rachel and Micah as she pondered those Sundays at the coal camp.

After several more minutes of meandering through the Israelites' history, Preacher Collins said, "Now I'm gonna close with this question."

The word *close* turned Zetta's thoughts away from the coal camp.

"David wudn't just talking about the Israelites demanding a king," he said. "He was talking about us today. Have you ever hankered after something that you reckoned was a good thing, but it turned out to be the worst in the world?"

Zetta lowered her eyes as the preacher looked from face to face. Lord, Asa was determined that working coal would give us a better life. But look at us now.

Preacher Collins cleared his throat. "Yes, I reckon we all been there a time or two. But that just means we gotta ask the Lord to guide us in every little thing."

Mable's sudden shout rolled over the final words of her husband's sentence. "Yes! Yes! Help us listen, Jesus!"

Preacher Collins ran his hand through his hair and waited as though to make sure Mable was finished.

"You'll notice I cut the sermon short today because we got two important announcements to tend to," he said finally. "First, let's close in prayer. Brother Luttrell, will you lead us?"

Zetta sucked in her breath, knowing Luttrell never prayed in public. Why hadn't the preacher asked him privately if he would be comfortable doing that?

As Zetta fretted over Luttrell's discomfort, he stammered a quiet "Beg to be excused."

"Oh. Well, Brother Luttrell, that's all right. Brother Jim, would you close us in prayer?"

Jim Reed stood and raised his right hand. "Father God, we thank you for being here with us today and every day and for helping us bear our many burdens."

Then he began to name specific people who were carrying burdens, beginning with Brother Jeems with the leg ulcers. As the list grew, Zetta held her breath. But he didn't name her.

He paused then as though pondering if he'd forgotten anyone. "Lord, you know many here carry a heart hurt nobody knows about but you. So we ask you to help as only you can. In your son's name. Amen."

Amen, Zetta thought. Yes, a heart hurt pretty much sums up how I feel.

"Thank you for that fine prayer, Brother Jim," Preacher

Collins said. "Now I want Loren Davis and Sarah Webb to come up here and be by me."

Zetta turned to watch the young couple stand. But as they stepped away from their seats, her brother caught his foot against the bench leg in front of them. Sarah turned to smile at Loren, but he didn't notice.

A few of the women who saw his awkwardness put their hands over their mouths as though trying to stifle laughter. But Jesse Allen snorted.

Finally, Loren got his feet straightened out and hurried to stand next to Sarah. His shoulders were slumped.

Preacher Collins nodded. "This fine couple is gonna get married Sunday April 22 at noon. And they asked me to say that y'all are welcome. The wedding service will be followed by dinner on the ground right here at the church. With all the good cooks in our midst, I know there'll be plenty of good eating. And that'll give us plenty of time to celebrate with the new Mr. and Mrs. Davis and still get home in time for evening chores."

He raised his right hand. "Now let me pray a blessing over 'em."

While the others bowed their heads, Zetta tilted hers to look at the couple. Then she felt that same crawly feeling she'd had a few days earlier when she was near the chicken coop. She knew Jesse Allen was watching her watch Loren and Sarah. She quickly bowed her head as the preacher began to pray.

"Lord, we ask you to bless Loren Davis and Sarah Webb as they become one in a few more weeks. May you be first in their thoughts each morning. May they be faithful to you and each other every day. And as they serve you, may they live a long and happy life together."

Zetta sighed, pushing aside the rest of the prayer as she wrestled with her thoughts. *Lord, Asa and I was faithful to each other always, and we tried to be faithful to you each day. But we didn't get that long and happy life.*

Preacher Collins finished his prayer by bellowing, "Amen and amen!"

He turned to the young couple. "You can go back to your seats now."

Loren nodded his thanks and took a step. Suddenly he stopped and put his arm out for Sarah. For an instant, she appeared startled, but smiled and put her arm over his. Zetta found herself fighting tears again.

Preacher Collins watched Loren and Sarah return to their bench, then said, "Now we got another announcement, but not as happy as the first one."

He gestured toward Jesse Allen.

"Since I'm kindly new, and Mr. Allen don't worship with us regular like, I don't know him the way you folks do."

Zetta bit her lip. *Believe me, you don't want to know him the way we do.*

"But he's got some important news for us. Come right on up here, Mr. Allen."

Jesse strutted to the front of the church, then hooked a thumb over his belt.

"Thank you, Preacher," he said. "Some of you know I been over in Virginia helping a cousin cut his chestnut trees."

He let his gaze sweep over the group, but he didn't look at Zetta.

"After the cutting," he continued, "we had to burn 'em."

The responses from his listeners included gasps and challenges of "Burn 'em?"

"Yep, burn them big ol' trees trying to stop a bad disease that's killing 'em left and right," Jesse continued. "The disease seems to be carried by the wind. It starts a kindly orange-brown mark on the trunk of the tree, but quickly turns into a canker that eats through the bark and into the wood. Then the tree dies."

Jesse waited as though to let his listeners absorb the news.

"My cousin and his neighbors heard about the disease coming in from up north, so they tried to stop the mark from growing into a canker by spraying the bark with new-fangled bug spray. But it didn't do a thing."

Jesse shifted his weight as he looked at the men. "And the disease is here now. All you have to do is look at your trees."

Zetta saw several people nod as Jesse continued. "You know none of 'em leafed out good this year. And if you study the bark, you're gonna see that orange canker on the trunk. Maybe we can save some of the trees if we get busy now. But we're gonna have to work together."

He waited for a moment then turned to Preacher Collins. "Since we had the closing prayer, I reckon we're done with church?"

At the preacher's nod, Jesse said, "Well then, I'm gonna stick around so we can decide what we're gonna do about our trees. So come on up."

As several of the men hurried toward Jesse, Zetta reached to take Isaac from Sally. Before she could thank her friend for helping, Luttrell was beside her.

"I'm ready to go if you are," he said quietly.

Zetta nodded. "More than ready. But don't you want to talk to the men about the trees?"

Luttrell shook his head. "Loren will tell me later. Right now, I'd just as soon not hang around."

And he picked up Micah and headed for the door.

Chapter 5

The next morning, Loren lifted the white cloth covering the applesauce cakes as Zetta entered the kitchen.

"Looky at all them sweets," he said. "Cakes and two kinds of cobblers. You was busy yesterday. And it being a Sunday at that."

"I thought I'd better get a head start. It never would do to be stingy when folks is here working. Go ahead and cut into one if you want."

Loren lowered the cloth. "Nah, I'll wait for your biscuits. The babies up?"

"No. And it's just as well," Zetta said as she added kindling to the stove's fire pit. "All of us tossed about all night. I was pondering feeding everybody tomorrow, and I reckon the youngins was wound up from Preacher Collins hollering so. But Rachel and Micah are sleeping good now. Isaac, too, now that his stomach's full."

"I barely had time to say hidy to you since I got here so late," Loren said as he pulled out a chair. "But me and Paw and Luttrell was talking about the trees. And then Sarah about had a fit when I started to leave her place early. I don't know why. Her and that Naomi was busy talking girl talk again. And now Naomi and her mother decided to stay longer to help when the men do the plowing. I'm telling you that girl wears me out."

45

"Looks to me like she's more interested in Luttrell than helping cook," Zetta said.

Loren grunted. "No argument there. I'm plumb sorry I let Sarah talk me into trying to get her and Luttrell together. I should be taking better care of my brother than that."

He watched Zetta pour spring water into the coffee pot. "Speaking of Luttrell, he told me about giving Jack to you."

"I tried to talk him out of it, but to hear him tell it, I'm doing him a favor."

"We been talking about how you got your head set on not depending on us much longer. So tomorrow morning, you'll have you a gentle mule in the barn before the men arrive."

"Reckon how many will show up?" Zetta said as she spooned coffee grounds into the pot.

"Probably five or six, plus me and Luttrell and Paw. And the women to help you. By the way, Paw planted extra seeds in the tobacca bed for you the week after we buried Asa. The plants come up good. So we'll put them in tomorrow, and you'll be all set for a cash crop."

Zetta swallowed hard, fighting tears. "Y'all take such good care of me."

"Now don't go crying. That's what kin do. Besides, after Maw died, you took care of us. Me and Luttrell kindly could do for ourselves. But Hobie was just a couple weeks old, and you did everything for him. Even after Paw brung Becky into the house."

Loren rubbed his forehead. "Well, I reckon I better think on something else. By the way, I been meaning to tell you the snakes is bad this year. Me and Luttrell killed four copperheads already near Paw's tobacca bed. Them critters is mean. They'll hunt ya down if ya ain't watching."

"I watch every time I'm outside," Zetta said as she dumped three handfuls of flour into the yellow mixing bowl. "In fact, the hens ain't laying like they usually do. And they ain't taking to the broody boxes yet. I'm wondering if a snake is getting the eggs."

"Or a varmint. We had a possum a while back stealing eggs 'til I finally caught him. I'll check your hen house before I go. Unless you need me around today. Becky said you turned down hers and Mable's offer to come over today and help."

Zetta smiled. "Are you offering to help me with women's work?"

"Huh! You know that's not what I mean. But I figure you've got a lot to do."

"I'm just fooling," Zetta said as she set a cup of coffee before her brother. "Sally and her girls will be over directly to help. The four of us will do fine, and I'll be free of hearing Becky and Mable telling me to get another man. Well, at least 'til tomorrow."

Loren frowned. "I don't blame you there. Say, Jesse Allen didn't show up yesterday afternoon, did he?"

"No. Why?"

"Well, whilst I was talking to the men before church about who brings his mules and who does what with the corn planting and the tobacca dropping, Jesse stepped into the conversation like he's planning to be here for all that. So I told him he better not show up tomorrow. Or any other day for that matter."

"What'd he say?"

"He just shrugged real cocky like and said I best not be telling him what to do. Then he jerked his thumb in the direction of that so-called sheriff brother of his and said he had legal rights to go wherever he wanted. How in the world that outlaw ever got elected is beyond me."

Loren took a long drink of coffee then said, "But I sure told him off, so we're done with him,"

Zetta sighed. Jesse Allen wouldn't be dismissed that easily.

* * * * *

After breakfast, Loren checked the hen house and, with a

wave, let Zetta know nothing was amiss.

Something's still not right, she thought as she watched him go. Then she turned to spoon gravy over the scrambled egg on Rachel's and Micah's plates.

"In a few minutes, Miz Sally and her girls are gonna come help me get ready for tomorrow," she said. "And you both better be good. You hear me?"

As Rachel and Micah nodded earnestly, Sally's call of "Hello in the cabin" sounded.

Zetta hurried to open the door. Locking doors had become an unfamiliar habit lately.

"Come in. Come in."

Sally stepped inside with Abigail and Deborah behind her. Both girls, tall and autumn-haired like their mother, clutched aprons filled with polk stalks.

"I hope you ain't tired of polk," Sally said. "Jim gathered a right smart this morning, thinking maybe you'd like it for tomorrow."

"Polk don't stay in season long enough for anybody to get tired of it," Zetta said. "Tell him I appreciate that. Better yet, I'll tell him myself when he's here tomorrow."

Sally turned to her daughters and gestured toward the kitchen table. "Put the polk there 'til we can wash it and get it ready to fry."

Then she pulled an envelope from her apron pocket as she and Zetta followed the girls into the kitchen. "This here letter is for you," she said. "I hope you don't mind I asked for your mail whilst I was at the store."

"No, I appreciate that," Zetta said. "And you was already there getting yours."

"I *was hoping* to get ours," Sally said as she handed the envelope to Zetta. "But we didn't get a thing. That's worrisome since Jim ain't heard from his sister in a while."

"Norrie? How's she doing since the baby?" Zetta said.

"Not good," Sally said. "Jim worries about her a right smart. Always has ever since she was a little bitty thing. He about had a fit when she run off to get married to that no account Calvin Risner. He was all sweet talking before, but soon as they was married, he showed his true colors."

Zetta watched Abigail hug Rachel and Micah. Then she lowered her voice and asked, "How so?"

Sally huffed. "Treating her real ugly like. Complaining about every little thing and calling her addlebrained and fat because she gained weight after the baby. It's all Jim can do to keep from punching his face every time he has to be around him. I hope she's all right."

"She's probably too busy with the baby to write much," Zetta said as she turned the envelope to check the return address. Then she smiled. "This here is from Dosha, one of the women at the coal camp."

"Well, you go right ahead and read it whilst the girls and I wash the polk," Sally said as she took the dishpan from its hook on the wall.

Zetta pulled out a chair. "Dosha has the brightest red hair I've ever seen. And she helped make being at the camp tolerable for me, so I'd like you to know her a little. Would you mind if I read the letter out loud?"

Sally smiled. "You know I love hearing other people's business, so go ahead."

Rachel took the final bite of biscuit then scurried to lean against her mother. "Miz Dosha stayed with me and Brother when Baby Isaac was born, huh, Mama?"

"She sure did, Sweetie. Micah, do you want to listen to what Miz Dosha has to say, too?"

But Micah shook his head and hurried to his blocks near the fireplace.

"All right, Sister. Let's read Miz Dosha's letter. 'Dear Zetta. I hope this finds you and your sweet babies doing all right. I'm glad your brothers is helping. Jack still talks about being in the mine with them. And he sure does miss Asa and how good he was to him.'"

Zetta looked up. "Jack's her husband. He's the one I told you about who got hurt and wudn't driving the mantrip when Asa got kilt."

Sally nodded solemnly as she poured spring water into the dishpan filled with the polk stalks. Zetta turned back to the letter. 'Every day, Jack's foot is getting better. Thanks to Clarie showing me how to wrap it with the right medicine.'" Zetta looked up again. "Clarie's the camp granny woman that helped bring Isaac into the world. She knows a right smart about cures, and she showed Dosha how to make a poultice for Jack's mangled foot."

"I'm looking forward to meeting her one of these days," Sally said. "I wish we had somebody like her around here. Seems like the doctor is always tending folks on the other side of the county, and Poxy don't know nothing other than birthing babies. Where's your best knife?"

Zetta pointed to the drawer in the nearest cabinet then returned to the letter. 'I'm still having me a big time cooking for the students. And every day I thank the good Lord for Clarie making a way for us here.'"

She looked up again. "Dosha and Jack didn't have any place to go after he got hurt, so Clarie wrote her cousin who teaches over there."

"Family sure makes a world of difference in tough times," Sally said. "Which would you druther we do? Fry the polk now and reheat it tomorrow? Or wait and fry it up fresh?"

"The kitchen's gonna be crowded either way," Zetta said. "But maybe let Becky fry it tomorrow. If she's busy maybe she won't be telling me to get over my grieving."

"Next we'll have to find something to keep Mable busy so she don't eat everything before the dinner," Sally said. "Read some more."

Zetta rubbed Rachel's back as she read. "'One little feller here stutters, too, so he likes to hang around Jack. Maybe more good things will come from our being here.'"

Zetta looked up again. "Jack stutters something awful. A lot of the miners teased him, but Asa never did."

"Asa was a good man all around," Sally said. "When I see God, I wanna ask him why he took a good man. And that's not the only thing I want to ask him about."

Zetta saw Abigail and Deborah nod and sadly glance at each other.

"I ponder Asa's dying all the time," Zetta said. "And Mama dying after Hobie was born. And your little Mary dying when she wudn't even three years old."

Sally wiped her eyes with her apron before speaking. "Thank you for including Mary. As of today, she's been gone twelve years."

"Oh. I'm sorry I didn't remember the exact day," Zetta said. "And here y'all are working and helping me. Wudn't you druther be home?"

"No. Helping you is helping me," Sally said. "If I was sitting at home, I'd just be thinking about that sweet child every minute. Did I ever tell you Jim was making her a grown-up bed since she was getting too big for her crib?"

Zetta shook her head and pulled Rachel closer.

"He'd work on it in the toolshed every chance he got, and Mary would smile and clap her little hands as she watched. When he smoothed the wood, she'd pick up the shavings. Then about the time the bed was almost finished, that fever come on quick like and took her."

Tears sprang to Zetta's eyes.

"Men don't grieve the way women do," Sally said as she wiped her eyes again. "So whilst he was trying to be strong and comfort me, I thought he was being hard-hearted. I didn't understand how bad he was hurting 'til he didn't come in for supper one night. I was aggravated at him, so instead of sending one of the boys after him, I went myself."

She paused as though remembering. "He wudn't in the barn, but I could hear the awfullest sounds coming from the workshop. When I hurried up there and pulled the door open, Jim was leaning against Mary's bed and sobbing the worst in the world. We cried together then for the first time. Things was better after that."

Sally took a deep breath. "So that's what I'd be remembering if I was home," she whispered. "I'm glad I'm here."

Tears rolled down Zetta's cheeks. As she put both arms around Rachel, Abigail and Deborah hugged their mother. In the next room, Micah loudly stacked his blocks and knocked them down again.

Moments passed before anyone spoke. At last Sally patted her daughters' backs and stepped away. "Well, there I go again," she said. "Doing what I seem to do best lately. Making us all cry. But crying don't get a thing accomplished."

She wiped her eyes with her apron again and took a deep breath. "All right now. Deborah, you finish washing the polk and wrap it in a damp towel. Abigail, you scrub the potatoes. When you finish, put 'em in a pan of clear water."

She turned back to Zetta. "I'm over my crying jag for now, and I'm enjoying listening to what your friend wrote. So keep reading whilst I wash the cabbage."

Zetta continued. "'Are your chestnut trees in trouble? Ours is. And folks here is worried. The school needs the nuts for the students and to sell. We are hoping nothing bad is wrong.'"

Sally stopped pulling wilted outer leaves from the cabbage heads. "Jim had the boys up in the woods again yesterday to look at our trees," she said. "He's saying our trees won't produce anything this year, but he's not about to burn 'em. Or let anybody else."

"I sure don't want to lose my trees, neither," Zetta said. "One more thing to worry over."

"True enough," Sally said. "But I shouldna stopped you from reading. What else does she say?"

Zetta looked back at the letter. "That's about all since she says she needs to get to the school kitchen and fix supper. She's the best hand to cook."

"And so are you," Sally said. "What all you got planned for tomorrow?"

Zetta hugged Rachel and said, "Sister, you and your rag baby go play."

As the child ran to the front room, Zetta put Dosha's

letter on the sideboard and reached for the pad of paper holding her menu.

"I thought we'd have chicken and dumplings, boiled eggs, soup beans with ham hocks, raw onion slices, cornbread, canned green beans, baked sweet potatoes, cooked cabbage, fried Irish potatoes and gravy, fried apples, canned beets, coffee, sweet milk and buttermilk. And churned butter and blackberry jam, and the sweets I made yesterday. And now your good polk."

"Lands! All that food will feed an army," Sally said.

Zetta looked up from the list. "Mama always said when it come to food, she'd druther have a bushel too much as a teaspoon not enough. I reckon I'm just trying to do what she would've done."

"She'd be right proud of you," Sally said. "I sure do miss her." Then she took a jagged breath as though fighting more tears. "Where's your cabbage chopper?"

* * * * *

As Zetta and Sally and the girls tidied the kitchen at the end of their busy day, Luttrell opened the back door. Abigail was sweeping the floor nearby and gave a startled yelp as the door swung toward her. Zetta saw Luttrell's face redden as he quickly pulled off his hat.

"I'm right sorry," he stammered. "I wudn't looking."

Zetta fought a smile as Abigail blushed and stammered, "I'm fine. I was just surprised," and she scurried away from the door.

For an awkward moment, everyone was quiet. Finally, Luttrell nodded at his sister.

"Whilst y'all finish up in here, I'll get Jack settled."

And he hurried down the back steps to tend the mule.

Zetta and Sally looked at each other, then laughed.

"Well, that was a sight," Zetta said. "What do you reckon it will take to get these two to actually talk to each other?"

Sally winked at Zetta. "Probably a miracle since neither

one of them favors Jim or me when it comes to courting. Why, him and me couldn't keep our hands to ourselves."

Abigail gasped. "Mama! I don't need to hear that!"

But Deborah laughed. "Aw, come on, Sis. How you reckon we all got here?"

As Abigail rolled her eyes, Sally smiled. "We needed that laugh. This sure beats crying!"

* * * * *

A few minutes after Sally and her daughters went out the front door, Luttrell quietly came up the back steps.

"I reckon it's safe to come in now," he said as he slowly opened the door.

Zetta smiled. "You coulda stayed before, you know. Like Abigail said, you just scared her a little, that's all."

Luttrell tossed his hat onto the nearest chair and hugged Rachel and Micah as they ran to greet him. "Well, I felt right foolish," he said. "Y'all finish everything?"

"As much as we could," Zetta said. "We'll do the main cooking in the morning."

"Paw and them are planning to arrive early," Luttrell said. "Loren will bring the wagonload of manure for the garden. Hobie and Frankie will take care of the mules that ain't plowing. Paw will be his usual self and be in charge, so be prepared."

"And Becky will take over my kitchen," Zetta said. "I appreciate everybody's help, but I'm already looking forward to having the day over and done."

Luttrell sat at the table and pulled Rachel onto his lap as Micah ran back to his blocks in the front room. "Is Jim Reed planning to be here?"

"Of course. Their biggest boy is working at the train station, but Sally said their boy Bernard is coming."

"If Paw don't run them off," Luttrell said.

Zetta reached for her favorite cast-iron skillet. "I wish Paw would get over his grudge toward Jim. By the way, did

Loren tell you Naomi and her mother will be here tomorrow?"

"Yep. He warned me all right. I'll just stay out of her way."

"I hope you can," Zetta said. "Did you get Jack settled in the barn? I appreciate you giving him to me."

"Like I told you, you taking him helps us both."

"When you gonna get another mule?" Zetta said as she spooned lard into the skillet.

Luttrell frowned. "I'm not ready to get one yet. In fact, I'm not ready for a lot of things folks seem to want me to do."

Zetta took a deep breath. "Believe me," she said. "I sure know that feeling."

Chapter 6

The sun was barely up the next morning as Zetta finished milking Brownie and gathering eggs. As she started back to her house, she looked toward the oak tree. No one was there.

She reached the kitchen steps just as two wagons entered the yard. Her father, Becky and Mable Collins were in the first one. Zetta raised her hand in greeting then took a deep breath as she saw Paw's set jaw. He was not in a good mood.

Loren guided the second wagon, filled with manure to spread into the plowed soil. Hobie and Frankie sat on the wooden seat next to him, grinning and waving at Zetta.

Even as she smiled at them, she breathed a prayer. "Lord, I appreciate everybody helping, but I'm dreading today. Asa should be the one plowing our land. So please help me."

As both wagons stopped beyond the back steps, Hobie and Frankie jumped down and ran to help the women from Paw's wagon. As Mable put her hand on Frankie's thin shoulder to steady herself, her weight threatened to take him to his knees. As Zetta watched, she willed him to use all of his eleven-year-old strength to keep Mable and himself upright.

When Mable had gained her footing, both boys turned to hold out their hands to Becky. She waved them away.

"Can't you see I'm already mostly down?" she said. Then she jerked a basket from the back of the wagon and left the boys looking small and solemn.

As Becky stomped past Mable and up the steps, Zetta followed her into the kitchen.

Inside, Luttrell drank the last of his coffee as Becky plopped a dish of butter on the table. She ignored his greetings and turned to Zetta.

"I churned that last night since I figured you wouldn't have enough," Becky said.

Zetta bit her tongue to keep from saying she wished Becky had stayed home. Instead, she watched Luttrell hurry out the back door. Then she managed to say, "I appreciate you thinking of extra butter."

Becky shrugged as she looked around the kitchen. "Well, where do you want me to start? We're here to help even though we got plenty enough to do at our own places."

Zetta slowly handed the egg basket to Becky. "If you'd like to boil the eggs, that'll be a big help. The bucket of spring water is there on the bench to wash them."

"I reckon I know to wash 'em first," Becky said as she grabbed the basket.

This is going to be a longer day than I figured, Zetta thought.

Mable pulled herself up the final step and opened the back door just as Rachel and Micah entered the kitchen. As they rubbed the sleep from their eyes, Mable nodded.

"There you are. You poor little fatherless babies."

As both children scurried beside Zetta, she put her hands on their heads and breathed a prayer for patience.

"Good morning, Mable," Zetta managed. "Thank you for helping today."

"I'm glad I can help a poor widow and her little fatherless babies," Mable said as she reached toward Rachel, who pushed even closer to her mother. "My husband said to tell you he's right sorry he can't be here. He's visiting Brother Jeems over a ways. You know, the one with the leg ulcers."

Lord forgive me, but I wish Mable wudn't here, either, Zetta thought.

"Well, give me something to do," Mable said.

Zetta forced a smile. "How about frying the polk? My best skillet is on the sideboard next to the cornmeal. Or would you druther do something else?"

Mable dropped into the nearest chair. "I'll cut the polk for ya or slice them potatoes over there, but it bothers me to stand on my feet too long."

Zetta nodded and reached for the bowl of water holding the potatoes. Just then Sally and her daughters appeared at the back door. Sally and Deborah each were holding a large cast-iron skillet. Abigail held a small covered basket.

"After hearing all the food you planned for today, I figured we might need an extra skillet or two," Sally said.

"I'm sure you figured right," Zetta said. "Come on in."

As they stepped inside, Sally raised her eyebrows at Zetta as she saw Becky and Mable bent over their tasks. But she greeted them cheerfully.

"Hidy, ladies. Here ya are, hard at work. We're gonna have us a fine time today."

"Yes, it's good to help those who are less fortunate," Mabel said without looking up. But Becky merely shrugged.

Zetta frowned at the two women, but Sally patted her arm as though to say it's okay. Then she smiled at her daughters.

"You know from yesterday what's to be done," she said. "Deborah, you stir up the cornbread. And Abigail, I know you brung egg gravy for the youngins."

Abigail nodded and held out her hands toward Rachel and Micah. "Let's get some breakfast in you and get you dressed. Then we'll play."

She turned to Zetta. "Isaac still asleep?" As Zetta nodded, Abigail leaned closer.

"I'll take care of the youngins, like at the quilting. You got enough to deal with today."

Zetta nodded her thanks as the two children ran ahead of Abigail into the bedroom.

Sally gestured beyond the back door. "Here's Jim and Bernard," she said. "They was so long at breakfast, I was afraid they'd be late."

As Zetta looked outside, she saw Sally's husband take off his hat as he greeted her father. Jim's voice reached her as he gestured toward his son.

"Mornin' Mr. Davis. You remember my boy, Bernard. We appreciate helping work Asa's ground today. My other boy, Albert, wanted to come but he's working at the train station."

John Davis merely grunted as he turned to direct other wagons pulling into the yard.

* * * * *

Within minutes, the last of the helpers had arrived. While the men greeted one another in the yard, the women crowded into Zetta's kitchen and asked about each other's families. Soon they were adding dumplings to the chicken pieces boiling in the largest kettle, frying potatoes, adding ham hocks to the soup beans and opening jars. And they laughed as they bumped into each other in the small space despite Becky's frowns at each giggle.

Sarah and her cousin Naomi set the table, using all of Zetta's plates. As they poured spring water into the pint jars, which served as glasses, Naomi kept looking out the window to where the men were plowing.

Zetta looked up from cutting the applesauce cake into generous pieces and sighed as she followed Naomi's gaze. The girl was watching Luttrell.

Sarah's mother, Blanche, interrupted Zetta's thoughts. "You care we ain't planting by the signs today?"

Before Zetta could answer, Sally spoke. "The full moon just passed so this is a good time, especially for the corn."

"But we're planting potatoes, too," Blanche said.

"They're under the ground. You don't want black spots all over 'em."

Naomi turned away from the window. "What's planting by the signs?"

"The moon phases and the place of the stars in the eastern sky control the growing of crops," Blanche said. "So if we plant in the right time, we get a good harvest."

Naomi shrugged. "Sounds like extra work. We don't follow that, do we Mommy?"

Her mother, Agnes, looked up from slicing onions. "Your daddy don't pay the signs no mind. But my daddy followed 'em and said it come from the Bible. I can't quote chapter and verse, but he always said when God was creating the earth he declared the lights in the heavens to be for signs and for seasons. Come to think of it, I recollect he got better crops than us."

Becky nodded as she peeled the boiled eggs. "I always plant beans when the star sign is in the arms. I just hope the peas we plant today grow good. They should've been planted last month. But Zetta was so worked up over her man dying she couldn't think about nothing else."

His name is Asa, Zetta thought. How I wish you'd just go away.

Mable Collins reached for the dish of canned beets on the table. "None of that planting by the signs matters long as you pray whilst you plant everything."

Finally she's saying something I can abide, Zetta thought as she watched Mable plop a beet slice into her mouth.

* * * * *

At noon, Zetta poured water into two wash pans on the porch bench as Sally hollered at the men to come eat.

The men released the teams of mules from the plows and gave the reins to Hobie and Frankie before starting for the house. The boys led the animals to the shade of the oak tree.

Zetta stood on the porch and held the extra water pitcher as the men pulled off their dusty felt hats and slapped them against their thighs. She studied her father's face as he waited his turn to splash water on his face and run the brown lye soap over his dirt-crusted hands. His jaw still was set in his grumpy way.

Loren shook the water from his hands and reached for the towel beside the wash pan.

"Hey, Sis. We got your garden all plowed and ready. And with the extra teams plowing the main field, we're 'bout done. This is going faster than we reckoned."

Jim Reed nodded. "This is how work should go."

As the men entered the kitchen, the women placed bowls of hot food on the table. The men waited until Paw Davis pulled out the chair nearest the door. Then the others sat.

Loren leaned over the nearest bowl of chicken and dumplings. "Jim, you're a good hand to pray," he said. "But this time say something quick like so's we can eat."

The women stood quietly as Jim pushed back his chair and raised one hand. "Father God, thank you for this bounty and for the loving hands that prepared it. Bless it to our bodies and help us serve you well. In Jesus' name. Amen."

At the end of the blessing, the men reached for the bowls of food before them. Mable had slipped from the hot kitchen into the front room, fanning her face with her apron as she went. The other women watched the table. As each bowl emptied, they picked it up and set a filled one in its place.

Sarah's father reached for the cornbread. "One time, when I was a youngin, me and my paw and the neighbors was helping a widow woman harvest her crop. At noon dinner, she brung a platter of roasting ears to the table and set them down. Then right there in front of us, she took each one in her hands and broke them in two."

He took a big bite of the bread, then talked as he

chewed. "I don't need to tell you none of us ett much after that."

Zetta nodded in sympathy as she set more baked sweet potatoes on the table. As she looked up, she saw Naomi pushing her bosom against Luttrell's shoulder as she refilled his coffee cup. Luttrell's face reddened, and he quickly leaned forward.

Ben grinned as he watched. "What's the matter, Luttrell?" he said. "Don't you like a little female nudging?"

Loren frowned at Naomi as she smiled at Ben's remark. Then he turned to Zetta.

"After we finish dropping the tobacca plants, we'll get the corn in. Then come harvest time, we'll have another day like today."

Ben thrust his fork into a boiled egg and pointed it at Loren. "Hanging tobacca is a tedious job, but I'll be here. Sure would be nice, though, if you helped out by passing around some of the moonshine you've been known to have. You gonna have some at the wedding?"

Zetta grimaced as she saw her father lift his head to glare at his son. But Loren was watching Sarah as she put a bowl of beans on the table then placed both hands on her hips.

Loren puffed out his cheeks. "Now y'all heard the preacher say we're getting married at the church. So even if I had moonshine, which I don't, it wouldn't be at the church no how."

Ben shrugged. "Well, I wish you had some. My mother-in-law come to live with us a couple weeks ago. She's not sleeping good and is giving June fits."

Loren appeared relieved to change the subject. "What's she doing?" he said.

"Oh, she gets up in the middle of the night and starts cooking up a storm," Ben said. "That wakes June up. We're both afraid she's gonna burn the house down around us. Yessir. Some moonshine would help her sleep better."

"Like I said, I ain't got no moonshine," Loren said. "And right now I'd druther talk about what we're gonna do about our chestnut trees. I sure don't want to start cutting 'em."

Zetta glanced at her father. Why was he so quiet?

"Well, you heard our buddy Jesse Allen tell what's happening over in Virginia," Ben said. "If we cut a few of the ones hit with that canker now, maybe we can save the rest."

Then he turned to grin at Zetta. "Besides my nephew Silas will come to help. He's not been married. Maybe you and him will hit it off. You need a man to help you run this place."

As Zetta took a step backward, Loren spoke. "Listen here, Ben. Jesse Allen is no buddy of ours. And Zetta's doing all right. She don't need one of your sorry kin hanging around."

Ben dropped his fork onto his plate. "You got no call to badmouth like that," he said through clinched teeth. "If it wudn't for the women here, I'd punch you right in the mouth."

Everyone was quiet, tense and waiting. Loren took a deep breath and let it out slowly.

"Ah, come on now, Ben," he said at last. "Can't you take a joke? I ain't even met your nephew. I'm sure he's a fine feller."

As Ben glared at Loren, Zetta looked at her father, silently willing him to speak.

He returned her gaze. "How 'bout serving me that good-looking cake over there?"

Zetta hurried to the sideboard. But as she reached for the cake, she pondered the canker mark on the chestnut trees. They were marked by disease. She was marked by widowhood.

* * * * *

The women sat down to eat only after the men had returned to the field. Zetta was grateful Isaac loudly demanded his own meal in the bedroom. Zetta stroked the baby's head as he gulped the milk, and she smiled as Abigail spread a towel on the floor and treated Rachel and Micah to an indoor picnic.

Once the children were asleep for their afternoon naps, Zetta and Abigail went to the kitchen for their own meal. Despite Becky's frowns, Blanche, Agnes and Sarah were laughing about scenes from their childhoods as they washed dishes. Sally and Deborah were putting the leftover food into smaller dishes and covering them with clean cloths. Mable still was at the table reaching for more cake. Naomi was filling a pitcher with spring water.

"Well, 'bout time y'all decided to help clean up this mess," Naomi said as she tucked a strand of unruly hair behind her ear. "I'm taking drinking water to the men."

"To Luttrell, you mean," Abigail whispered as Naomi headed out the door.

Zetta turned to the young woman and mouthed a sympathetic *I know* as they reached for empty plates.

As Abigail thrust a serving spoon into the dumplings, Jim jerked open the kitchen door.

"Quick! Get me salt and onion! Luttrell got snake bit!"

Chapter 7

Zetta heard the other women gasp as she grabbed a salt dish from the table, along with the plate of sliced onion. She started toward the door, but Jim stopped her.

"Stay here," he said as he grabbed the dishes. "Loren's sucking the poison out. Get the bed ready."

Zetta and Sally hurried to spread Luttrell's pallet in its usual spot in front of the fireplace while the women watched the men from the window. Zetta hurried back to the kitchen as the men carried Luttrell up the steps. Paw Davis and Loren held Luttrell under his arms. Jim and Ben held his legs. Hobie and Frankie scurried behind them.

As Zetta held the door for them, she saw a red bandana tied above Luttrell's ankle.

She took a deep breath to steady herself as she looked at Luttrell's gray face. *Please, Lord, don't take my sweet brother* was her inward cry.

Sally gestured toward the front room. "In here. Be careful now."

Zetta saw the men ease Luttrell onto the pallet. Then Jim quickly pulled Luttrell's boot off. As Zetta started for the front room, Loren came back into the kitchen and grabbed another salt dish from the table. He tossed the contents into his mouth and followed that with a dipperful of spring water. Then he stepped onto the porch and spat the salty water into the yard.

Zetta waited for him to come back inside.

"How'd this happen?" she said.

Loren started to answer but suddenly muttered a curse and hurried into the front room.

As Zetta followed, she could see Naomi bending over Luttrell.

"Get your feisty self away from him," Loren said as he grabbed her arm. "In fact, leave. You're why he got bit."

"What?"

"That's right. I saw you sashaying up to him whilst he was clearing brush at the field edge. And when you put your hand on him all flirty and silly like, he backed up instead of watching where he was stepping. Now get out of my sight!"

As Naomi stomped into the kitchen, Sarah turned on Loren. "Don't you talk like that to her! This ain't her fault."

Loren leaned close to Sarah. "I'm the one that seen her silly prancing. So you can get out of my face, too." And he turned back to his brother.

"Loren!" Sarah said. When he didn't look at her, she slapped her hand over her mouth and ran from the room, followed by her mother and aunt.

Sarah's father stepped close to Loren. His voice was sharp.

"Don't talk like that to my girl, Loren."

Loren didn't look at him. "Now's not the time to talk on this. So I reckon y'all better leave right now."

As Sarah's father tightened his fist, Zetta knew he wanted to hit Loren. Instead, he suddenly turned and followed the women into the kitchen.

Asa never let anyone leave here angry, Zetta thought as she hurried after them.

"Folks, please don't go," she said as they opened the door. "Loren's worried is all."

They ignored her as they hurried down the steps.

Stunned, Zetta watched them leave. Lord, this day just keeps getting worse, she thought. We need your help more than ever.

She put her hand to her forehead and looked around the kitchen for something helpful to do. Then she poured spring water over a clean cloth.

As Zetta knelt to put the damp cloth on Luttrell's forehead, Becky clenched and unclenched her hands.

"I can't have him back at the house with all I've got to do already," she said.

Zetta forced herself to answer calmly. "He's staying right here," she said. "After all he's done for me, I won't have anybody else tending him. Especially one who don't want him around. I appreciate your help today but you can go now."

Becky turned to Frankie and Hobie. "Bring our wagon. I know when I ain't wanted!"

Zetta didn't follow them. Instead, she turned the cloth to the cooler side and put it back on Luttrell's forehead. Her father watched her for a moment

"I appreciate you taking care of my boy," he said. Then he touched her shoulder and left.

* * * * *

Ben left as soon as Paw Davis did. Now only Loren and the Reed family remained. As Sally brought another cool cloth for Zetta to place on Luttrell's forehead, Loren untied the bandana to pour fresh salt on the bite. Jim handed him more sliced onion and studied the leg for signs of swelling. Luttrell's eyes remained closed.

Abigail and Deborah, along with their brother Bernard hovered near the door, waiting to see how they could help.

"I wish I could talk to Clarie Farley," Zetta said. "She'd know what to do."

"Let's do that," Sally said. "Bernard, go have Albert send a telegram."

As Bernard stepped forward, Sally turned to Zetta.

"What's the name of the camp? I know it's near Hazard."

"Rusty Hinge. No. No. That's what the miners called it. Uh, the Golden Gate Camp. That's it. Ask her what we should do."

Sally gripped Bernard's shoulder. "Now listen close. Send the telegram to Clarie Farley at Golden Gate Camp near Hazard. Say this: Luttrell snake bit. What best poultice? And then you wait right there 'til you get her answer."

Bernard headed for the door before Sally finished the sentence.

Jim finished tying fresh onion slices over the salt then stood up. For a moment he and Sally watched Zetta on her knees beside Luttrell.

"It hurts me to see him like this," Jim said. "And I'm worried the leg is starting to swell. I wish I could do more."

Zetta looked up just as Sally whispered, "You can, you know. And our little Mary would be pleased."

Jim's eyes filled with tears as he answered Sally. "I reckon I can at that."

He leaned toward Zetta. "I'll be back directly. Please let us do this for him."

Zetta nodded. But as soon as Jim left, tears rolled down her cheeks as she looked at Sally.

"Don't get me started," Sally said. "That bed has been taking space in the workshop all these years. It's time to put it to good use."

Then she and Zetta embraced and cried together as Loren solemnly watched.

* * * * *

Before Jim had time to bring the bed, Bernard returned. He was breathless from running.

"I got her answer quick like," he said. "The telegram said, 'Raw onion to start. Will arrive morning train.'"

"Thank you, Lord," Zetta said. Then she looked at Sally. "I didn't expect her to show up. But I'm glad."

"Dang, that's good news," Loren said. Then he leaned close to Luttrell.

"You hear that, Brother? Clarie's coming. So you hang in there. You're gonna be all right."

Zetta's next breath was a prayer. *Oh, Lord. Please. May that be so.*

Chapter 8

Jim Reed arrived with little Mary's unused bed, and his son Bernard and Loren helped unload it from the wagon. On Zetta's front porch, Sally jerked off her apron and slapped away twelve years of dust. Finally, with an approving nod, she allowed the men to carry the bed inside.

Zetta stood from wiping Luttrell's sweaty face as Sally held the door open.

"Where you want this?" Jim said.

"Here by the window," Zetta said as she quickly pulled a straight-back chair aside. Then she hurried to her bedroom and returned with extra bedding.

As she came back into the front room, Zetta saw Jim run his hand over the headboard in what appeared to be a goodbye caress. After Zetta and Sally spread the sheets over the thin mattress, Jim nodded to Bernard and Loren.

"All right now," he said. "Let's lift him up gentle like."

Loren put his hands under Luttrell's shoulders while Bernard lifted Luttrell's healthy leg. Jim put both of his hands under Luttrell's injured leg.

"Together now," Jim said. "Careful."

Luttrell's eyes remained closed as they eased him from the floor and onto the bed. But he whispered, "Thank you."

Zetta clutched two pillows, unsure whether to put them

under Luttrell's head or his leg.

Jim pointed to Luttrell's injured leg. "Put one of 'em here, to keep him comfortable," he said. "The other pillow goes under his head. Gotta have his head higher than the bit leg to keep the blood from rushing to his heart."

As Zetta eased the pillows into their proper position, she glanced toward Loren. He was rubbing the scar on this chin.

He's worried sick, she thought. So am I. Lord, please help Luttrell. Please help us all.

* * * * *

For an awkward moment, everyone stared at Luttrell. Then Jim turned to Bernard.

"Well, we better finish the job we come to do today," he said. "The little bit of corn left ain't gonna plant itself."

Sally nodded at Deborah and Abigail. The girls had remained huddled near the door.

"Let's finish cleaning the kitchen and then get a few rows of beans planted," Sally said.

Then she looked at Zetta. "And we'll be back over tomorrow to finish the garden," she said. "I'm glad your Clarie Farley is coming. But I'm right sorry to have to meet her this way."

Zetta stepped toward the kitchen, but Sally pointed toward Luttrell. "No, you're needed in here. We'll take care of the rest."

Zetta gripped her friend's arm. "I don't know what I'd do without y'all. Every time I turn around, you're helping me."

"Think of it as me just repaying your sweet mother for all she done for me over the years," Sally said. And she hurried to the kitchen as though fighting tears.

Zetta looked toward the bedroom, grateful the children still were napping despite the commotion. Then she flipped the washcloth on Luttrell's forehead to the cooler side.

* * * * *

As Zetta gently stroked Luttrell's arm, Loren untied the bandana on his brother's leg and put a fresh slice of onion over the bite.

They both studied Luttrell's face. His eyes remained closed.

"I don't like that grayish color," Loren whispered. "But his breathing is good and steady."

Luttrell right arm was lying across his chest. Slowly he moved his thumb upward in an encouraging gesture.

"Atta boy," Loren said. "You just lay there good and quiet. And remember what I said about Clarie being here come morning."

Luttrell gave another slow thumbs-up.

Loren watched him for a moment, then said, "This sure wudn't the way the day was supposed to go."

Zetta sighed. "Seems to be a lot of that happening lately."

They watched the gentle rise and fall of Luttrell's chest. Then Zetta looked at Loren.

"Are you and Sarah going to be okay after what you said to Naomi?" she asked quietly. "Y'all won't call off the wedding?"

Loren frowned. "Nah. It'll happen like we said."

"But they all stormed out of here, real mad like."

"They'll cool down after a while," he said.

"You sure?"

Loren ran a hand through his hair. "Yah, I'm sure. Sarah can't call everything off. Look, I might as well tell you. She's in the family way."

Zetta gasped. "What? She's gonna have a baby?"

Loren shrugged. "Last I heard, that's what being in the family way means."

"Do Paw and Becky know?" Zetta said.

"Sure enough. That's why they was in such mean moods today."

"Do Sarah's folks know?"

"You better believe it," Loren said. "I was all set to have us just go to the preacher and get everything taken care of now. But they said we done told everybody a date, so we have to abide by that."

Zetta gestured toward Luttrell. "Does he know?"

"Well, he does now. If he ain't asleep."

Luttrell wiggled two of his fingers. He had heard.

"When is she due?" Zetta tried to keep her voice steady.

"In a little over seven months," Loren said. "So these hills will see another fat baby that just come early. Won't be the first one that ever showed up like that."

"But I wanted you and Sarah to have time to get used to each other before the youngins started showing up," Zetta said.

Loren shrugged again. "Hey, that reminds me. Whilst you was trying to get Sarah and them to stay, Becky asked if we killed the snake."

"That so?" Zetta said. She knew her brother was through talking about the baby.

"Yep. I told her it got away since I was more worried about Luttrell than the critter."

Loren gently retied the bandana over Luttrell's leg as he continued. "Then she told me that if I find it and kill it, I'm to make sure everybody stays away from it because a snake won't die 'til sundown even if the head is severed."

"I hope that copperhead is in the next county by now," Zetta said.

"Me, too. But before I bothered to answer Becky, Mable Collins had to add her two cents' worth by telling about her sister chopping a copperhead to pieces with her garden hoe. Later, she went past the snake parts and poked a stick at the head. And the head bit the stick even though it had been cut off a bunch of hours before!"

Zetta shivered. "Mama told stories like that. But I never set out to prove them true. I cannot abide a snake."

Loren jerked his thumb in Luttrell's direction. "I reckon we all can agree to that," he said. "But right now we need to get this boy well."

Chapter 9

Zetta went to bed reluctantly that night as Loren insisted she rest.
"Your youngins need you," he said. "And you ain't gonna be no use to nobody, if you wind up sick."
Then he grinned. "Besides, I want you making your good biscuits come morning."
But even in her familiar bed, Zetta couldn't get comfortable as she relived the day's awful events. Sleep came in short snatches as she fought images of the copperhead's fangs sinking into Luttrell's flesh. Each time she awakened, she pulled her gray shawl around her gowned shoulders and quietly slipped into the front room to check on Luttrell. Each time, in the soft glow of the kerosene lamp, she found Loren sitting beside their brother. And each time he gave her a thumbs-up and then motioned for her to return to the bedroom.
Finally, just before dawn, Isaac stirred. Zetta quickly opened her gown so his whimpers wouldn't turn into howls that would awaken Rachel and Micah.
As Isaac gulped the milk, Zetta stroked his downy head.
"Father God, you know I'm awful worried about Luttrell," she softly prayed. "Please pull the poison out of his leg.

Please don't take him from us."

She listened, wanting some heavenly sign. But she heard only the taunts of blue jays and the calls of doves awaiting the rising sun.

Suddenly, the birds were silent.

As Zetta turned toward the window, she saw a shadow move.

She jerked her shawl over Isaac. Was Jesse Allen watching me nurse this child? she wondered.

With the shawl still over the baby, Zetta stood up to look more carefully out the window. No one was there. Soon the birds resumed their cries.

*****

With a full tummy and a dry diaper, Isaac quickly fell asleep again. Zetta smiled as she watched his little chest rise and fall with each breath.

I'm glad you sleep good now, she thought. Soon as you start getting teeth in a few months, these easy nights will be long gone.

She tucked the faded green crib quilt around him then reached for her dress from yesterday. She looked out the window again, but saw no one.

With her back to the window, Zetta dressed quickly and pulled her dark hair into a tight bun. As she stepped into the front room, she was startled to see Jim Reed retying the bandana on Luttrell's leg. He greeted her with a raised hand then pointed to Loren who was sprawled on the floor and snoring softly.

She motioned for Jim to follow her into the kitchen.

"When did you get here?" Zetta whispered.

"Couple hours ago," Jim said quietly. "I was worried about Luttrell and figured Loren could use some sleep. Sally and the girls will be along directly."

"Y'all are all the time helping me," Zetta said. "Thank you. How's his leg?"

Jim stepped toward the back door as though not wanting to be overheard.

"Loren's been doing a good job keeping onion and salt on the bite, but the swelling ain't going down," he said. "When I was a boy, one of my uncles got bit. The swelling got so bad, they had to cut open his leg to release pressure. Still didn't help."

Zetta slapped her hand to her mouth to keep from crying out.

"I shouldna told that," Jim said. He glanced around the kitchen as though searching for something encouraging to say. "Well, I'm glad your granny woman friend is showing up today."

Zetta rubbed her forehead. "Yes. Clarie. She'll be on the morning train. I better get y'all some breakfast now."

* * * * *

As Zetta pulled the skillet of browned biscuits from the oven, Loren came into the kitchen.

"Where's Jim?"

"He took care of the animals for me, then went home," Zetta said as she turned the biscuits onto a plate. "I couldn't get him to stay for breakfast."

Loren reached for a biscuit. "I ain't staying neither," he said. "Paw's heading this way, and I'm in no mood to talk. Tell him I'm meeting Clarie's train."

Loren hurried to the front room just as Paw Davis dismounted from his mule at the kitchen steps. Zetta opened the door for him.

"Morning, Paw," she said. "You doing all right?"

"I reckon," he said as he stepped inside. "How's your brother?"

"Leg's still bad," she said. "You can check on him whilst I'm fixing his breakfast."

Paw frowned. "This is a sorry mess," he said. "Loren with him?"

"No, he's meeting Clarie's train," Zetta said as she heard the front door close.

"Who's Clarie?"

"The granny woman from the coal camp," Zetta said. "She knows cures."

"You telling me you're letting a stranger tend your brother?"

Zetta tried to keep her hands from trembling as she reached for the eggs. "Clarie's no stranger."

* * * * *

Zetta's father strode out the back door before she finished scrambling the eggs.

"His leg is worse than I figured," he said.

Zetta frowned as she watched him go.

I don't know what ails him at times, she thought. Good thing Luttrell's here instead of with him and Becky.

Zetta spooned the eggs onto a plate and added a buttered biscuit. Oh, Lord, Please help, she prayed as she carried the food into the front room.

There Luttrell was propped up on his elbows and staring at his swollen and discolored flesh.

"Have you ever seen a more useless leg?" he said.

Zetta held out the plate, but remembered Asa's mangled leg as he and her brothers waited for the camp train to take him to the Lexington hospital. The journey he didn't survive.

"Let me help you sit up a little more," she said. "Or would you druther I feed you?"

Luttrell shook his head. "I shouldna said that. Especially since you surely remember Asa's leg. But I'm supposed to be taking care of you. Not the other way around."

"I reckon we always been taking care of each other," Zetta said. "It's just my turn to take care of you now. But you gotta eat a little something before Clarie gets here."

Luttrell nodded. "True enough. Once she shows up, there won't be no arguing."

Then he smiled weakly. "Not that I'll want to."

* * * * *

As Zetta handed coffee to Luttrell, the call of "Hello in the cabin" rang out.

Luttrell frowned as he turned to his sister.

Zetta nodded. "That's Jesse Allen all right. I'll see what he wants. But I'm tired of him thinking he can show up like this."

Jesse was standing in the yard. He pulled off his hat as Zetta stepped out the door.

"What'da want this time?" she said.

"Now is that any way to greet somebody who just come by to offer help?" Jesse said. "I was at the store and heard Ben telling about Luttrell. How's he doing?"

Zetta put her hands behind her back, wishing Loren hadn't left. "He's getting along good. And your help ain't needed. Or wanted."

"Well, what about the plowing?"

"Finished yesterday," Zetta said. "When you was skulking around the house this morning, you should've seen it was."

"Zetta, why you always accusing me like that?" Jesse said. "I told you before I come to the front yard when I come calling."

"And I told you before you ain't welcome here."

"You're still carrying a grudge," he said. "And from childhood at that. Now we gotta help each other. Especially as we figure out what to do about the chestnut trees."

"Nobody's gonna bother my trees," Zetta said. "They're sluggish now. But they'll be better next year."

Jesse slapped his hat back onto his head and pulled a small white pouch from his shirt pocket.

"You think your trees are just sluggish?" he said as he fumbled in the same pocket and found a pack of thin papers. "Have you looked at 'em? I have. Every single one has that orange canker eating into the wood."

With narrowed eyes, Zetta watched Jesse pour a line of crushed tobacco into the paper and lick one edge to seal the cigarette. As he twisted the ends of the paper, he frowned at Zetta.

"I'm telling you, cutting them might save the rest of your trees up the mountain."

Zetta looked at the white blossoms of the apple and pear trees Asa had planted near the gate in honor of Rachel's and Micah's births. She pulled in a deep breath, wishing he was the one dealing with this problem.

"And I'm telling you, nobody is cutting my trees," she said, feigning calmness. "Now you and me is done talking."

Jesse snapped his thumbnail against a matchstick and lit the cigarette before answering.

"You're wrong, Zetta," he said. "You ain't getting rid of me that easy."

He smirked as he took a long draw off the cigarette. Just then, Sally and her daughters opened the gate. Each one carried a small bucket.

Jesse touched the brim of his hat in greeting.

"Morning, lovely ladies," he said.

Sally and Abigail ignored his comment, but Deborah giggled. She was quickly silenced by her mother's frown.

Jesse took another deep pull from the cigarette before flicking it onto the ground in front of the women.

"Whilst y'all are here, try to talk some sense into Zetta about the trees," he said. And he strode out the gate.

Without comment, Sally crushed the smoldering flame with her shoe.

* * * * *

Zetta stepped back and gestured toward her front door.

"I'm glad y'all come over just now," she said to her visitors. "I don't know why Jesse Allen thinks he can all the time show up."

"Some men think *no* don't apply to them, I reckon," Sally said.

Then she held up her bucket. "We brung seed beans and onion sets, so we'll go around the back and finish the garden, if that's all right. Jim said for us not to be disturbing Luttrell."

Zetta smiled. "I told him this morning, y'all are all the time helping. And here ya go again."

"Well, between him worrying over Luttrell and fretting about Norrie not answering letters, he wudn't sleeping a bit," Sally said as she motioned Abigail and Deborah forward. "Coming over here give him something he could do."

I understand needing to *do*, Zetta thought as she watched them go. I just wish my *doing* turned out better.

Chapter 10

As Zetta spooned gravy over scrambled eggs for Rachel and Micah, she looked out the window. Sally and her daughters were dusting off their hands as they stepped from the garden. She quickly opened the kitchen door.

"Don't tell me y'all are finished already," Zetta said.

Sally smiled. "Three women know how to get things done! And we finished before the bees got too ambitious."

Zetta gestured toward the porch bench. "I already got a pan of water waiting," she said. "After y'all wash your hands, come on in."

"Sure enough," Sally said as she started up the steps. "How's Luttrell?"

"About the same," Zetta said. "But he didn't eat much. Maybe he will with Clarie here."

"I'm looking forward to meeting her," Sally said as she dipped her hands into the water and reached for the chunk of lye soap. "I'm just sorry it's because of a copperhead."

"I don't like how his leg is still swelling," Zetta said as she handed a towel to Sally. "But Jim probably told you."

"In fact, he did," Sally said. Then she saw Abigail and Deborah put their hands into the pan of water at the same time.

"Y'all know better than that," she said. "Wait your turns.

And don't be wiping your hands on the same towel at the same time. Otherwise, y'all will get in a quarrel."

Abigail quickly pulled her hands from the water. "I'm sorry, Mama. I forgot."

But Deborah rolled her eyes. "Those old tales don't mean a thing," she said.

"What you think about 'em don't mean they ain't true," Sally said.

Then she turned back to Zetta. "We was talking about Jim. He told me to tell you he saw a stray cat go in your barn this morning. She's about to have kittens, but your two little cats didn't have any problem with her being there."

"I hope she meanders on," Zetta said as she held the kitchen door for Sally. "I've got enough critters for the time being."

* * * * *

As Sally and her daughters pulled out chairs from the table, Abigail smiled at Rachel and Micah before she sat down.

Zetta gestured toward the stove. "The coffee's still hot if you want some," she said.

Sally shook her head. "We're just fine. So don't think about waiting on us. Go see if Luttrell needs anything."

Just then Zetta saw Loren guiding his wagon to the side of the cabin. Clarie was beside him. Her silver hair was in its familiar braid and tightly bound at the nape of her neck.

"They're here!" Zetta said as she hurried to the back porch.

As the wagon approached the steps, Clarie returned Zetta's smile.

"There's my girl," Clarie called. "I've been missing you."

As Zetta watched the wagon come closer, she saw the worn black satchel on the bench beside Clarie. The same bag she'd had when she helped Isaac come into the world.

Thank you, Lord. Everything's gonna be all right now, Zetta silently prayed as Loren set the brake and jumped down to help Clarie from the wagon.

As Clarie thrust her walking stick into the dirt and leaned on Loren's arm, Zetta was struck at how the older woman had aged in the less than two months since they had parted. But she hurried down the steps and threw her arms around Clarie as Loren reached for the black satchel. Her hug was heartily returned.

But before either woman could speak, Loren yelled.

"Dadgummit!"

"Loren! Watch your mouth!" Zetta said.

"Watch my mouth, nothing!" he yelled. "I just got stung by a dadgum bee!"

Clarie surveyed the yard and gestured to a small patch of weeds beside the cabin.

"Loren, hush! Get over here!" she said. "Grab you a leaf from three different plants."

"What'd ya talking about?"

Clarie pointed to the weeds again. "Do like I said. That sting is gonna start swelling."

Loren shrugged. "How big of leaves?" he said.

"Don't matter. Just get three different ones and crush 'em together," Clarie said. "Then rub the juice on the sting."

As Loren followed Clarie's instructions, Zetta watched amazement cross his face.

"This beats all," he said. "Clarie, you ain't even in the house yet, and your cures is working already. So you tend Luttrell whilst I tend my mules. And I'll bring your other satchel in directly."

Zetta held Clarie's arm as the woman thrust her walking stick forward and hauled herself slowly up each step.

As Clarie entered the kitchen, Sally and her daughters stood to greet her. But before they could say hello, Rachel threw herself against the woman.

"Miz Clarie!" Rachel shouted.

Clarie wrapped both arms around the child.

"I've missed you a right smart, honey," she said. "That old camp just ain't the same without y'all."

Then she smiled at Micah as he solemnly stared at her. "And look how big you're getting," she said. "I declare!"

Even as Rachel pulled herself out of the hug, she continued to grip Clarie's hand.

"Are you gonna live with us, Miz Clarie?"

"No, honey. I'm just here for a little while to help your uncle," she said. "But first I need to meet these folks."

Zetta pulled Rachel to her side and gestured toward Sally and her daughters.

"Lands, Clarie! I was so busy grinning at you for being here I plumb forgot my manners," Zetta said. "This here is my good neighbor, Sally Reed and her girls, Abigail and Deborah."

As the women smiled and nodded, Sally gripped Clarie's hand.

"I'm right proud to finally meet you, Clarie," she said. "Zetta brags on you all the time."

Clarie patted Sally's hand. "I don't know if I deserve such praise," she said. "But I'm glad to meet y'all, too. Right now, though, I reckon I better get busy."

She stooped awkwardly to pick up the satchel. "Show me where Luttrell's at," she said to Zetta. "And make sure that kettle's got plenty of hot water."

"He's in here," Zetta said as she started toward the front room.

Sally stopped her.

"Y'all are gonna be busy for a while," she said. "So how about we take the youngins back to our place? I'll bring 'em back directly."

As Zetta looked at Rachel and Micah, Abigail leaned toward them. "And I'm fixing to make some coco milk," she said. "Reckon you know anybody who might like to help me?"

Both children nodded eagerly and took her outstretched hands.

Zetta looked at Sally. "Thank you. Again. Maybe one of these days I can do something for y'all."

Sally patted Zetta's arm and pointed toward the front room.

* * * * *

Clarie's slow steps allowed Zetta to catch up with her. Even as the older woman approached Luttrell, she was looking at his leg.

Then she smiled at him.

"Ain't you a sight. I hear tell you tangled with a copperhead."

Luttrell nodded. "Yep. But I got the raw end of the deal."

"Well, I'm here now," she said. "How'd you sleep last night?"

"Not good," Luttrell said. "I reckon I kept thinking about everything that happened. And wondering what's ahead."

"I figured as much," Clarie said. "Whilst I'm tending to the bite, you're gonna drink some of my sleeping tea."

"You ain't gonna cut my leg open?" Luttrell said.

"Not if I can help it," Clarie said as she pulled her familiar blue apron from the satchel. Then she smiled as she unwrapped the bandana covering Luttrell's wound.

* * * * *

When Zetta gave the requested cup of hot water to Clarie, the older woman pushed a small white pouch in.

"When this here is the right color, you need to drink it right down," she said to Luttrell. "It'll let you sleep and let me concentrate on your leg."

"The tea reminds me of what you give me after Isaac was born," Zetta said. "I never in my life slept as deep as that night."

"It gets the job done, all right," Clarie said. "Sleep's a great medicine, so I always start with that."

"What all is in it?"

"Oh, this and that," Clarie said. "Things like wild roses from up the mountain. And lavender. I had to send away for the seeds. And mums and geraniums from my garden, along with some other petals."

"I can't imagine flowers in that dirty old camp," Zetta said.

Clarie nodded. "Y'all weren't there long enough to see my summer patch," she said. "I planted everything behind my cabin trying to keep the coal dust down. I don't reckon planting my flowers back there really helps, but at least I feel better about trying."

She glanced at the tea. "It's plenty dark now," she said.

As Zetta helped Luttrell sit up and drink the tea, Clarie gently touched the skin around the snake bite. Then she pulled a pouch about the size of her two hands from her satchel. Holding it above a wash pan, she poured hot water over it.

"Is that the same poultice you used for Jack's foot?" Zetta asked.

"Some of the plants are the same, like the ginseng and wild rose for pain and swelling," Clarie said. "But for snake bite I've always put in violet plants from my garden and tobacca leaves from a farmer over near Hazard."

"All we did was use salt and onion," Zetta said as she helped Luttrell lie down again.

"Doing that first was the right thing," Clarie said.

She nodded at Luttrell. "Soon as I took off the bandana and saw the onion black as coal, I knew it had been pulling the poison out. It'll take a few days, but you are gonna be all right. Now quit worrying and go to sleep."

* * * * *

By the time Clarie finished retying the bandana over the poultice, Luttrell was sleeping soundly. Zetta watched as the older woman put her hand on his forehead.

"He's doing good so far," Clarie whispered as she turned toward the kitchen. "We'll keep doing what we can and leave the real healing up to the good Lord. Now whilst he's sleeping, I reckon I could do with some coffee. The train left the camp pretty early."

"I'll fry a couple eggs," Zetta said. "And biscuits and gravy's left from this morning."

"I won't say no to that," Clarie said as she pulled out a chair. "Being in your kitchen again reminds me of those camp mornings when you'd serve sweets to me and Dosha and Polly. I know you hated being there, but I'd give anything to have those days back."

Zetta sighed. "I just wanted us home. Well, I'm here. But Asa ain't. And nothing is ever gonna be the same."

Before Clarie answered, Loren opened the back door.

"Here's your other satchel, Clarie," he said. "How's Luttrell?"

"Sleeping good," she said. "And the poultice is doing its job. How's your bee sting?"

Loren showed his arm. "Can't even tell it happened," he said.

"Just remember about crushing three different leaves," Clarie said. "I reckon bees is all fired up since they ain't got the chestnut blossoms this year."

Loren nodded. "Yep, we're gonna have to make some decisions on our trees soon."

Then he turned toward the front room. "But right now I'm more interested in getting Luttrell well."

* * * * *

Isaac awakened just as Zetta served Clarie a hearty breakfast. As the two women talked, Zetta nursed Isaac and asked questions about the camp. But Clarie's answers were vague.

"You know I wrote you about there being less and less work," she said between mouthfuls. "Things is going on that I don't like. And I'm still trying to figure everything out."

Zetta watched her friend wipe the plate with the last bite of biscuit. *Clarie's not telling me something,* she thought as she put a well-fed Isaac against her shoulder. As Zetta patted the little back, Clarie smiled.

"I'm sorry Luttrell got snake bit, but seeing you is doing me a world of good," Clarie said. "And I love it when I see my girls with plenty of good milk for their babies."

As Isaac released a hearty burp, Zetta saw Abigail coming up the back steps. The young woman looked frightened.

Clutching Isaac with one arm, Zetta jerked open the door. "Are the youngins all right?" she asked, trying not to panic.

"Yes. Yes. They're fine," Abigail stammered. "But Mama asked if Miz Clarie could come help us. If Luttrell don't need her."

"What's wrong?" Zetta asked.

Abigail's eyes filled with tears.

"Daddy's sister just showed up. With her baby."

"Norrie? Here?"

Abigail nodded. "They're both bad off. Especially the baby."

Chapter 11

Zetta looked to Clarie for an answer as the older woman pulled herself up from the table.

"Tell your mother we'll be there quick as we can," Clarie said.

Then she turned to Abigail. "No, you come in for a minute whilst I check Luttrell's poultice. Then you can tote my satchel to your house. It gets kindly heavy when I'm trying to hurry."

Zetta shifted Isaac to her other arm and held the door open.

"Will Luttrell be all right without y'all here?" Abigail asked as she stepped inside.

"He's sound asleep right now," Zetta said. "Besides, Loren's with him. Come see for yourself."

Abigail timidly followed Zetta into the front room as Clarie repositioned the poultice.

"He's coming along good," Clarie whispered. "His leg ain't as swollen as before. In fact, when he wakes up in a few hours, I bet he's gonna be hungry. That'll be a good sign."

Loren motioned Abigail forward. "No need to hang back," he said. "Luttrell sure ain't dead."

Zetta saw new tears in the young woman's eyes. "I know," Abigail said. "But snake bites are awful. Daddy's been telling us about one of his uncles that got bit."

"His uncle didn't have Clarie around," Loren said. "This here boy is gonna be just fine."

"Don't be giving me undeserved credit," Clarie said as she handed her satchel to Abigail.

"We'll just keep doing what we can do. And keep asking for the good Lord's help."

* * * * *

As the three women approached the Reed's kitchen steps, Sally jerked open the door.

"Norrie showed up out of the blue, plumb puny," she said. "And the baby is worse off."

"We're here now," Clarie said as she pulled herself up the steps. "Boil me plenty of water."

As they stepped into the kitchen, Zetta took in the scene in one glance. Norrie, disheveled and dirty, sat at the table holding the too-quiet baby wrapped in a soiled blanket. Jim stood next to his sister, gripping her shoulder.

As Zetta said, "Oh, Norrie," Rachel and Micah ran in from the front room to clutch their mother's legs. Deborah and her brother Bernard followed them.

Clarie turned to Abigail and gestured toward the table. "Put my satchel right here," she said. "And fill your largest wash pan with warm water."

Then she reached for the baby. Norrie hesitated for a moment, but released her hold as she looked into Clarie's kind face.

As Sally and Abigail scurried to follow orders, Clarie began to unwrap the baby. "What's this child's name?" she said.

"Adah," Norrie said as she looked at Jim. "Calvin wanted a boy, so he didn't care what name I give her. So I named her after our mother."

"How's your milk?" Clarie asked as she continued to unwrap the baby.

Norrie began to sob. "I'm all dried up from the walking

and hiding from Calvin," she managed. "Adah cried at first, then got all quiet like this."

Holding the now naked baby in her left arm, Clarie pulled a glass jar from her satchel and held it toward Norrie.

"Your milk is gonna come back in after you drink some of this," she said.

She handed the jar to Sally. "Make the tea strong. Now where's that wash pan?"

Abigail pointed to the gray pan on the bench near the stove. "I filled it with warm water, like you said."

Clarie nodded and put her elbow into the water to check the temperature.

"That's just right," she said. "Now get me a dipper of water and a spoon."

As Clarie lowered dirty little Adah into the pan, she gently sloshed water over the listless body.

"The tea's ready," Sally said. "Strong, like you said."

Clarie turned to the still sobbing Norrie. "Quit your crying and drink every bit of this."

"What is it?" Norrie asked between jagged breaths.

"Red raspberry and other plants to make your milk come in," Clarie said. "Drink it all."

As Norrie began to drink, Abigail held the dipper toward Clarie. She put the spoon into the water and then to Adah's mouth. She smiled as the baby swallowed the few drops.

"Her little lips is moving, wanting more," Clarie said. "Somebody get me a towel to wrap this child in. She's gonna be all right."

Clarie turned to Zetta, who held a sleeping Isaac as his siblings still clutched her leg.

"Zetta, sit down," she said. "You're the one who can help this youngin now."

Then she turned to Jim. "I reckon you and your boy got things to do in the barn."

He looked bewildered. But as Clarie tapped her own chest and then pointed at Zetta, Jim stammered, "Yes. Come on, Bernard. This is up to the women now."

He pushed Bernard out the door despite the boy's question of "What they gonna do?"

Tears rolled down Norrie's cheeks. "I can't feed my own baby," she wailed. "I'm a no account mother."

"No. You're a good mother because no matter what, you want your baby's life saved," Clarie said. "Now you finish that tea and go to bed. Sleep will help your milk come in faster, and you won't have to see another woman nursing your baby."

As Sally and Deborah led Norrie from the room, Zetta handed Isaac to Abigail. The young woman smiled at Micah and Rachel.

"Let's all go play in the front room," she said. "I've got a brand new story to tell you."

Both children scrambled after her.

Zetta watched them go as she unbuttoned her dress. "But I just nursed Isaac," she said. "What if I ain't got enough milk yet?"

"You've got enough to fill this tiny belly," Clarie said. And she placed the baby in Zetta's arms.

* * * * *

Sally came into the kitchen as Zetta pulled Adah close. She took a deep breath. "I can't begin to tell you how much you doing this means to us."

"It's about time I helped," Zetta said as she stroked the baby's head. "Goodness knows y'all been helping me plenty."

Sally gestured for Clarie to sit. "And you knowing just what to do," she said. "I wish we could do something for you."

Clarie sank into the chair. "I'm doing all right. My old bones need to be useful now and again," she said. "How's Norrie? She's had a time."

"She's asleep. And about as soon as her head hit the pillow," Sally said. "All she muttered was they was safe. Jim couldn't believe it when he saw her stumbling toward him."

"How long's she been walking?" Clarie asked.

"I don't rightly know," Sally said. "She hid with the baby in a cave near their place for a while, trying to figure out what to do. She'd put some food and diapers there, knowing Calvin was getting meaner. Finally, she come here."

Clarie nodded. "There's no better place than with folks who love you."

* * * * *

Loren stepped from the spring house as Zetta and the others approached the back porch. Rachel and Micah ran to hug their uncle, and he set the water bucket down.

"Well, don't y'all look like a ragtag bunch," he said. "Sis, you brung more folks back than you left with."

"This here is Norrie's baby," Zetta said as she gestured toward the sleeping bundle in Abigail's arms. "And Deborah's here to help, too. How's Luttrell?"

"Awake and wanting cold water and something to eat," Loren said. "I'm glad you're back. I was starting to think I was gonna have to conjure up a meal for him."

Zetta smiled. "You saying you was fixing to do women's work?"

"Don't be accusing me of that," Loren said. "I just was gonna get some vittles in him."

He nodded toward Adah as though wanting to change the subject. "Hey, Clarie. How come you brung that youngin back here?"

"Norrie's wore out. So the baby is better off with Zetta for a while," Clarie said. "Did Luttrell use the chamber pot yet?"

"Yep. I helped him when he woke up," Loren said. "I thought he never was gonna stop."

"Good. His body is healing," Clarie said. "Soon as we take care of him and the babies, I need some time with Zetta. We been so busy I ain't yet told my sad news from the camp."

Zetta looked at her quickly. But Clarie shook her head. "Bad news can wait," she said. "Now help me up these steps."

Chapter 12

As Zetta and Abigail lowered both babies into Isaac's crib, Adah awakened and made mewing sounds. Zetta reached for her and settled into the rocker near the window.

"You know my kitchen about as good as I do," she said as she unbuttoned her dress. "You can help Clarie get some food in Luttrell."

"But what if he don't like what I fix?" Abigail said.

Zetta smiled as she saw Abigail blush. "He'll be glad for anything. Just follow whatever Clarie says."

"We can hear you out here," Clarie said. "And Luttrell said eggs will do, and a biscuit, if they's any left. I know you can fry eggs."

Abigail took a deep breath. "I sure enough can," she said. "I'll be right there."

And she smoothed her hair before she left the bedroom.

* * * * *

Zetta nursed Adah for just a few minutes before the baby drifted into exhausted sleep.

"You poor little thing," she said as she placed Adah next to Isaac again.

As Zetta stepped into the front room, Abigail came from

the kitchen with a plate of eggs and a biscuit. They both waited as Clarie poured hot water onto the poultice and repositioned it over the bite.

"Where's the youngins?" Zetta asked.

"Deborah's got 'em out in the yard, looking for feathers," Loren answered. "I swear, these Reed girls are as handy as a pocket on a shirt."

Zetta smiled at Abigail. "Y'all are at that," she said. And she was pleased Abigail blushed again.

Clarie gestured for Loren to step closer to his brother. "Luttrell, we're gonna help you sit up now," she said. "But a copperhead bite makes a person plumb weak, so don't move too fast."

"My leg burns like fire, so I'm not arguing," Luttrell said as Loren slowly pulled him into a sitting position.

"Well, you're on the mend now," Clarie said.

"How long's he gonna have to lay low?" Loren asked.

"I don't righty know yet," Clarie said. "But it helps that the snake had to bite through his pant leg to get to the skin."

She touched Luttrell's shoulder. "Even so, don't get any notions about running footraces. You still need to rest."

Luttrell nodded. "Like I said, I'm not arguing."

* * * * *

Zetta and Clarie watched Abigail give Luttrell the plate of food before she hurried outside to join Deborah and the children. Then Clarie turned to Loren.

"We'll let you tend your brother whilst he eats," she said. "But holler if he needs us." And she motioned for Zetta to follow her into the kitchen.

As Clarie eased into a chair, Zetta poured coffee for them both. "You said you have bad news from the camp."

Clarie ran her hand across the worn wood of the table. "Yes. I guess I'll start with Polly."

"Is she all right?" Zetta asked as she sat across from her friend.

"I'm afraid not," Clarie said. "Right after I wrote you, her baby come too early. A tiny little boy that didn't live two minutes. He died right in my hands."

"Oh! That's awful."

"Polly knew the baby wudn't crying, and she kept begging me to tell her everything was all right," Clarie said. "Instead, I just put that little body in her arms and told her Jesus was taking care of him now."

Tears rolled down Zetta's cheeks. "Oh, Clarie. I'm so sorry."

"And it just got worse," Clarie said. "Perton come in from the mine about then, so I had to tell him. But instead of going in to comfort his wife, he just did a lot of cussing and took off on a drunk."

"That sure sounds like him."

Clarie stirred her black coffee. "Remember the morning I brung Polly by to meet you?" she said. "She asked me if I ever had a baby die. It was like she knowed things wudn't right."

"I remember," Zetta said. "Dosha was all happy, but Polly seemed worn out even then."

Clarie nodded. "And when her little baby died, she was ready to give up. Perton wudn't around to help her, so I took that poor girl up to my place. Fed her good and made sure she had plenty of sleeping tea. And I let her talk about the baby. About how she loved it right from the start. And how happy she had been that she was gonna have somebody to love her back."

"Does Dosha know?"

"Yes. In fact, when I sent her the news, she wrote right away and insisted Polly stay with her and Jack for a while over at the Hindman School," Clarie said. "I got one of the men to take us over there. Seeing Dosha and Jack was a good tonic for Polly. For me, too. Now that she's there, I'm hoping she grows a backbone and stands up to Perton."

"I hope so, too," Zetta said as she wiped her eyes. "Who took y'all over there? Leroy?"

"No. With the mine not doing good, he was let go," Clarie said. "Him and all the other colored men. They always get the short end of the stick. I wrote you about things being bad. Well, they keep getting worse."

"What about LeRoy's mother?"

"Ruthie had to leave, too. There weren't no colored babies to help into the world at the camp, so she couldn't stay. She was the closest friend my age I had there. I sure do miss her."

"What about the other miners?" Zetta asked.

"More and more of them is out of work, too," Clarie said. "Some go home to their mountain kin. Some try to get on at another mine or find pitiful jobs in town since they still owe the camp store. And some of 'em work with a company that's coming through and cutting the blighted chestnut trees. They think cutting some trees will save other ones. But I don't see it's making any difference."

"What'd ya gonna do if the mine closes?" Zetta said.

Clarie smoothed her apron across her lap. "I don't rightly know," she said. "All my adult life I've been taking care of miners' wives. Now and again, I ponder going over to Hindman. I need to be around young folks, and maybe the school can use me somehow. Besides, it would be good to be with Dosha and Jack again."

"I can't picture you not being in your sweet cabin," Zetta said.

Clarie took a deep breath. "Me neither. I don't like the way things are going, and I probably won't like how they finally turn out," she said. "But I notice the good Lord ain't in the habit of asking me how things should go in this tough life. So I'll keep putting one foot in front of the other and trusting him to somehow bring his good out of our troubles."

* * * * *

Their noon dinner that day consisted of leftovers from the previous day's plowing. As Zetta covered the remaining food with vinegar dampened cloths, the Reed sisters washed the dishes.

"I can't believe everybody was here just yesterday," Zetta said. "With everything that's been happening, it seems like a week ago now."

"Daddy's always saying the older he gets, the faster time goes," Abigail said.

"I agree with him on that," Clarie said as she stepped into the kitchen with Rachel and Micah. "In fact, some days I get up in the morning and don't much more than turn around and it's time to go to bed. But that sure beats sitting by myself and staring at four walls."

"You'd never do that," Zetta said.

Clarie smiled. "And I sure don't want to ever start."

She nodded toward the front room. "Luttrell's sleeping now, and Loren's still sitting right there with him. We best go check on Norrie. I know she's fretting about her baby."

"That's good timing," Abigail said as she dried the last plate. "I'll get Adah."

As Abigail left the room, Deborah tossed the dishpan of water into the patch of weeds near the back porch. She hung the pan on the kitchen wall, then turned to Clarie.

"Want me to carry your satchel?"

Clarie shook her head as she put a pint jar of herbs into her apron pocket.

"Milk tea is all I'm taking this time," she said. "I'm hoping I won't need it, though."

* * * * *

As the women headed for the Reeds with both babies, Rachel and Micah ran ahead, giggling as they stooped to pick up feathers.

As the group neared the porch, Jim nodded and opened the door. Then he gestured for Bernard to follow him to the barn.

In the kitchen, Norrie, freshly bathed and wearing one of

Sally's dresses, pushed aside her plate of soup beans and cornbread as Abigail held the baby toward her.

"Is she all right?" Norrie asked as she unwrapped the quilt.

"Doing real good," Clarie said. "And you look a right smart better than when we saw you this morning. I reckon you slept good, too."

"I sure did," Norrie said as she kissed Adah. Just then, the baby awakened and cried.

"That's the strongest sound that sweet child has made all day," Zetta said.

"Oh! My milk is back," Norrie said. "Soon as she cried, I felt it drip."

Clarie nodded. "You both are gonna be just fine now."

"Y'all saved our lives," Norrie said as she opened her dress.

"No, honey. The good Lord done that," Clarie said. "We're just glad he let us help."

Tears filled Norrie's eyes. "I been talking to the Lord plenty when I was trying to get here," she said. "Now I need to thank him proper like."

She turned to Sally. "Calvin wouldn't let me go to church. I miss it a right smart. Can I go with you come Sunday? I need to be there and thank the Lord for saving us."

Sally put her hand on Norrie's shoulder. "There's nothing I'd like any better."

* * * * *

After their supper, Zetta lit the kerosene lamp in the front room. Clarie blinked in the brightness then turned to Loren.

"I'm gonna stay with Luttrell," she said. "So you go home and get a good night's rest."

Loren frowned. "Now, Clarie, I can't let you be sleeping on the floor."

"I've spent plenty nights on a pallet tending a birthing

mother," Clarie said. "I don't reckon this will be any different."

"I agree you ain't sleeping on the floor, " Zetta said. "But I got me a idea."

She turned to Loren. "Let's bring Brother and Sister's little bed out here. They can sleep with me in the big bed. If I had half a brain, I would have thought of this before. And kept you and Luttrell off the floor."

"That makes sense," Loren said. "I'll get y'all settled and be back in the morning. But tonight I reckon I better go make amends with Sarah and her folks. I'm dreading that. It'll help if Naomi and her mother ain't around. I hope they had the good sense to hightail it home."

He started toward the bedroom then turned back to Zetta.

"Hey, I forgot to tell you Ben was downright contrary this morning when I stopped at the store for the mail."

"I've seen him get that way a time or two," Zetta said.

"Well, he sure was like that today," Loren said. "He's still sore about my calling his nephew sorry kin yesterday. That man can't take kidding to save his life."

"Are you gonna apologize to him, too?" Zetta asked.

"Nah. Having to grovel to Sarah and her folks is bad enough," Loren said. "I ain't got it in me to do it twice in one day. I'll just stay out of Ben's way for a while. Maybe do something nice for him later. He'll get over it after a while."

"I hope you're right," Zetta said. But her stomach tightened. Ben would not dismiss an insult easily.

Chapter 13

Early the next morning, Zetta was awakened by two-year-old Micah leaning just inches from her face and smiling.

"Hi, sweet boy," she whispered. "Be real quiet so we don't wake everybody else up."

Zetta pulled the quilt over Rachel's shoulders then eased from the bed with Micah. She wrapped her gray shawl over her gown as she watched Isaac's chest rise and fall in deep sleep.

"We'll get ready in the kitchen," she said as she grabbed her dress and Micah's little shirt and overalls. As they stepped into the front room, Clarie was preparing a fresh poultice.

"Morning," she said. "Luttrell had a good night. Didn't even need sleeping tea."

Luttrell raised his hand in greeting as Zetta stepped closer. "Morning, Sis. I'm sorry I'm not much use yet. But I'm getting there."

Zetta put her hand on his shoulder. "Don't be in too much of a hurry. The important thing is you're moving in the right direction."

And she turned away before her brother could see her tears.

* * * * *

Zetta dressed herself and Micah quickly in the kitchen then grabbed the milk bucket and small egg basket before they stepped outside. As she took Micah's hand and started down the porch steps, movement near the oak tree caught her attention.

She turned quickly, but saw no one.

I'm getting tired of Jesse Allen's shenanigans, Zetta thought as Micah pulled away and ran toward a fallen log near the chicken coop.

She was close behind him as he scrambled to stand on top of the log.

"Micah, remember what I showed you and Sister before. Don't be jumping off 'til you look on the other side," Zetta said. "Snakes like being near logs, so always look for 'em."

The toddler studied the ground then turned back to his mother. "No 'nake."

"Good for looking, sweet boy," Zetta said. "Now come back this way so we can milk Brownie and take care of the other critters. Pretty soon you'll be doing this all by yourself."

"Me a big boy."

"Yes, you're Mama's big boy," Zetta said as she clasped his hand. But she took a deep breath. Asa, you should be here to teach him how to watch for copperheads and take care of farm critters, she thought. How am I gonna teach our little boys to grow into men all by myself?

* * * * *

When the barn chores were finished, Micah took wobbly steps as he kept his eyes on the few eggs in the small basket he carried. His mother carried the bucket of milk.

"Keep your eyes on what's in front of you, not on what's in your hands," Zetta said. "You'll be less apt to stumble that way."

Micah nodded, but kept staring at the eggs.

As they reached the steps, Zetta took the basket from the child.

"You worked hard," she said. "I reckon you're ready for some breakfast now."

Micah smiled and bounded ahead. Then he waited for Zetta to nudge open the kitchen door with her hip.

Clarie straightened from putting a skillet of biscuits into the oven as they entered.

"I hope you don't mind I started breakfast," Clarie said. "I figured I can't feed little Isaac but I can fix biscuits and fry eggs."

"There's not a thing you could do that I'd mind," Zetta said as she set the egg basket and milk bucket on the sideboard.

Rachel ran into the kitchen as she heard her mother's voice.

"Come look, Mama," she said as she tugged on Zetta's hand. "I'm helping Uncle tend Baby Isaac."

Clarie chuckled as she pointed beyond the door.

"Wait 'til you see what's going on in there."

With Micah gripping her other hand, Zetta allowed Rachel to pull her into the front room. There Luttrell was sitting up with Isaac in one arm and Rachel's rag doll in the other. Isaac was staring at Luttrell instead of howling for his breakfast.

Zetta smiled at her brother. "You're a sight. I'd give a pretty if Loren could see this."

Luttrell returned her smile. "I'd sure appreciate you not telling him. He'd never let me live it down."

"I'll keep your secret," Zetta said as she reached for Isaac. "But I'm gonna remember this sweet scene."

Then she turned to her toddlers. "Let's go visit with Miz Clarie in the kitchen, and let your uncle be for a while."

"I'm feeling better, Sis," Luttrell said. "Let 'em play in here. They'll be good company."

Zetta studied her brother's face. The skin's color was back to normal. "All right. But if they get too rambunctious, holler."

Zetta watched Micah scurry for his blocks and Rachel

reach for her rag doll. Then she took Isaac into the kitchen.

"Clarie, you've made all the difference in the world for us," Zetta said as she settled into a chair and opened her dress. "Luttrell's coming along real good, thanks to you."

"Like I said before, I'm glad to be here," Clarie said. "Especially since I'm not much use at the camp right now. Besides, I'm happy to help a good man like Luttrell."

Zetta pulled Isaac close. "He's that, all right. Did I tell you he give me his mule when I said I can't keep letting him and Loren tote our mail and carry us to church?"

"You tried all riding together yet?" Clarie said.

"No. But I got it all figured out," Zetta said.

"Tell you what," Clarie said. "After we eat, and Isaac sleeps, you try it with Rachel and Micah."

Zetta listened to Micah noisily knocking down his stacked blocks. And she nodded.

* * * * *

After breakfast, Zetta led the mule to the front porch where Micah and Rachel, clutching her rag doll, stood next to Clarie. Both children bounced with excitement. An old brown quilt covered the animal's back.

"This here is Jack," Zetta said to the children as she climbed the steps with the reins in her hand. "And this is his first time having all of us ride him, so I need you to be good. You hear?"

Both children immediately stopped wiggling.

Zetta gently took Rachel's rag doll from the child and handed it to Clarie.

"Sister, I'm gonna put you on Jack's back first," Zetta said. "And you are gonna sit real still whilst I hand you your rag baby and you play like you are holding Isaac real careful."

The child looked at Zetta with wide eyes.

"You're gonna do just fine," Zetta said. "Then whilst you hold your rag baby in your lap, I'm gonna put Brother up right behind you. After that, I get on behind him and take your rag baby from you just like I'll be taking Isaac when we do this for real. You ready?"

At Rachel's somber nod, Zetta swung her onto the broad back of the animal.

"Good. Now use one hand to hang onto Jack's hair on the back of his head," Zetta said. "It's called a mane."

"You're doing a good job explaining," Clarie said as she held the rag doll toward Zetta.

"I appreciate that," Zetta said as she took the doll and handed it to Rachel. "But all this already is wearing me out."

Clarie nodded. "Well, life's rigamarole is a little easier, especially for children, when we know what's around the next bend."

Zetta turned to Micah. But he took a step back.

"Don't be that way, Brother. Come here."

Micah slowly approached his mother, and she swung him up behind Rachel.

"You hold tight to Sister. Don't squirm now."

Zetta studied both children then thrust her left leg over the mule's back and pulled herself upright.

"No, don't be turning around," she said as both children twisted toward her. "Just keep holding on. Now Sister, I'm gonna take your rag baby from you just like I'll do when you're holding Isaac."

When Zetta placed the rag doll in the crook of her left arm, she turned to Clarie. "This is harder than I reckoned it would be."

"That's like most things in life, honey. But you're doing a real good job," Clarie said. "Where you headed now? The store?"

"No. I'll wait on that for a while," Zetta said. "I don't want a bunch of folks watching us this first time."

"I sure understand that. And when you get back, we'll do a washing," Clarie said. "When I changed Isaac this morning I seen he's about out of diapers."

Zetta smiled. "We'll be doing a washing like we done together at the camp. All we need now is Dosha."

And she gently nudged the mule's sides with her heels.

* * * * *

As Jack eased forward, Rachel grabbed his mane with both hands. But Micah looked back at his mother and grinned.

"Brother, you better be hanging on Sister real tight," Zetta said. "Don't be falling off!"

Micah uttered a quiet noise that sounded like a complaint, but he leaned against Rachel as they plodded past the Reed's cabin. Zetta glanced toward the front porch, grateful no one seemed to witness their first trip. But as the mule neared the cemetery, a black stallion roared toward them. Jesse Allen was on his back.

Zetta quickly pulled on Jack's reins with one hand and thrust her other arm around the children. As she did so, Rachel's rag doll fell to the ground.

As Jesse pulled his horse to a stop, Zetta felt Jack quivering beneath her knees. But he remained quiet.

Jesse, still holding his horse's reins, quickly dismounted, swooped up the rag doll and handed it to Rachel.

"Here you go, little 'un," he said. "You better be hanging on to this a mite tighter."

Zetta bit her lower lip before saying, "Sister, what'da say to Mr. Jesse?"

"Thank you, Mr. Jesse," came the child's whisper. But she turned back toward her mother and frowned.

Zetta, knowing the child was upset that her rag baby had been dropped, tried to keep her voice level as she turned to Jesse.

"You liked to have scared the living daylights out of us," she said. "What'd you doing riding like that?"

"Blacko likes running," Jesse said as he pushed back his hat. "Besides, I wudn't expecting to find y'all out and about. Where you heading?"

"I don't reckon that's your business."

"Like it or not, Zetta, everything you do is my business."

Zetta pulled in a long breath through her nose, then pushed it out through her mouth as she pondered scolding him for spying earlier that morning. But she decided he would deny such action. Again.

Thus, she forced herself to say calmly, "Well, I reckon we both got places to be."

Jesse held up his hand. "Don't be so quick to run off," he said. "Actually, I was on my way to your place to tell you a tree crew is in Floyd County. After they finish with the blighted trees there, they'll be moving this way. Probably won't be for three, maybe four weeks, though. Me and some of the men already started cutting my trees and burning the worst ones. You better be thinking about cutting yours, too."

"I told you nobody's touching them," Zetta said. "Whatever is ailing them will clear up next year. Besides, I hear tell trees is being cut near Hazard, and it ain't helping a bit."

"Well, I sure was giving you credit for more sense than that," Jesse said. "But I reckon you are about as shortsighted as Asa was."

Zetta stiffened her back. "You got no business saying that, Jesse Allen."

"Is that a fact? There y'all are on one sorry-looking mule," he said. "I recollect how Asa sold his wagon and team before he went to work coal. Said he'd buy even better when he got back. He ought to see you now."

As Zetta struggled to respond, Jesse mounted Blacko and slapped his hat against the horse's flank.

Chapter 14

As Zetta and the children approached their cabin after the ride, they could see Clarie sitting on the front porch. She stood as the mule plodded into the yard.

"Isaac and Luttrell is still sleeping, so I reckoned I'd wait out here," Clarie said. "How'd y'all do?"

Zetta guided the mule closer to the porch. "It went all right, I reckon," she said as she dismounted and pulled Micah from the animal's back. As she reached for Rachel, the little girl frowned at her then looked at Clarie.

"Mama dropped my rag baby."

Zetta set Rachel onto the porch and knelt in front of her.

"Sister, I told you I'm sorry that happened. But Mr. Jesse's horse scared me pretty bad when he come at us like he did. Your rag baby ain't hurt none. So don't be complaining so."

"But you dropped her right in the dirt," Rachel said.

Clarie sat down again and held out her arms. "Come here, Child. Let me make sure your rag baby is all right."

Rachel rushed to Clarie and gently put her doll into the woman's lap.

Clarie smoothed the doll's dress. "See now? Your rag baby ain't none the worse for wear. She just needs you to rock her real gentle like for a while. You feel like doing that?"

As Rachel smiled and pulled the doll close, Clarie looked at Zetta. "Sounds like y'all had some excitement," she said.

Zetta nodded. "There's this feller that's all the time hanging around. When he rode up on his fancy horse like he did, I grabbed Sister and Brother to make sure they didn't fall. That's when I dropped her rag baby."

"Who's this feller?" Clarie said as she pulled Micah onto her lap.

"Just somebody me and Asa went to school with. And the whole time we was growing up, he was always pestering and picking fights."

"This feller sweet on you?"

Zetta's face reddened. "He says so. But I don't trust him as far as I can pick him up and throw him."

Clarie rubbed Micah's back as she looked at the young mother. "You've heard me say that when your mind ain't sure of something then listen to what your gut is saying. If your stomach hurts every time you think of that person, listen real close. But…."

Zetta waited a moment then said, "But *what*? Go ahead and say what you're thinking."

"All right. But you are early in your grief, so you don't want to hear this," Clarie said. "Yes, trust your gut when it comes to knowing the truth about folks, but in the same breath I don't want you to build a fence so high around your heart that you rob yourself of a sweet future."

"You ain't even met this feller, and you're taking his side!" Zetta said. "I'm telling you, he ain't to be trusted."

"I ain't taking his side," Clarie said. "Like you said, I don't know him at all. I'm just saying that whilst you're fending off this feller now, don't be shutting out another good man."

Before Zettta could respond, Abigail Reed stepped into the yard.

"Hidy. I hope it's all right that Mama sent me over to see if there's anything I can help with," Abigail said. "She seen you going by on the mule. She was plumb nervous about y'all riding like that, but was glad Baby Isaac wudn't with you, too."

"Well, I thought I'd see how a ride would go," Zetta said as she studied the reins still in her hand. "But I don't rightly know if that was such a good idea."

"Mama said to tell you we still got the pony cart Daddy made when we was little," Abigail said. "She'd sure like you to have it. Daddy can fix up the harness."

"That's a better idea than mine, I reckon," Zetta said. "If y'all are sure you don't need the cart, I'd be much obliged."

Abigail smiled. "Mama said to tell you the cart ain't doing nothing right now but collecting dust in the barn."

"Like always, y'all are a big help," Zetta said. But she was eager to change the subject from the disastrous practice ride. "How's Norrie and little Adah today?"

"They's both eating good. And Aunt Norrie is smiling and talking about being free of Calvin. But that makes Daddy right nervous. He's all the time telling her to stay in the house in case he shows up."

"You reckon Calvin would actually do that?" Zetta said.

Abigail shrugged. "Aunt Norrie says he won't because he knows Daddy will run him off quick. She mostly talks about going to church with us come Sunday since she ain't been allowed since she married. She says the only good that come from Calvin is sweet little Adah."

The three women were silent for a moment but Zetta's thoughts were on what a good man Asa had been to her and their children. Not like Calvin.

"I can understand her longing for church," Clarie said at last. "We ain't had real services at the camp ever since the owner let Preacher Howard go. I miss being together like that a right smart, too."

She tapped her upper lip then said, "Luttrell's getting along good now, so my work here is about finished. But I'd like to stay on a couple more days and go to church with y'all."

She turned to Zetta. "That is if I ain't done wore out my

welcome by saying things I got no call to."

"I'd be right pleased to have you stay as long as you want," Zetta said. "And anything you say always comes from a good heart."

Clarie smiled. "Then let's get that washing going. Where do you keep your kettles?"

* * * * *

Abigail helped fill the two copper kettles—one for washing and one for rinsing—with well water as Clarie built a fire under the larger one. After Zetta brought the dirty clothes and diapers into the side yard, she shaved slivers from a chunk of brown lye soap and sprinkled them into the wash kettle.

After one woman had used a wooden paddle to plunge the clothes up and down in the hot water, another used a second paddle to transfer them to the cold water. From there, two women lifted out the items one by one, rung them out and hung them on the narrow rope lines strung between two nearby trees. Without comment, the women worked quickly while the children sat watching from the kitchen steps. Rachel held her rag doll close, and Micah studied the ants crawling over his bare toes.

When the work was finished, Clarie and Abigail took Rachel and Micah inside as Zetta tipped the rinse water into the fire under the first kettle. Just then Loren walked toward her.

"You sure timed that right," Zetta said. "Ten minutes earlier, I'd asked you to help."

"I'm in such a good mood, I might even have jumped right in with women's work," Loren said as he smiled. "You know why? Because that silly Naomi and her mother went back home, just like I hoped. And they ain't coming back for the wedding neither."

"Sarah okay with that?" Zetta asked as she started up the steps.

"I reckon. She didn't say otherwise," Loren said as he followed. "Me and her is trying to get past all that happened when Luttrell got snake bit."

As he opened the door, Loren looked at his sister. "But Naomi being gone means Sarah needs somebody to stand up with her, and she told me to ask if you'll take Naomi's place."

"Me?"

"Yep. She knows she should be asking in person proper like, but she's staying close to home for now, trying to keep peace with her folks. I don't mind saying that I can't wait for us to be married and living in her granddad's old place, away from her folks."

When Zetta didn't comment right away, Loren ran his hands through his hair.

"Look, I know I shouldn't be so all fired up to get on the mountain," he said. "What with you needing help and all. But I'll try to get down here plenty."

Zetta put her hand on Loren's arm. "You've already got enough to tend to without worrying about me and the youngins. Yes, I'll miss having you around like before, but we'll get by. Right now you need to be thinking about being a good husband to Sarah and a good paw to y'all's coming baby."

Loren grunted. "The baby. I kindly forget about that now and again."

"Well, once Sarah starts showing more, you won't be forgetting," Zetta said as she reached for the door. But Loren stopped her.

"I got something else to tell you," he said. "Whilst I was at Sarah's, she showed me this week's paper."

"So?"

"Well, we're more than a month from when Asa got kilt, but the news is just now being printed. And not even on the front page. Know what is? A women's fancy hat show and who was visiting home folks."

Zetta pulled in a deep breath, remembering that rainy day in the coal camp when Loren had told her Asa was dead.

Loren looked beyond Zetta's shoulder as he continued. "You know Paw ain't never hankered to pay that war price of a dollar-fifty a year for a subscription," he said. "But I still been watching for news about Asa. I even asked Green Wilson a while back how come he ain't wrote nothing about that. Know what he said?"

Zetta merely looked at her brother.

"He claimed Paw didn't want a big write-up," Loren said. "But that's not Paw's call. That's yours."

Zetta forced herself to shrug. "Everybody that cares about us was at his funeral," she said.

But she knew Loren was right. And she wished her father would stop making decisions that should be hers.

Chapter 15

Saturday morning, as Zetta hurried to gather the eggs, she glanced toward the oak tree. No one was there.

But inside the barn, she felt the familiar crawly feeling of being watched. With heart pounding, she looked toward Jack's stall. But a movement in the back corner caught her eye.

Lord, thank you Jack ain't been stole, she inwardly prayed. But this business with Jesse Allen has got to stop. If he's back there, please keep me safe.

Suddenly Rachel and Micah's two kittens bumped against Zetta's ankles, startling her.

Determined to appear calm, she bent to pet the cats.

"Well, little critters, you must be hungry if you're coming out of hiding," she said. "Let's see how much milk Brownie has for us today."

After running her hand along the cow's back in greeting, Zetta positioned the gray enamel bucket and reached for the three-legged stool. Just then a large calico colored cat sauntered by with a dead mouse dangling from its mouth.

"So you're the stray Jim saw before," Zetta said. "Well, I'm glad you're making yourself useful around here."

She glared toward the back corner. "That's more than I can say for some around here."

* * * * *

As Zetta opened the kitchen door after finishing the chores, a sudden wind puffed out the bottom of her dress.

Clarie looked up from washing Rachel's and Micah's hands.

"That wind's carrying rain," Clarie said. "But my knees was telling me the same thing this morning."

Zetta nodded as she hugged the children. "The rain'll be good for the garden. And the tree blossoms. Sarah wanted the redbuds and dogwoods to be in full bloom for the wedding. I reckon she's gonna get her wish."

She nodded toward the front room. "Is Luttrell playing nursemaid again?"

Clarie smiled. "Yes. But he made me swear not to tell Loren. Speaking of Loren, reckon he'll show up today? He acts like he's all barbed wire and gristle, but he sure cares about y'all."

"He does at that," Zetta said. "I just wish him and Sarah hadn't started their family before starting their marriage."

"I've seen that happen more times than I can count," Clarie said. "But getting things twisted up one time don't mean folks will keep twisting 'em up."

Before Zetta could answer, she saw Abigail through the window. She jerked open the door.

"Come in. Come in," Zetta said. "You're out awful early. Norrie and the baby all right?"

Abigail smiled. "They're both doing real good. And Aunt Norrie is all excited about going to church tomorrow. Daddy just sent me over to say he's about got the pony cart all slicked up. And he's added an extra piece of wood in one corner to make a place for Baby Isaac. He'll bring the cart over directly before the rain starts."

Then the young woman looked toward the front room.

"How's Luttrell this morning?" she said quietly.

"He's getting there," Clarie said. "I was about to take

him some breakfast. You can do that whilst I conjure up grub for the rest of us."

Clarie smiled at Zetta. "But I reckon you want to feed Isaac first."

* * * * *

With Clarie and the children bent over eggs, biscuits and gravy, Zetta was in her bedroom nursing Isaac and listening to the conversation in the front room.

"When y'all was at my house talking to Daddy about the plowing day, Loren somehow started talking about battles fought right here, like at Ivy Point," Abigail said to Lutrell. "So I got to thinking about that again and wondered if I could ask you a question."

"I reckon."

"Did any of your people fight back then?"

"A Davis kin," Luttrell said. "Confederate side."

"Did you ever hear tell of him talking about what happened?"

"All I ever knowed was that he made it home all in one piece."

Zetta heard Abigail clear her throat as though unsure how to continue.

"Well, last night after supper, Daddy and Aunt Norrie got to talking about their granddaddy losing his arm at Perryville," Abigail said. "They was telling about him seeing the pile of arms and legs outside the medical tent and begging the doctor not to toss his'n away like that. But that's exactly where his arm wound up."

Zetta heard Luttrell answer slowly. "They ought not tell such things in front of you."

"Oh, if I don't say anything, folks tend to forget I'm around," Abigail said. "Anyway, I wanted to talk to somebody about that war."

Luttrell remained quiet as Zetta heard Abigail rush on.

"When I was in school, all I heard was how the northern

books call it the Civil War, but how it actually should be called the War Between Brothers," she said. "And how Kentucky didn't take official sides, but that didn't stop battles from being right here."

Zetta listened as a moment of silence hung between the couple.

"Them is good things to get settled in your mind," Luttrell said at last. "But don't you reckon you should talk to your paw?"

"I know Daddy won't talk to me about it," Abigail said. "He still thinks of me as his little girl. I appreciate you letting me wonder out loud. I'll be quiet now."

To Zetta's surprise she heard Luttrell say, "You don't have to be quiet around me."

Zetta didn't hear Abigail answer. But she was convinced the girl blushed.

* * * * *

Shortly after Abigail left for home, Jim Reed guided his mule toward Zetta's back steps. The animal was pulling the yellow and green pony cart.

Zetta, still holding Isaac, stepped onto the porch with Rachel and Micah close beside her.

"This beats all, Jim," she said. "I don't know that I've ever seen a finer looking cart. You sure outdone yourself."

Jim grinned. "This is the least I can do after what you and Miz Clarie done for Norrie and the baby," he said. "So let's get your mule in this here harness and see how it goes."

Clarie had followed the little family onto the porch and reached for Isaac.

"I'll tend him whilst y'all switch out the mules," she said. "That's a fine contraption!"

Rachel and Micah wiggled and jumped as their mother started for the barn.

"Are we going for a ride now, Mama?" Rachel called from the porch.

"Sure enough," Zetta said. "Soon as me and Mr. Jim get everything squared away. And this time we won't have to worry about your rag baby."

* * * * *

Concern for Rachel's rag doll quickly became the least of Zetta's worries. With both youngins smiling and sitting cross-legged behind the wide plank serving as the driver's seat, Zetta guided Jack onto the road. As they passed the Reed's cabin, she smiled at the family waving back from their porch.

Then as the cart approached the cemetery, Jesse Allen showed up again.

Zetta ignored him as she tugged on Jack's right rein to direct the animal closer to the side of the road. But Jesse turned his stallion in front of the mule, stopping it.

"Well, now. This sure beats what I seen the other day," he said. "Yep, this will do the job for now. Least ways 'til we're married."

Zetta squared her shoulders. "You're right sure of yourself. Just like I got no say in this."

Jesse smirked. "You won't need to say nothing. My job will be to do the talking."

"And I suppose my job will be to keep quiet and take care of your every little whim?"

"Yes, ma'am," Jesse said. "But we can figure out the details later."

"I doubt that," Zetta said. "Now I'd appreciate you getting out of my way. I want to take the youngins back home before the rain starts."

Jesse pushed back his hat. "I'll see you tomorrow at church. Me and Thorn."

Thanks for the warning, Zetta thought. I wish the rain had showed up before you did.

She gripped her mule's reins as Jesse spurred his stallion into a showy gallop. Then she turned the cart toward home.

* * * * *

Loren arrived at the house just as the rain did.

Zetta was stirring the kettle of beans as he came through the back door, slapping his hat against his thigh.

"I hope you've got your good cornbread to go with them beans," Loren said. "These last two days I was working as hard as Paw's mules as we finished his plowing. And I even helped Becky with her garden since me and Sarah will be eating out of it this first year. But she was grouchy the whole time and never once made cornbread."

"She still mad about the baby coming early?" Zetta asked.

"I reckon. She was even growling at our little brothers. And them working hard."

"Their names are Frankie and Hobie."

"I know that. How's Luttrell today?"

Zetta shook her head at Loren for changing the subject, but reached for the dipper.

"Every day he's doing better. Clarie's just changed the poultice," she said.

As they headed to the front room, Zetta paused at the doorway. Luttrell was propped up as Rachel folded her rag doll's blanket across this forehead. Micah was lining a row of wooden blocks across his uncle's stomach. And Clarie was smiling as she gently bounced a cooing Isaac.

"This sure don't look like a sick room anymore," Loren said as he looked at Luttrell. "Don't you reckon you're about ready to get up out of that bed?"

"Can't," Luttrell said. "Clarie's saying I gotta keep my leg propped up a while longer."

Loren turned to the woman. "He's doing good. And he needs to go to church tomorrow and show folks he ain't dead," he said. "When I stopped by the store I had to hear stories from everybody who ever lost a relative to snake bite or even heard tell of one."

Clarie shook her head. "The poultices is still pulling the last of the poison out," she said. "Besides, if he rests now, he'll be able to stand up with you at the wedding. So which do you want? Showing folks he ain't dead? Or having him at your wedding next week?"

"I guess I ain't got much of a choice," Loren said. "I reckon this just ain't my day."

"Meaning what?" Zetta asked.

Loren shrugged. "At the store, some of the fellers got to asking when you're gonna take down your trees to help stop the blight. So I told 'em I've been hearing of fires getting out of hand from some of the burnings and that your trees ain't none of their business."

Zetta put her hand to her forehead. "Oh, Loren. I wish you hadn't said it like that."

"Then Ben got all stirred up again over my joking about his nephew the other day," Loren said. "June was busy trying to keep her mother from putting foodstuff on the wrong shelves, but she tried to smooth things over. Ben just told her to hush. I swear he wears me out."

Suddenly, Loren thrust his hand into the pocket of his overalls. "Hey, I about forgot your mail," he said. "You got a letter from that carrot-topped gal. Maybe after you read it, you can stir up your cornbread."

Zetta reached for Dosha's letter. "Cornbread's coming. Soon as me and Clarie read this."

* * * * *

Clarie carried Isaac as she followed Zetta into the kitchen. "Listen to this little feller telling a big story," she said. "And him barely three months old."

Zetta smiled. "He started that the other day. I'd give a pretty to know what he's saying."

"I wonder if babies ain't trying to tell us about heaven since they just come from there," Clarie said as she settled into the nearest chair.

Before Zetta could comment, Loren called from the front room.

"Save that wondering for church tomorrow," he said. "Today I'm waiting on cornbread."

"It's a good thing you're one of my four favorite brothers," Zetta said. "Otherwise, I'd put you outside in the rain. Hollering ain't gonna make me move any faster."

"All right," Loren answered in a quieter voice. "But my stomach's caving in."

Zetta handed Dosha's letter to Clarie. "How about you do the reading for us whilst I do the stirring?"

Clarie shifted Isaac to her other arm and opened the envelope as Zetta dumped cornmeal into her favorite bowl.

"'Dear Zetta, I'm writing to give a happy report about Polly being here,'" Clarie read. "'She stayed in bed for a while, but finally got up and helped me and Jack plant our little garden out back of the school. I reckon seeing him hobble around but still working give her something to think on. She even went to the kitchen with me the last couple of days and helped make dumplings for the students. Remember at the camp how she said Perton claimed she couldn't cook? Well, he ain't here now. So I brag on her a right smart. And not just for her cooking. And I let her talk about her baby that died. I even cry with her seeing how I wish me and Jack had a little feller. And every day I see color coming back in her cheeks. Perton ain't tried to get in touch with her. But she's welcome to stay with us until she makes up her mind what she wants to do. I know it's wrong of me to wish this, but I wish she wouldn't go back to him. All he does is hurt her heart. Well, I shouldn't be complaining. But my life is so sweet that I want everybody to have a good man like Jack and good work each day and good friends like you. I'm going to write Clarie next and let her know how Polly is doing. Don't forget that me and Jack pray every day for you and your sweet babies. Your friend, Dosha Conley.'"

Clarie looked up from the letter. "In all the excitement of getting here, I plumb forgot to write her about Luttrell. I'll do that first thing when I get back to the camp."

Zetta straightened from putting the cornbread skillet into

the oven. "You called it the camp instead of home," she said.

"I reckon I did at that," Clarie said. "I guess it don't seem much like home these days. If I have to move, I'll miss my little cabin. But not much else."

"You're welcome to stay here as long as you like," Zetta said. "You're what I miss most about the camp. I know Luttrell wouldn't be getting along this good without you. And look at what you did for Norrie and little Adah."

"It does feel good to be some use," Clarie said. "But I might as well get on back. I reckon Monday is as good a time as any to leave. That is if Loren is willing to haul me to the station."

"I heard that," Loren called from the front room. "But I'd druther keep you here a while longer. At least 'til after the wedding. Better yet, 'til the baby comes."

"I can't stay for the wedding, much as I'd like to," Clarie said. "But, Lord willing, I'll try to come back to help bring y'all's little youngin into the world. Now why don't you come in here instead of us hollering back and forth."

Loren immediately appeared. "I was on my way. Me and Luttrell's been talking about church in the morning. I was fixing to bring my wagon over for y'all. And I'll stay with him."

"But like you told them fellers at the store, I ain't dead," Luttrell called from the front room. "I don't want you missing church on my account."

"I know that," Loren said. "Let me finish my story, will ya?"

He turned back to the women. "So me and Luttrell talked it over. Since he's bound and determined to stay by hisself whilst we're at church, I'll bring my wagon around and get y'all."

"I appreciate that," Zetta said. "But there's no need. Jim brung over the pony cart he had for his youngins years ago. It's plenty big."

"Well, that beats all," Loren said. "Pretty soon you gonna be downright independent."

"That's not it," Zetta said. "I'm just trying to keep from wearing you and Luttrell out. I've got to stand on my own two feet one of these days. Might as well start now."

Loren stared at her for a moment. Then he shrugged. "Well, Sis, Asa would be right proud of you."

He rubbed the scar on his chin then said, "That cornbread about ready?"

Chapter 16

The next morning, Zetta awakened from a bad dream long before dawn. Heart pounding, she put her hand on Rachel's and Micah's chests as she fought images of nightmare crows with red, evil eyes. Both children were sleeping peacefully.

The gentle rain had stopped hours earlier, and lazy moonlight allowed Zetta to see Isaac's little chest rising and falling as he slept. She wrapped her shawl around her shoulders and stepped into the front room. Luttrell was snoring softly, but the quilts on Clarie's bed were hastily pulled together. A soft glow came from the kitchen.

Zetta quietly approached the doorway and found Clarie sitting at the table. The light from the kerosene lamp poured over the writing paper in front of her.

"I hope me stumbling around didn't wake you," Clarie whispered as she looked up. "I don't know what ails me. Maybe I'm just excited about getting to go to church this morning. But I sure had trouble sleeping, so I figured I'd write Dosha."

Zetta eased into a chair across from her friend. "You didn't wake me up. A bad dream about crows done that," she said softly. "I haven't had such dreams since we left the camp."

"I recollect them dreams," Clarie said.

"The Lord was warning us about what was ahead, but Asa wouldn't listen to me," Zetta said. "He was bound and determined I was worrying about nothing. And look how that ended."

"I know, honey," Clarie said as she put her wrinkled hand over Zetta's. "But you and the youngins is here now. And we can't let worry take away the good things in each day."

Zetta took a deep breath. "How come you always know the right thing to say?"

"I don't know that I always come up with the right thing," Clarie said. "But I reckon living a long time brings a few benefits to offset the aches and pains."

Zetta gently squeezed Clarie's hand. "More than a few. In fact, you're one of the best women most of us know. And if you ever doubt that, all you have to do is think on what Loren said last night when he was hauling the water for our baths."

Clarie laughed then smothered the sound with her hand to keep from waking Luttrell.

"That did beat all," she said. "Talk about a left-handed compliment! I hope his Sarah never hears tell about him saying if I was forty years younger he'd marry me in a heartbeat."

"You'll meet Sarah at church," Zetta said. "Normally, she's kindly shy around strangers, but I know good and well Loren's been bragging on you. So she'll warm right up."

"I'm so tickled to be going to a real church again that I won't care one bit if she don't even bother to say hidy."

"Oh, I better warn you about the preacher's wife, Mable Collins," Zetta said. "She's a big woman who always says the same thing every time she sees me, no matter who's around. So even before I get a chance to introduce you, she'll say 'there you are with your poor little fatherless youngins.' She wears me out."

Clarie smiled. "It sounds like we're gonna have us a big time even before we step through the door."

"That's the truth," Zetta said. "Well, I'd better put on my

working dress and take care of the critters before everybody wakes up."

"Whilst you're doing that, I'll fix breakfast," Clarie said. "This is going to be quite a day."

* * * * *

Luttrell nodded his thanks as Zetta poured a second cup of coffee for him after breakfast.

She watched him take a sip of the hot beverage then asked, "Are you sure you're going to be all right being here all by your lonesome this morning?"

"Aw, come on, Sis," he said. "We already discussed this. Y'all are gonna be gone just a couple of hours. And I'm gonna keep my leg propped up and stay out of trouble."

"All right," Zetta said. "I've got Jack hitched up, and Clarie and me is ready to load up the youngins. But something still don't feel right."

Luttrell smiled. "It'd be a different matter if this was the day I got bit," he said. "But I'm doing good now. So go on. Then when you get back you can tell me all the news I missed."

Zetta touched his shoulder and turned to Clarie. "Well, we might as well go."

* * * * *

As Zetta guided the cart under the redbud and dogwood trees at the churchyard, she nudged Clarie and nodded to the group of women gathered to the left side of the church door.

"The big woman in the black dress is Mable, the one I told you about," Zetta said. "She's standing next to the store owner's wife, June, and my stepmother, Becky. I'll introduce you to them right off. Might as well get that over with."

As Zetta picked up Isaac, and Clarie helped Rachel and Micah from the back of the cart, Jesse Allen and his brother, Thorn, rode their stallions into the churchyard. Jesse tipped his hat to Zetta, but she turned away and continued toward the women.

Zetta still was several steps away when Mable waved at her. "Oh, bless your sweet heart. There you are with your poor little fatherless youngins."

Zetta tossed Clarie an *I told you so* look then said, "I want y'all to meet Clarie Farley. She's the camp granny woman that brung Isaac into the world. Now she's here for Luttrell."

Clarie nodded at the women. "I'm glad to finally meet y'all," she said. "And I'm looking forward to worshipping the Lord with y'all this morning."

Zetta waited for Becky to return the greeting or at least ask how Luttrell was getting along. But her stepmother was too busy frowning at Clarie.

June smiled and stepped toward Clarie. "I sure could've used you yesterday at the store," she said. "Hazel, the youngest girl of poor old Brother Jeems, had her baby die of fever Friday night. And him not even two months old." She took a deep breath. "Anyway, Hazel's mommy come by the store to ask if I had anything to dry up her milk. Of course, we don't carry such a thing, so I told her to bind her bosom. That's all I knowed to say."

Clarie nodded. "You said right. But I've got tea to help even more. I know you ain't open on Sundays, but we can drop it off at your house sometime this afternoon."

"If that's all right," Clarie said as she turned to Zetta.

At Zetta's nod, Clarie turned back to June. "Does that suit your day?"

"I appreciate your help," June said. "That family's been through enough already."

Suddenly she gestured forward. "Here comes Sarah. Good thing they're getting married next week. She's starting to show."

At least June ain't being ugly about it, Zetta thought as she turned to receive Sarah's hug.

Sarah giggled and pointed toward the flowering trees as she released Zetta. "Them blossoms is gonna be perfect for the wedding. Oh, I can't believe I'll be Mrs. Loren Davis in just seven more days."

Then Sarah smiled at Clarie. "You must be the one Loren's been talking about. Me and him sure do wish you was staying for the wedding."

Clarie wrapped her arms around Sarah. "Oh, honey. I wish I could. But I told the woman that's taking care of my cow and chickens I'd be back tomorrow. I reckon I'd better do as I said. But I'm sure happy for y'all."

Zetta touched Clarie's sleeve. "The Reeds are here," she said. "Look at Norrie. She's grinning from ear to ear."

As the women turned to watch Jim and his sons help the women down from the wagon, Zetta was happy to see Norrie wearing Sally's best lavender dress and holding little Adah confidently against her shoulder. Her light auburn hair framed her rosy cheeks, and she barely resembled the exhausted woman who had appeared just a few days before.

With Abigail and Deborah following, Sally guided Norrie toward the women.

"This here is Jim's sister, Norrie Risner," she said. "Her and her baby, Adah, is visiting us for a while."

As the women clustered about Norrie and admired the baby, a tall dark-haired man suddenly was at Zetta's side.

"So you're the pretty lady that's been keeping me in vittles," he said as he put his right hand into his overall pocket. "And always accusing me of being some other feller."

Zetta's mind raced as she looked into the man's angry eyes and realized this was the one who had been skulking around her farm, stealing eggs and vegetables. And watching her.

But before Zetta could untangle her thoughts, Norrie turned quickly at the sound of the man's voice. Her face went white.

"Calvin," she gasped.

"That's right," he said as he leaned toward her. "I been waiting for you to show up in these parts ever since you run off."

Norrie pulled the baby tightly against her right shoulder as she backed up, bumping Sally.

Sally saw the man and immediately shoved Abigail toward the men.

"Run get your daddy," she shouted.

Calvin leered at Norrie, ignoring everyone else.

"Ain't you a sight. Coming here looking all smiley and proud when you ought to be home where you belong," he said. "Well, we're leaving for there this minute."

Norrie trembled as she whispered, "I ain't never going back with you."

"Then I reckon I'll have to teach you a lesson right here." And Calvin jerked a pistol from his pocket and immediately fired at her heart.

As women and babies screamed, and mothers grabbled for their children, Zetta saw Jim Reed sprinting across the churchyard at Calvin.

But he was too late.

Jim hollered, "No!" as he wrestled Calvin down, his fists bloodying the man's face.

Norrie turned in slow motion toward Sally who was reaching for her.

As the young mother thrust her baby into her sister-in-law's arms, she muttered, "Sally, I'm kilt." She fell to the ground.

As the men ran toward their women, Clarie awkwardly knelt to press her hands against Norrie's chest. But the wound poured blood and life between her fingers.

Horrified, Zetta clung to Isaac with one hand as she pushed Micah and Rachel behind her with the other. And all the while red blood flowed across Norrie's borrowed lavender dress and onto the sparse green grass.

Zetta was aware of Sally sobbing and the women hurrying their children to the wagons. But she couldn't take her eyes off Jim as his fists repeatedly pounded the man's face.

Still holding the pistol, Calvin struggled to lift the weapon. But Sheriff Thorn stomped on Calvin's arm and kicked the pistol away.

"That's enough!" Thorn shouted as he displayed his own weapon.

He turned to the men standing nearby. "Pull him off."

Several strong hands, including Loren's and Jesse Allen's, grabbed Jim by his arms and pulled him to his feet. Blindly, he pushed against them with fists covered in blood.

As Calvin staggered to this feet, Thorn pointed his pistol at the man's face.

"Don't be moving," he said. "I'm taking you to jail."

The man closest to Zetta said, "No, we'll take care of this feller right now. I've got me some rope in the wagon."

Thorn hooked his thumb over his belt and faced the men. "Boys, there'll be no hanging here today," he said. "I'm the law, and we're gonna do this thing the right way."

At Thorn's declaration, Jim lunged toward Calvin again. But his friends pulled him back.

"Let me finish him," Jim yelled at the men holding his arms. "He done kilt a woman that never showed him no harm. What if this was your sweet sister?"

"It ain't up to us," someone muttered as they released his arms. "You know we gotta abide by the law."

Thorn pointed to one of the men. "Bring your wagon around," he said. "And use that rope to tie him up. And I'll need three or four of you other fellers to follow us."

Jim immediately stepped forward, but Thorn waved him aside. "You know you ain't going," he said. "Take your sister on home and get her ready for the laying out."

Jim turned slowly to Sally as she clutched Norrie's baby. Her tears were dripping onto little Adah's head.

He looked at Clarie, who remained kneeling next to Norrie's bloody and frail body.

"I was supposed to protect her," he whispered. "Now look."

"I know," Clarie said quietly.

Jim wiped his bloody hands across the front of his overalls then pulled his bandana from his pocket and put it into the granny woman's stained hands.

As Jim helped Clarie to her feet, Preacher Collins appeared at his side.

Where was he all this time? Zetta wondered.

"Brother Reed, this is indeed sad," Preacher Collins said. "We're all gonna be praying for you. And I'll stop by directly to talk about the funeral."

Tears rolled down Jim's face as he looked at the preacher. "Nothing ain't ever gonna be right again," he said.

Preacher Collins licked his lips as though trying to come up with something to say. Then he looked at the others standing awkwardly near Norrie.

"Well, I reckon we better call off church," he said. "We need to get ready to offer what help we can to this dear family."

He turned away, and most of the others standing nearby followed. But as his wife passed Sally, she put her hand on her shoulder.

"Here you are left with this poor little motherless youngin."

Chapter 17

Rachel and Micah clutched Zetta's skirt as she pulled Isaac against her heart and watched Jim carry Norrie's lifeless body to the wagon his sons had pulled around.

Sally started to follow him, but managed only one step before sobs overwhelmed her.

Abigail and Deborah threw themselves against their mother and cried with her. Clarie and Zetta each put a hand on Sally's shoulders as tears rolled down their own cheeks.

"Everything about this is wrong," Sally finally managed. "Y'all shoulda heard Norrie talking to little Adah this morning as she nursed her, telling her about church and the singing folks would be doing and how God was gonna give them a new life. Now this!"

At that moment, Adah whimpered and made smacking sounds.

"How am I gonna keep this child alive?" Sally was close to wailing.

Clarie took Adah from the woman's hands. "For now, we're gonna take her home with us, and Zetta is gonna feed her whilst I check on Luttrell's leg," she said. "Then we're gonna go to your house. Have your girls ever helped lay out a body?"

Sally swiped at her eyes. "Not 'til now," she said.

Clarie turned to Abigail and Deborah as they huddled close to their mother.

"This is the last loving thing anybody can do for somebody else," she said. "Y'all will wash her and dress her and brush her hair. And there ain't nothing to be afraid of."

Zetta pulled a handkerchief from her sleeve and wiped her tears. "And me and Clarie will be over soon as we can."

"I reckon you've got salt," Clarie said gently. "I'll bring camphor when we come."

Sally nodded. "Yes, I got plenty of salt. But I'll appreciate the camphor."

Deborah looked puzzled, but Abigail shook her head as she put her hand on her sister's arm. In that moment, their brother Bernard stepped forward.

"Mama, we need to get to the house," he said as he gestured toward the wagon. Jim was in the back, gently rocking Norrie as he held her in his lap. Albert jumped down from the front bench, ready to help his mother and sisters.

Zetta and Clarie, each clutching a baby, watched the beleaguered family settle into the wagon.

Rachel tugged on Zetta's skirt. "That mean man hurt Miz Norrie," the child said. "Is he gonna come hurt us?"

Zetta pulled Rachel close. "No, honey. The mean man is in jail now," she said. "And he won't ever come hurt us."

She saw Micah watching her with wide, frightened eyes. Please, Lord, she inwardly prayed. May that be so.

* * * * *

At the cabin, Zetta and Clarie entered the front room, each carrying a hungry baby, as Rachel and Micah ran to their Uncle Luttrell.

"Well, y'all are back sooner than I expected," he said as he put an arm around each child.

"A mean man hurt Miz Norrie," Rachel said.

He looked at the women. "What happened?"

"Norrie's husband showed up and kilt her," Clarie said.

"Right in front of everybody. Let me wash my hands and help with these babies first. Then I'll tell you what all."

Luttrell closed his eyes and pulled Rachel and Micah close.

* * * * *

After Isaac and Rachel were changed, Zetta settled into her rocker with a baby at each breast. Clarie returned to the front room.

"Your mommy is needing her two big youngins to keep her company," Zetta heard Clarie say to Rachel and Micah. "Then after I check your uncle's leg, I'll fix us all something to eat. That okay?"

Zetta heard only Rachel's "Yes, ma'am" but knew Micah nodded.

"We've got soup beans and cornbread from last night," Zetta said. "We can fry some taters to go with 'em."

And thank you, Clarie, for getting the youngins out of earshot about Norrie's killing, Zetta thought.

Rachel ran into the bedroom, hugging her rag doll. Micah followed, carrying his blocks, dropping two, picking up one and dropping two more. Finally, he joined his sister.

"Brother, stack your blocks quiet like, and don't be knocking them down," Zetta whispered. "I'm trying to get these babies to sleep. You hear me?"

As the toddler nodded, Zetta smiled. "That's my good boy."

Then Zetta heard Clarie start to tell Luttrell about the killing. She turned to Rachel and Micah. "Let me put a kiss into your hands for you to hold the rest of the day," she said.

As the children held out their hands, Loren stormed into the living room.

The children turned, but Zetta stopped them.

"Y'all can hug him in a minute," she said, not wanting the children to hear Loren's account of the morning. "For now, I need to keep looking at your sweet faces," she said.

"Sister, you and your rag baby sing me a song."

As Rachel launched into a whispered rendition of "Jesus Loves Me," Zetta could hear what was happening in the front room.

"How's our boy's leg?" Loren asked.

"See for yourself," Clarie said. "When I took the poultice off, there wudn't one bit of color on it. So, Luttrell, it's time for you to take a step or two. Don't get ambitious, though."

"Like I always tell ya, I ain't gonna insist on a foot race," Luttrell said.

"Good for you," Clarie said. "Now me and Loren is gonna help you take two steps to that chair. Let me know if your leg hurts extra when you put weight on it."

"Wait," Loren hollered. "First, let me tell about getting that durn Calvin to jail."

"I didn't know you helped take him in," Clarie said. "When we left, men was putting him in the wagon, and Sarah was sobbing against you."

"She was a sight all right," Loren said. "I had to send her with her folks because she's afraid seeing Norrie kilt like that marked her baby."

He paused then added, "Well, *our* baby. Anyway, with her going on like that, anybody that didn't know about her being in the family way sure knows now!"

"Don't worry. Folks usually are forgiving when it comes to the arrival of babies," Clarie said. "So how'd it go with getting Norrie's man to jail?"

"He set in the wagon real cocky like all the way to town," Loren said. "Never showed one bit of remorse. And even smirked. Hanging's too good for somebody like him."

Father God, I know it's wrong to think that way, but I sure agree with Loren, Zetta thought as she thumped both babies' backs and urged sleepy burps. *I'll never understand why good men die whilst bad ones keep pulling in breaths.*

"Well, there. I've had my say," Loren said. "Let's get this boy in a chair."

"Whoa! Is that moonshine I'm smelling?" Clarie said.

"So what? Taking a swig kept me from punching Calvin right in the mouth because of his smirking. But Jim already done a pretty good job on his face. I gotta give it to Jim. I didn't know he had that much fight in him."

"Well, you're gonna see some more fight if you drink around me," Clarie said. "And you better not let it mess with your wedding day. Now help me with your brother."

Zetta heard only a subdued "Okay" from Loren.

* * * * *

After a hurried noon dinner, Zetta stacked dishes into the wash pan as Clarie pulled a bottle of camphor from her satchel.

"I sure wudn't planning on using this during my time here," Clarie said. "That killing come right out of the blue."

"I ain't so sure," Zetta said as she turned to her friend. "You and me both didn't have a good night what with my bad dream and you not sleeping. Was God warning about trouble?"

"Makes a person wonder, don't it?" Clarie said.

"And if God was warning us about bad things, why didn't he stop 'em?" Zetta said. "Or if he wudn't gonna stop 'em, why didn't he tell us what to watch out for so we could stop 'em?"

"Them's good questions," Clarie said. "And I don't have answers. All I know is God ain't in the habit of running things by me first. He give humans the choice to do right. But I reckon there's plenty of times when he's crying right along with us when he sees such a choice used in wrong ways."

"Well, giving us free rein is one of the things I'm gonna ask him about when I get to heaven," Zetta said.

"Oh, honey. I reckon when we finally stand before him, we're gonna be so caught by his glory we ain't gonna care anymore."

Zetta shook her head and finished stacking dishes.

*****

With both babies sleeping, and Rachel and Micah playing in the front room near their uncles, Clarie and Zetta hurried to the Reed's house in the pony cart.

As they entered through the kitchen door, they saw Norrie lying on the sturdy table and in the lavender dress. A matching piece of material was folded over the blood stains.

"Is it wrong to bury her in the dress she was kilt in?" Sally said without greeting the women. "I sewed it last month, so I still had material left. She was so happy when I offered it to her this morning. She said she'd never had anything so pretty since she'd been married."

"You done right by deciding on this dress," Zetta said. "Y'all done a good job of making her look like she was this morning."

"You did at that," Clarie said. "And I see you got the bowls of salt ready. I brung the camphor. If you got a little rag, I'll take care of that now."

As Sally tore a clean dish cloth in two, Zetta saw Deborah turn to Abigail.

"What's salt and camphor for?" she whispered.

"Camphor keeps the face and hands from turning dark too fast," Abigail said.

"And the salt?" Deborah asked.

"We'll put the bowls next to her in the coffin when folks ain't visiting. That helps her stay looking nice. If the weather was real hot, we'd leave the bowls with her all the time."

Deborah looked in awe at her sister. "How come you know such things?"

"At school, I heard the big girls talk about helping with laying outs. I mighta forgot some of my lessons, but I sure didn't forget that."

As the women watched Clarie gently wipe the camphor over Norrie's skin, Sally leaned against Zetta's shoulder.

"I keep thinking about her handing Adah to me even as she was dying," Sally said. "How she loved that baby to have the strength to do that. And now she won't ever feed her again or kiss her goodnight or watch her grow up."

Zetta nodded somberly. "I know. It's awful to think about."

Sally took a jagged breath. "Know what's eating at Jim? He was watching for Calvin to show up here. He never figured on him showing up at church."

"Oh, Sally," was all Zetta managed as her eyes filled with tears.

Sally took another deep breath and straightened her shoulders before turning to her daughters. "Well, better change to mourning clothes," she said. "Folks will start coming in pretty soon."

Zetta touched Sally's arm. "Me and Clarie will be back later. I need to check on the youngins, and she promised June she'd give her some milk-drying tea for the Jeems girl."

"I heard about her baby," Sally said as she rubbed her temple. "What if she don't dry up her milk? What if she took care of Adah, instead?"

When neither visitor answered, Sally hurriedly continued. "I know Zetta's doing a good job. But she's already got her hands full. This might be the Lord's solution."

"When it's the Lord's solution, he'll let us know." Clarie said. "But we got to be careful about running ahead of him and guessing what he's about. The girl's milk is drying up already. Anyway, she might be grieving too much to nurse a stranger's baby."

Sally responded slowly. "You're right. I reckon I was just trying to take this off Zetta."

"I know you got a good heart," Clarie said. "And to ease your mind, I hear tell some city stores sell newfangled milk just for babies. I'll take a look at the catalog when I'm at the store. If that don't work, we can always sweeten cow's milk with a little honey."

Zetta looked at Sally. "Don't you worry. Adah's gonna be taken care of. For now, she's gonna stay with me 'til after the funeral. We'll figure this out later."

Before Sally could reply, heavy footsteps sounded on the front porch.

"That'll be Jim and the boys with the coffin," she said. "I better get the door for 'em."

Zetta followed her friend into the front room. There, two straight-back chairs were facing each other, ready for what would be placed on their sturdy seats.

As Sally held the door open, Jim and Bernard struggled to get the pine box into the room without bumping the wall. Inside, they positioned the box, propped the lid beside it, and stepped back as Sally put a pillow into the left side and draped a flowered quilt over the rough wood.

As they stood back to look at their work, Jim gripped Sally's shoulder. "Thank you for making it pretty," he said. "I was feeling bad about having to get the box ready so quick like."

"We're doing what we can for that sweet girl," Sally murmured.

Then Zetta saw her friend look around as though wanting to talk about something else.

"Where's Albert?" Sally asked. "I thought he was helping you."

"He was. For a while," Jim said. "He had to get to the station. But he's gonna have trouble keeping his mind on work after all this."

Jim puffed out his cheeks. "Well, now for the next hard part," he said. And he turned toward the kitchen. Clarie still held the bottle of camphor and stood by Norrie's body.

Jim's steps were leaden as he moved forward.

* * * * *

Zetta and Clarie watched as Jim gently placed Norrie in the coffin, and Sally refolded the lavender material over the blood stains.

Then Jim pulled Norrie's cold hands together across her stomach and put his trembling fist on them.

"Little Sister, I ain't never gonna get over this," he said. "You come to me for help, but I failed you. I ain't never gonna forgive myself. And I ain't never gonna forgive that man. But I'm gonna take care of your baby."

Zetta watched Jim's jaw tighten moment by moment.

"She looks like I remember before she give in to that man's fancy talk and run off," he said to Sally. "She didn't even finish school. And never got her picture took the way I did when I was done with book learning."

The women were silent, waiting.

"Know what I'm gonna do?" Jim's voice suddenly was harsh. "I'm gonna go get Green Wilson to bring his picture maker out here and get one of her looking all pretty. A picture like the city folks get when their people die."

Sally looked helplessly at Zetta as Jim grabbed his hat from the rack. But as he jerked open the front door, Preacher Collins was standing there.

And he was frowning.

Chapter 18

Zetta started to tell Sally that she and Clarie would leave to allow privacy with the preacher, but Sally already had joined Jim at the door.

"Preacher Collins! Come on in," she said. "Can I get you a glass of buttermilk or maybe some spring water?"

Preacher Collins glanced at the nearby coffin as he muttered, "No. I just come to talk about the burying."

Why's he being so standoffish? Zetta wondered. A person just don't go around refusing hospitality. And not even offering appreciation.

Jim remained standing by the door, but Sally gestured toward the row of straight-back chairs awaiting the afternoon's visitors.

"Set down here, Preacher. We appreciate you coming to talk to us."

Preacher Collins cleared his throat as he moved toward the chairs.

"I'd like to talk to just Brother Jim," he said. "Since this here was his sister."

This here? Zetta thought. She has a name. Norrie. Norrie Reed Risner.

"Well, I'll be in the kitchen then," Sally said. "Holler if I can get anything for you."

Zetta and the others followed Sally, but stood awkwardly near the sturdy table where Norrie had been just minutes before.

"That beats all," Sally whispered. "I ain't never been told I can't be part of whatever matters to Jim."

"You want we should leave?" Zetta said. "Me and Clarie will be back directly, though."

"No. I'd appreciate you staying," Sally said. "I got a bad feeling about this."

"All right, then," Clarie said. "Where do you keep your lye soap? Whilst we're here, we'll help scrub down the table."

Sally gestured toward the brown soap waiting on a pile of clean rags. "Everything's right here," she said. "And the water's on the stove."

Then she put her hand on the old woman's shoulder. "Please tell me you'll stay for the burying. You ain't been here long, but you're like family already."

Clarie slowly nodded. "I'm sorry all this happened, but I'm glad to be of some use," she said. "But I'll need to get word to the camp woman tending my critters."

Bernard had pushed himself against the wall farthest from the table, but stepped forward.

"Albert can send a telegram from the station like he done when they told you about Luttrell," he said. "Just give me her name and the message, and I'll take it right quick."

Sally handed Clarie a tablet of paper and pencil from the dish shelf. "And don't you worry about the little cost," she said. "The station manager lets Albert send important telegrams now and again."

Clarie wrote the woman's name and Golden Gate Coal Camp then handed the paper to Bernard. "The message ain't long," she said. "All I'm saying is 'Trouble here. Staying longer.' And you don't need to wait for the answer."

"No, I'll wait there," Bernard said as he hurried out the kitchen door.

"That boy sure was glad to get out of here," Sally said as she picked up the lye soap. "And I don't blame him one bit."

But as she reached for the dishpan, she frowned and motioned toward the front room. Zetta could hear Jim's voice growing louder.

"Preacher, I ain't got no quarrel with you putting the burying for the Jeems baby tomorrow morning since the youngin died first."

"And his mother's folks is members and all," Preacher Collins said.

"I hope you recollect me and my woman's been members ever since we was married," Jim said. "And that was long before you showed up."

"Yes, but the baby was innocent and deserves a Christian burying," Preacher Collins said.

"Whata you saying?" Jim demanded.

Preacher Collins cleared his throat. "Well, none of this woulda happened if your sister obeyed her man," he said. "I hear tell he didn't just show up and shoot her. First, he asked her to go home where she belonged."

The women in the kitchen glanced at each other. "Lord, help Jim," Sally whispered.

"Listen, Preacher. He didn't ask her, he ordered her," Jim said. "You're telling me a good Christian woman was supposed to go back to a man that beat her, badmouthed her and wouldn't claim their baby because it was a girl and not a boy?"

Preacher Collins cleared his throat again. "If she was a good Christian woman she wuda followed the Bible and not her own wishes."

"Now you're gonna say women is supposed to submit to the man," Jim spluttered. "I heard that plenty when I was growing up. My paw couldn't read, but he sure knowed that verse."

"You don't need to get all riled up," Preacher Collins said.

"Riled up? Preacher, you ain't seen how riled up I can get," Jim said slowly. "I'm just trying to get you to see that sweet Norrie here is an innocent woman that's been wronged time after time and then was murdered because she wouldn't go back to the one causing the torment."

"You're arguing with God, not me," Preacher Collins muttered.

"No, I'm trying to figure how a man who claims to give forth God's word pulls out just one piece of it," Jim said. "I heard my paw holler that part every time he hit my ma. I'd try to stand up for her, and then he'd hit me a while."

"Now, Jim, this has nothing to do with you and him."

"It has everything to do with men like that who pick and choose what God says," Jim said. "My paw couldn't read, but I sure can. And I wonder why preachers don't talk about the part just in front of that verse. The verse that tells folks to submit to one another. It says submit to each other in the fear of God. And another verse tells husbands to love their wives even as Christ also loved the church. How come you ain't applying all that to what happened to Norrie?"

From the kitchen the women saw Preacher Collins quickly stand up.

"Well, I reckon our time here is done," he said.

"It is at that," Jim said as he gestured toward the door. "And we'll do our own burying early tomorrow afternoon without you preaching Norrie into hell."

Stunned, Zetta and the other women watched Preacher Collins hurry out the door. Before they could comment, Jim called from the front room.

"Sally, you and the girls set with Norrie. I'm gonna get Green Wilson and his picture maker now."

"Jim, it's Sunday," Sally said as she hurried to him. "He ain't gonna come out here now."

Jim shoved his hat on. "Believe me. He's gonna take that picture today whilst Norrie's still looking pretty."

And he strode out the door.

*****

When Zetta and Clarie returned home, Loren and Luttrell

were on the front porch watching Rachel and Micah chase each other around the fruit trees blooming near the gate. Luttrell raised his hand in greeting then pointed to his leg propped on another chair. Loren jumped down to help the women.

"Hey, Sis. I'm glad you're back," Loren said. "The babies ain't been fussing yet, but they're bound to start a ruckus pretty soon. Y'all go on in, and I'll take care of ol' Jack here."

Zetta nodded her thanks to Loren as Rachel and Micah ran to hug her, but she looked at Luttrell. "I hope you ain't pushing your luck."

"Not pushing a thing," he said. "I just had to set in the sun for a while."

"I planned to have us inside before y'all got back," Loren said as he held out his hand to Clarie. "But he's been in that bed since Tuesday."

"You don't need to worry," Clarie said as she remained seated in the cart. "The good steps he took this morning tells me that."

"So you gonna just sit there grinning?" Loren asked.

"No. I need you to take me to June's store," Clarie answered. "I promised her special tea for the Jeems girl before all this happened to Norrie. Zetta can't take me now, so I'd appreciate you taking me since I don't know the way."

Loren hooked his thumb over his belt. "I ain't never drove a girly pony cart," he said. "And I sure ain't gonna start now. I'll just take you there on my mule."

Clarie chuckled. "These old bones ain't climbing on the back of no mule," she said. "How about I drive the cart, and you go along for the ride and tell me which way to go?"

"You know better than that," Loren said. "There's no way I'm gonna let a woman hold the reins with me just sitting there looking all foolish."

"Well, I always say there's more than one way to skin a cat," Clarie said. "So how's this? You ride your mule, and I'll follow you in the pony cart."

"We're gonna look a sight, but I reckon this will work,"

Loren said. "But you sure are stubborn."

Clarie slapped her thigh in delight. "Look at the cooking pot calling the kettle black," she said. "All righty. Let's get this done."

Zetta bit the inside of her cheek to keep from teasing Loren as he reluctantly walked to where his mule waited under a shade tree. She and Luttrell watched their brother and Clarie leave. Then she gestured for Rachel and Micah to start up the steps.

"After I check on the babies, I'm gonna cook for the Reed family," she said. "Do you know two youngins that want to lick the bowl when I make applesauce cake?"

As both toddlers scrambled ahead of her, Zetta turned to Luttrell.

"Can I get you anything?"

"Just some news," Luttrell said. "Whilst me and Loren was setting here, we seen Preacher Collins on his way to the Reeds and then go back again pretty quick. When's the burying?"

Zetta took a deep breath. "Tomorrow about one o'clock. But Jim and the preacher had a falling out, so Jim told him they'll do their own burying."

"A falling out? What over?"

"The preacher said Norrie wouldn't be dead if she'd been a good wife and gone back with Calvin," Zetta said.

Luttrell shook his head. "And I bet Jim don't want Norrie preached into hell."

"That's exactly it."

"I don't blame him one bit," Luttrell said. "You and me heard plenty such preaching when we was growing up. Well, when word gets around that the preacher ain't gonna be there, not many folks will show up. But I sure will."

"Plenty folks will still come," Zetta said. "Everybody knows Sally and her girls are good cooks."

* * * * *

Both babies still were asleep, so Zetta quickly stirred up her applesauce cake and poured the batter into two cast-iron skillets. As Micah and Rachel scraped the leftover batter from the mixing bowl, Zetta glanced out the kitchen window and saw Loren jump down from his mule and hurry to help Clarie down from the pony cart. Then Zetta smiled as she saw Loren lead Jack to the barn and Clarie slowly climb the kitchen steps. Loren was leading the mule instead of driving the cart to the barn.

Zetta opened the door. "Y'all are back quicker than I figured," she said. "Everything go all right?"

Clarie nodded as she eased into the closest chair. "About as good as could be expected, I reckon," she said. "The biggest problem was June's mother walking between us whilst we was trying to talk. I give June the milk-drying tea for the Jeems girl and then offered her mother some of my sleeping tea."

"I bet she appreciated that," Zetta said.

"Not exactly," Clarie said. "That poor woman knocked the tea pouch right out of my hand and told me to keep my witchcraft to myself. Then she stomped to the house part of the store."

"Witchcraft! Knowing plants for doctoring ain't witchcraft," Zetta said. "What ails her?"

"I know. Plumb pitiful," Clarie said. "And you should have seen Loren standing there all flabbergasted."

"Loren? Flabbergasted?"

"It was a sight all right," Clarie said. "June felt bad her mother did that, of course, and wouldn't let me pay for the two feeding bottles she had on her shelf."

"Feeding bottles?"

"Yep, I got 'em right here," Clarie said as she opened her satchel. "See? They got little nipples that ought to suit Adah just fine."

"I don't know," Zetta said. "You ever use anything like this at the camp?"

"A time or two when a mother was sick," Clarie said.

"They do all right. And I looked at the store catalog about the baby milk some companies is offering. But I don't reckon we'll have to go that route. We'll try cow's milk with a little sweetening for Adah first."

As Zetta reached for the bottle, she heard footsteps on the back porch. She opened the door, expecting to see Loren. But it was Bernard.

"The woman at the camp give her answer," he said as he held out the paper.

"Clarie's right here," Zetta said. "Come on in and read us the answer."

Bernard took a deep breath as he stepped inside.

"Okay, but it ain't good news," he said. "All the woman said was 'Mine closing. Come soon.'"

CHAPTER 19

Zetta spent another restless night as her mind replayed the day's events. Darting between vivid images of Norrie's murder were worries about how the closing of the mine would affect Clarie.

After Bernard had read the telegram, Clarie leaned her head into her hands. "I feel like poor ol' Job saying that what he feared had come upon him," she said.

But before Zetta could comment, the old woman straightened her shoulders. "Well, you and me talked before about this happening," Clarie said. "So I reckon I better start thinking on what I'm gonna do. I sure don't want to be living in a ghost camp all by my lonesome."

Now in the pre-dawn darkness, Zetta thought of Clarie's sweet cabin someday sitting on the hillside, empty and gradually sagging into the dirt. Then Norrie's bewildered look as she handed her baby to Sally jumped into Zetta's mind again and caused her to throw the quilt aside. She listened to Rachel's and Micah's breathing then eased out of bed and gently put her hand on the chests of both babies lying side by side in the crib. Wrapping her shawl around her shoulders, she quietly walked to the kitchen.

She wasn't surprised to find Clarie at the table in the glow of the kerosene lamp.

"So you couldn't sleep neither," Clarie whispered. "I figured I'd finish the letter I started to Dosha yesterday morning. I've sure got plenty more to add today."

"I keep pondering what you're gonna do with the camp closing," Zetta said.

"Me, too. Seems like I been taking care of folks all my life," Clarie said. "I learned birthing by helping my ma. Then when the camp took our land and moved in, there wudn't nothing for me to do but take care of miners' wives."

Zetta waited, listening.

"I tossed and turned for a long while last night," Clarie said. "Finally I told the Lord I was too tired to worry any more, and for him to untangle everything and let me know what I should do. And then I drifted right off to sleep."

"That's the best thing, I reckon," Zetta managed.

Clarie gestured toward the stove. "I made coffee and was fixing to stir up the biscuits. Little Adah sleeping good?"

Zetta nodded. "Slept all night, in fact," she said.

"I'm right pleased she took to the feeding bottle quick like," Clarie said. "I reckon it's because she wudn't fed by Norrie this whole time. Or maybe God showed special mercy to that child. And you."

"Whatever it was, I'm glad she's eating good," Zetta said. "Well, we got a busy day ahead. I best get dressed and take care of the critters."

* * * * *

As Zetta approached the cabin with the eggs and milk, Abigail, dressed in black, stepped through the front gate.

"I hope you don't mind me showing up early," she said as she approached. "Mama sent me over to help with the youngins. And she wants you to show me about the feeding bottle. She said her and Daddy used one a while back for a calf we had."

Zetta smiled at the young woman's breathy explanation. "You are always more than welcome here," she said. "Besides, I reckon you want to check on how Luttrell's doing."

Abigail blushed. "Well, when you brung over the food yesterday, I did hear you tell Mama he's planning to come to the burying. I hope he ain't overdoing."

"That's what he tells me," Zetta said as she started up the steps. "He's setting up all the time now. Come on in and see for yourself."

Luttrell was sitting at the table with his leg propped up on the nearest chair as the women opened the door. He nodded thanks to Clarie as she poured his coffee, but knocked over the cup as he tried to stand up when he saw Abigail.

Suddenly everyone was talking at once.

"Dang it," Luttrell said. Then quickly added, "I'm right sorry. I shouldna said that in front of y'all."

"It's all right," Zetta said.

"I got a rag here," Clarie said.

"Please don't stand up on my account," Abigail said.

Within seconds, the overturned cup was righted and the spilled coffee wiped up. In the silence that followed, Clarie grinned as she looked at the others.

"Ain't we a sight?" she said. "How 'bout we start over? Good morning. Y'all doing all right?"

No one spoke immediately, so Clarie continued. "Abigail, honey, you're out early. Can we do anything for you?"

Zetta smiled as Abigail blushed before answering. "I come over to thank y'all for all the food you brung over last night," she said. "And to help with the youngins before the burying."

"I checked on 'em a minute ago," Clarie said. "Ain't none of 'em awake yet. So how about you set down there, have a biscuit and tell us about the picture-making feller."

Abigail blushed again as she slid into the nearest chair. "Thank you on the biscuit, but we had breakfast extra early since none of us slept much last night," she said. "Me and Mama wanted to sit up with Norrie, but Daddy wouldn't have it. He said he needed to do that hisself."

"I reckon y'all put camphor rags over her skin and bowls

153

of salt around her after everybody left," Clarie said.

"Yes, ma'am," Abigail said as she took a deep breath. "But that bothered Daddy more'n I figured. He kept saying he was glad he got Green Wilson out there in good time."

"Did the picture-making go all right?" Zetta asked.

"Yes, it helped Daddy some," Abigail said. "Mr. Wilson come in the house quiet like and even put his hand on Aunt Norrie's and said he was sorry before he set up the picture maker."

Abigail took another deep breath. "He made one picture right away," she said. "One of her and the coffin. Then Daddy told him to make one just of her face so's he can show Adah in a few years how pretty her mama was."

Everyone was quiet for several moments before Abigail spoke again.

"Mr. Green offered to make a picture of us standing by Aunt Norrie, like the city people do. And he told how some folks even have him paint the person's eyes open on the picture. But Daddy said this was just for Adah later on. And he wanted Aunt Norrie's eyes closed so Adah would know her daddy kilt her mommy."

"I wish all this could be undone," Zetta said at last.

"Me, too. This is awful," Abigail said. "But me and Mama is worried about Daddy. He's always been gentle like, but now something bad is boiling around his heart."

"Is the grave all dug?" Luttrell asked.

"Yes. Daddy started on that soon as Mr. Wilson left," Abigail said. "Mama wanted him to wait 'til the boys got home from the station, but Daddy wudn't listen. Then your brother Loren showed up with a shovel."

Will wonders never cease? Zetta thought. Loren and Paw always carried a grudge against Jim for standing up for colored folks wanting to vote. And now Loren actually helped Jim with something as tender as digging Norrie's grave.

Luttrell interrupted her thoughts. "I'm right glad Loren done that," he said quietly. "I felt bad I couldn't, especially since your daddy helped me and Loren dig Asa's grave."

Zetta nodded, pondering that dreadful day not even two months earlier. Then she reached for the eggs and her favorite skillet.

* * * * *

The morning passed quickly with Abigail helping with the children, and Clarie showing her how much sweetening to add to the cow's milk and how to test the milk temperature by putting a few drops on the inside of her wrist.

After the simple noon dinner was over, and both babies were fed, Abigail insisted upon washing the few dishes while Zetta and Clarie dressed for the burying.

Zetta was surprised Clarie had brought a black dress.

"You packed that even before you left the camp?" Zetta asked.

"When I left for here, I didn't know what shape I'd find Luttrell in," Clarie said. "I'm sorry the dress come in handy, but I'm sure glad I ain't using it because of him."

As the two women stepped from the bedroom in their appropriate dresses, they were surprised by Loren.

"Hidy, pretty ladies," he said. "My wagon's all ready to take everybody to the Reeds. First, I stopped by Paw and Becky's to get a clean shirt and pants for Luttrell."

He turned to Abigail, who was standing in the kitchen doorway. "Ain't he gonna look handsome all slicked up?"

Even without looking at the young woman, Zetta knew she was blushing.

"Where's Sarah?" Luttrell quickly asked. "Ain't she going to the burying?"

"Nah. She says it's because Norrie wudn't none of her people," Loren said. "But the truth of the matter is she's afraid she mighta already marked the baby by seeing Norrie kilt, so she ain't taking any more chances."

Silence lingered for several moments. Then Clarie spoke.

"Luttrell, you go ahead and get changed in the bedroom," she said. "And Abigail, honey, since Adah's got a full tummy, you can take the feeding bottles now. I got 'em all washed and ready in the feedsack near the door. We'll be along directly."

* * * * *

As Loren guided the wagon to the Reed's side yard, Zetta turned to her toddlers. Rachel clutched her rag doll while Micah bounced his wooden dancing man against the wagon floor.

"Do you recollect what I said about being good?" Zetta asked. "I don't want to hear one word out of either one of you 'til we get back home. You hear me?"

Zetta smiled as the children nodded. "Now this is what's gonna happen," she said. "Both of you are gonna be in the bedroom with the babies whilst Mr. Jim talks. I'll have my chair right close to the bedroom door where you can see me. And I don't want you acting scared when you hear hammering going on. Y'all are gonna play quiet like and not wake the babies. You listening?"

Both children nodded earnestly again as Loren set the wagon brake.

"Well, I got everybody here in one piece," he said. "Luttrell, let me get the women and youngins down and then I'll help you."

Luttrell held up his walking stick. "I ain't no cripple," he said. "And I sure ain't about to fall on my face in front of folks."

Loren shrugged. "Well, suit yourself," he said as he held out his hand to Clarie, who was seated on the wagon's front bench.

"Here, you take Adah first," Clarie said. "Then I can get down easy."

Zetta smiled as Loren hesitated before reaching for the baby.

"Might as well get used to holding a youngin now," Clarie said. "You'll be holding yours soon enough."

Loren swallowed and carefully accepted little Adah.

As Zetta and the others started for the porch steps, two more wagons pulled alongside Loren's. Soon the men were slapping Luttrell on the back for being up and around after a snake bite while the women cooed over the four youngsters. Zetta smiled at their greetings, grateful she wasn't hearing "poor little fatherless, or motherless, babies" from Mable Collins.

Inside the cabin, Clarie and Zetta hurried Rachel and Micah past the coffin and to the bedroom, put the sleeping babies in the middle of the bed, and pulled two chairs across the doorway.

As Zetta settled into her chair, she studied the gallon jars filled with blooming dogwood and redbud branches at the head and foot of Norrie's coffin. Three graniteware dishpans were alongside the side and filled with dirt and violet plants. Sally had said the night before that later she and her girls would plant the violets on Norrie's grave.

As more folks arrived, Zetta nodded at them while pondering why they had come. Some came because they cared about the Reeds. Undoubtedly, some were there because they heard about Preacher Collins not giving the service, and they wanted to hear the reason straight from the horse's mouth. Zetta looked around the crowded room again, grateful Jesse Allen wasn't there.

Jim stood by Norrie's coffin and kept looking at his pocket watch. Finally, he cleared his throat as he faced the group.

"I appreciate y'all being here," he said. "To tell the truth, I didn't reckon this many would show up, us not having a preacher. I don't know what all you heard, but Preacher Collins and me agreed that since he didn't know Norrie, it'd be better if I did the talking today."

Clarie and Zetta glanced at each other, remembering the actual discussion. *Good for Jim for not badmouthing the preacher in public*, Zetta thought. *I hope the preacher returns the favor.*

Jim interrupted her thoughts. "Whilst I was setting up with Norrie last night," he said, "I was pondering our hard life as youngins and her even harder life when she married somebody that was better about making promises than keeping 'em. Well, you know such pondering didn't do me a bit of good. So I started reading the Bible. This verse pretty much tells how I feel. Let me read it to you."

Jim picked up the big Bible from a chair at his side, opened it and held it toward the light from the front window. "Here it is. Psalm 119, verse 169. 'Let my cry come near before thee, O Lord: give me understanding according to thy word.'"

Jim hugged the Bible close to his chest. "Most of you was right there when Norrie was kilt," he said. "And most of you saw how I tried to kill her man with my bare hands."

Many of the people nodded as Jim continued. "So you know this verse tells how I'm crying out to the Lord, trying to understand why that man took a sweet woman's life. The same woman he'd promised to take care of. And you know I wanted that man dead. Just like she was. And now I've gotta keep talking to the Lord about that festering in my spirit."

Hugging the Bible with one hand, Jim pulled a bandana from his pocket and wiped his brow. "And I'm asking for the Lord to help me and my woman raise Norrie's baby."

Jim looked at his wife seated with their four children. "I'm mighty glad you're with me, Sally," he said. "And I appreciate our youngins knowing this is the right thing to do."

Tears rolled down Sally's cheeks as she nodded.

Jim looked at Zetta before turning to the others. "I know most of you here had folks die," he said. "Folks you loved and figured you couldn't get along without. You know sorrow. But me and my family is gonna get through this just like y'all are. By hanging on the Lord. And asking for his help day by day."

Clarie patted Zetta's hand as tears filled the young widow's eyes.

Jim gestured toward the coffin. "I take comfort knowing

Norrie put her trust in the Lord as her Savior and that she's with him right now."

A jagged breath escaped from Jim. "Remember how Jesus was hanging on the cross and how the thief next to him asked Jesus to remember him?" he managed. "Remember how Jesus told the thief he would be with him that very day? So it helps to know Norrie is safe with the Lord right now."

Jim cleared his throat before continuing. "We know the Lord said that his father's house has many mansions, and that he would prepare a place for us," he said. "Norrie never hankered after a mansion. She just wanted a little place to tend where she was loved. But if anybody deserves a heavenly mansion, she does."

Zetta glanced at the people nearby who were nodding and, like her, wiping their eyes.

"Because of Jesus, I'm gonna see Norrie again one of these days. And our Mama. And the sweet little girl me and my woman lost a while back. That's what faith gives a person. We couldn't bear losing somebody otherwise."

Jim slowly put the Bible back on the chair. "Well, I reckon I better pray now," he said. "I'll finish with a few words at the graveyard."

Everyone bowed their heads and waited.

"Lord, we're gonna nail the coffin shut now," Jim began. But his voice faltered. Only when Sally stepped to his side and put her hand on his shoulder did he continue.

"We are grateful these nails ain't holding Norrie's soul in this box, Lord," Jim said. "She ain't here. She's with you. But we're still here, Lord, and missing her. So please help us. And please help her baby grow strong and learn to love you the way her mama did. In Jesus' name. Amen."

At their father's final word, Albert and Bernard stepped forward to lift the coffin lid and position it onto the coffin. As Jim picked up the hammer and nails beside the Bible, Sally held her arms toward the group.

"Won't y'all join me in singing 'Blessed Assurance'?"

Most the folks sang the familiar words loudly to drown

out the noise of sturdy nails going into the wooden box. But Zetta merely mouthed the words, remembering the sound of Asa's coffin being nailed shut. Then trying to shake that memory, she took a deep breath and looked out the window.

Jesse Allen was standing on the porch. And staring right at her.

Chapter 20

At the cemetery, Zetta stayed close to her brothers and Clarie as Jesse Allen positioned himself directly across from her at the grave. With Rachel, clutching her rag doll, and Micah close by her side, she pulled Isaac to her face.

Clarie, holding Adah, inclined her head toward Jesse. "Is that the feller we talked about?" she whispered.

Oh, Asa. I wouldn't have to deal with Jesse if you was here, Zetta thought as she looked toward her husband's grave farther up the hill. But she nodded.

"I seen him on the Reeds' porch," Clarie said as Jim pulled his wagon close to the grave.

After setting the wooden brake handle, Jim grabbed two coils of rope and jumped down to join his sons as they pulled Norrie's coffin slowly from the back of the wagon. Luttrell started to step forward, but Loren grabbed his arm.

"I'm helping," Loren said. "You stay put."

With three long strides, Loren helped steady the coffin as Jim looped the ropes around it.

Then the four of them lifted the narrow box and carried it the few steps to the grave.

"I'm at the head," Jim said quietly. As Loren nodded, Zetta knew Norrie would be buried correctly—facing east for the return of Jesus when he would call his beloved from their graves.

The four of them set the coffin down, and picked up the ropes to lower Norrie into the ground. When the box was just a few inches from the bottom, the men pulled the ropes up, causing the coffin to thud into the cold hole.

Jim stared into the grave for a moment and murmured, "Oh, my little sister."

Then he took off his hat, as did all the other men, and picked up a handful of dirt, which he held over the grave.

"Lord, your word says we started out as dust and that we will return to dust," he said. "So we return Norrie's body to the earth that she come from. And we ask for your strength to get us through the days ahead. Amen. Oh, Lord. Amen."

Zetta and the other women quietly cried as Jim tossed the dirt onto the coffin.

Thank you, Lord, that nobody is putting on a show like Becky and Mable Collins did when we put Asa in the ground, Zetta thought as she remembered their showy wails. Now she watched Jim shove his hat back on and grab one of the shovels stuck into the nearby mound of dirt. His sons and Loren reached for shovels as well.

Suddenly Zetta remembered how Rachel had sobbed at Asa's burying, begging for dirt not be thrown on her Poppy. With her free arm, Zetta gripped Rachel's shoulder.

"Take Brother's hand," she said and quickly turned away from the grave.

At Loren's wagon, the children climbed into the back.

"You still need to be quiet," Zetta said. "Set over in the corner. We'll go home directly."

But Rachel pointed toward Asa's grave. "Poppy's up there," she said. "Can we go?"

"Oh, honey. Not today," Zetta said. "But one pretty day we will. Be good now."

As both children scurried into the far corner of the wagon bed, Zetta rubbed Isaac's back and watched the men use the flat of their shovels to pack down the last of the dirt over the grave.

As they finished, Sally and her daughters spread the

flowering dogwood and redbud branches over the fresh dirt.

Suddenly Zetta realized someone was standing behind her. Jesse Allen.

"Whata ya doing here?" she demanded as she faced him.

"You're always badmouthing me even when I'm doing good things," Jesse said as he pushed his hat up.

"Well?"

"I'm here because I know how tight you are with the Reeds," Jesse said. "And I'm right sorry all this happened. You shouldna had to see Norrie kilt like that."

"Nobody shoulda seen that," Zetta said.

"Anyway, I come to give you some news," Jesse said. "Thorn wanted me to tell you he's taking that Calvin feller to another jail 'til the trial. He knew this would be a good time for the move, what with Jim busy burying his sister."

"So that sheriff brother of yours just up and made the decision to do that?" Zetta said. "Ain't he supposed to get a judge's say so?"

"Far as I know, he done exactly that," Jesse said. "But the point is he's having me tell you since I told him you're friends with the Reeds. He figured you can tell Jim the prisoner has been moved. And he don't need to come hot-footing around our jail and causing trouble."

"So how come he ain't telling Jim that hisself?" Zetta said.

"For crying out loud, woman. Ain't you listening?" Jesse said. "I done told you Thorn is moving the prisoner right now. Besides, he knowed I'd be here and could give you his message to pass on to Jim."

"All right," Zetta said. "You told me. You can leave now."

"Not so fast. I also need to tell you the crew is cutting and burning trees over near the river. Their boss was telling me they're having to be extra careful because of how dry the timber is. That little bit of rain we had a few days ago didn't do a thing to wet things down good."

"So now you're taking up my time to give me weather news?" Zetta said.

Jesse frowned. "No, I'll telling you the men will be getting to the trees here pretty soon."

"And I'm telling you we've had this conversation too many times before," Zetta said. "And I ain't changed my mind. I ain't giving nobody permission to cut my trees."

"We'll see about that," Jesse said.

Before Zetta could respond, Deborah Reed approached. Jesse made a dramatic show of pulling off his hat and winking at her, which caused her to giggle. Then Jesse turned back to Zetta, smirked and sauntered toward his stallion at the edge of the graveyard.

Zetta frowned as Deborah watched Jesse walk away. *That girl don't know he's just a wolf in sheep's clothing,* she thought. *But I wonder if it will do any good to try and tell her.*

Beyond Deborah's shoulder, Zetta saw Luttrell slowly take off his hat to Abigail as she stood up from putting the last flowering branch on Norrie's grave.

Now that's the way to greet a woman, she thought.

Deborah turned from watching Jesse. "Mama sent me over here to tell you she'll get Adah from you and Miz Clarie now."

"Speaking of the devil, here I am," Clarie said as she approached with Adah.

Sally appeared right behind Clarie and held out her hands.

"I'm ready to take our little girl home now," she said as tears threatened.

"I'm gonna miss you, Adah," Clarie said as she kissed the baby on the forehead before gently putting her into Sally's arms.

Zetta leaned forward to kiss the baby as well. "You're loved a bunch, little 'un."

Then Zetta and Sally looked at each other as tears ran down their faces.

"What's gonna become of this child?" Sally said.

"She's gonna be just fine because she's got y'all," Zetta said.

"I appreciate you saying that," Sally said. Then she tenderly smiled at the baby. "We're gonna do the best we know how."

She looked at Zetta again. "I'd like y'all to come back with us and the other folks and help eat up the vittles," she said. "We sure was surprised by all that was brung over."

Zetta shook her head. "That's good of you, but Clarie here needs to get packed."

"You ain't leaving us?" Sally said, quickly turning to the old woman.

"Afraid so," Clarie said. "I just found out I'm needed back at the camp."

That's so like Clarie, Zetta thought. Not telling her own troubles to somebody else with troubles. Becky should take a lesson.

"We're gonna miss you a right smart," Sally said. "I'm sorry Luttrell got snake bit, but I'm sure grateful that brung you here. You knowed exactly what to do when Norrie showed up like she did."

Clarie nodded. "God does work in mysterious ways, don't he?" she said. "Y'all are gonna stay in my prayers. And Zetta will send me news on little Adah."

"Thank you," Sally said. "I reckon I better go before I start crying again." And she and Deborah turned toward the wagon where the rest of the family waited.

Zetta bit her lip, dreading to tell Sally Jesse's news. But she knew she had to.

"Sally, wait," she said. "Jesse Allen just told me Thorn is moving Calvin to another jail right now. He don't want Jim going to the jail and causing trouble."

Sally took a deep breath and let it out slowly. "Jim's gonna be pretty mad," she said. "But I'm glad Calvin ain't here. Jim's not eat a thing since this happened, and he didn't sleep one minute last night. In fact, all he did was pace back and forth all morning as we was waiting for folks to show up for the burying. I'm right worried about him."

Sally glanced toward the wagon where Jim waited. "I

know this was hard to tell me," she said. "But I'm glad to know it. And I'll tell Jim. Now you and me can just pray about how he's gonna act at the trial."

* * * * *

After guiding his wagon close to Zetta's back steps, Loren jumped down to lift Rachel and Micah to the ground. Clarie already was clambering down, so he held out his hands for Isaac as Zetta stood.

"Well, I declare, Loren," Clarie said. "Don't tell me you're actually volunteering to hold a youngin."

Loren grinned. "Might as well get used to it, I reckon."

"Good for you," Clarie said. "You're coming right along."

Then she turned to Luttrell. "And you, young feller, had better spend the rest of the day in bed with your leg propped up," she said. "You got just five more days before you got to be fit as a fiddle and get Loren through his important day."

As Clarie mentioned the wedding, Loren frowned.

"I'm glad to be getting married," he said. "But I'm sure gonna be glad to get all the rigmarole over with."

"I wish I could watch you get hitched," Clarie said. "I'm missing a big time."

"Well, just stay then," Loren said.

Clarie sighed. "Can't. And I might as well save Zetta the trouble of telling you why," she said. "The mine is closing. I need to get home, take care of my critters and ponder what I'm gonna do."

"Well, now. I sure didn't figure ol' Rusty Hinge would ever quit," Loren said as he handed Isaac back to Zetta. "Too bad it didn't shut down before Asa got the notion to go work coal."

Sure enough, Zetta thought as she climbed the kitchen steps with the children. But he was bound and determined to pay off this farm. The farm he never lived to claim as fully his.

* * * * *

As soon as they entered the cabin, Rachel and Micah hurried to their toys near the fireplace, and Luttrell gratefully stretched out on his bed. After taking care of his mules, Loren headed to the straight-back chair by Luttrell's bed, tipped it back against the wall and put his hands behind his head.

"Clarie, you go on about packing your duds whilst Sis takes care of Isaac," he said. "Me and Luttrell will stay out of y'all's way. But I'm ready to take you to the station whenever you're ready to go. Sure am gonna miss you, though."

Clarie smiled as she picked up her satchel and clothing from the other bed.

"Whilst you fellers are out here, me and Zetta are gonna talk and solve the world's problems in her room," Clarie said. "And what we don't solve, we'll sure identify."

But once in the bedroom, Zetta and Clarie didn't speak for several minutes as Clarie changed out of her mourning dress and put on a more comfortable traveling dress.

Finally, Zetta cleared her throat. "Here I am saying goodbye to you again. And again wondering how I'm gonna get along without you."

"You're doing a better job of getting along without me than you give yourself credit for," Clarie said. "Besides, now that I know the train's easy schedule, I'll try to visit again. Especially since I won't be helping miners' babies into the world."

"I'm having a hard time wrapping my head around the camp not being there," Zetta said. "And you not being right there in your sweet cabin."

"I know. But you've heard me say time and time again that life is full of tough days," Clarie said. "But we still have a choice. We can go through those days with the Lord or without the Lord. But we'll still have to go through 'em. So the only good thing is to hang onto him."

Isaac finished eating just as Clarie closed the satchel.

"Well, I reckon that's it," she said as she opened her

arms wide. "When you get the crops laid by, come see me. I've got a feeling you'll find me at the Hindman School."

As the two women embraced, Loren stepped to the doorway.

"I'd like for you to stay forever, Clarie, but I also don't want you missing that train," he said. "How about you give me one of those hugs, and we'll be on our way."

The old woman gave Loren his requested hug, as well as hugs for Luttrell and the children. Then as Loren carried the medicine and clothes satchels to the wagon, Clarie hugged Zetta again.

"Remember what I said about you being stronger than you think you are," Clarie said. "The good Lord said he'd never leave us. We just gotta make sure we don't leave him."

"I appreciate you saying that," Zetta said as she walked onto the porch with her friend. "Seems like I got so much worrying to do that I think everything is on my shoulders."

"I know, honey," Clarie said as Loren pulled the wagon closer to the steps. "But the good Lord's shoulders are way stronger than ours."

From the porch, Zetta waved goodbye until the wagon was out of sight.

As she stepped back into the kitchen, she was struck at how empty the cabin felt even though she wasn't alone. Luttrell was resting, Isaac was asleep, Rachel and Micah were playing quietly. But Clarie's absence had added a hollowness to the walls.

Determined to shake off the sudden loneliness, Zetta reached for the pencil and paper on the dish shelf and pulled out a chair from the table.

Dear Dosha, she began to write. *I'm sorry to take so long answering your good letter, but we've had a lot going on here.*

She put the pencil down and stared at the paper. How am I gonna tell about Luttrell getting snake bit? she thought. And Clarie coming to tend him? And Norrie with sickly little

Adah? And me nursing that child? And then Norrie's man killing her at church of all places. How can I explain how much I miss Clarie already? And how much I miss her and Jack?

    Zetta looked at the few words on the page again. Then she put her head down on the table. And quietly cried.

Chapter 21

Zetta awakened before the others and was surprised she had slept well despite missing Clarie.

Maybe it's because I finally quit dreading answering Dosha's letter yesterday and just wrote it, she thought as she quietly dressed. And I was telling the truth when I told her I wished we could be talking over coffee and sweets like we done at the camp. Never in all my born days did I ever think I'd be saying that.

As Zetta put her hand softly on each child's chest to check the breathing, she again pondered Norrie's burying the day before. And Deborah's reaction to Jesse's wink.

I've got to talk to her and tell what he's really like, Zetta thought. But I don't want to be making a mountain out of a mole hill.

In the kitchen, Zetta lit the kerosene lantern then stepped onto the porch and into the morning air. As she looked toward the oak tree where Calvin had lurked earlier, she whispered a prayer.

"Lord, thank you he ain't hiding there," she said. "And thank you for this new day. Please let the sad times be behind us now."

As Zetta headed to the barn, she nodded as she passed the newly planted garden hidden in the pre-dawn darkness.

Can't wait to have fresh beans and new potatoes, she thought. Hard to believe it was just last week folks was here for the planting.

Zetta's gratitude for those who had helped was interrupted by the image of a copperhead sinking its fangs into Luttrell's flesh. To fight that thought, Zetta jerked open the barn door. In the lantern light, she saw the stray cat meandering by with another dead mouse dangling from its mouth. The two younger cats were following but scurried away at Zetta's appearance.

The mother cat's sides were smaller than before.

"You look like you done had your kittens," Zetta said. "Where you hiding 'em?"

The cat stopped and turned toward Zetta as though she understood the question.

"That beats all," Zetta said. "Are you actually gonna show me your babies?"

The cat blinked then walked to the back corner. Zetta followed quietly and watched as the cat dropped the mouse near a small mound of dry grass behind an old shovel.

Zetta lifted the lantern into the dark corner and realized she was staring at five wiggling lumps of fur.

"Well, little mama, you've got fine babies," Zetta said. "I appreciate you showing 'em off. I'll leave you be now, so we both can take care of our youngins."

* * * * *

With the barn chores completed and breakfast over, Zetta cleared the table as Luttrell drank his second cup of coffee.

"Now that Calvin ain't stealing the eggs, I've got extra," she said. "I'm thinking maybe I'll take some to trade at the store later when I mail Dosha's letter. You feel up to going?"

"Nah. I reckon I'll stay here," Luttrell said.

"You're being just like Loren and don't want to be seen riding in the pony cart."

Luttrell grinned. "You got me there," he said. "But

Loren's the only one I care about seeing me ride that way. I'm in no mood to have him fuss at me."

Zetta looked out the window as a wagon pulled into the side yard. "Well, here he is. He musta heard us talking about him."

As Zetta stepped onto the porch, Loren waved. "Come see what I brung you," he said. "Paw sent over the two piglets like he said. And I got lumber to build their pen. And pig feed."

"He's giving me the pigs even after I chased him and Becky off?" Zetta said.

"Yep. I kindly asked the same thing," Loren said. "He just said he's a man of his word. But I noticed he give you the runt. At least the other one will make good eating come fall."

"The coffee's still hot, so come on in," Zetta said. "I want to hear how Hobie and Frankie's doing."

"Can't. I'm moving my two pigs up to the cabin soon as I get yours taken care of," Loren said. "But to answer your question, our little brothers are getting closer to being men every day."

"You reckon you'll ever start using their names?" Zetta said.

Loren grinned. "Probably not," he said. "Hey, I almost forgot. Paw said Green Wilson's brother just got a new bull. He told me to tell you he'll take Brownie over there pretty soon to get serviced. The calf will bring cash money."

"Ain't he giving me a say?" Zetta said. "He knows Brownie's my only cow. We can't be without milk whilst we're waiting on her to have a calf."

Loren shrugged. "Tell him yourself then. Paw said you can buy the little bit of milk y'all use." And he turned away to guide the wagon closer to the barn.

Zetta frowned as she watched him go. When's Paw gonna stop making my decisions? she thought. She turned to go back inside, but Sally, Jim and Bernard came around the cabin's side.

The men acknowledged Zetta with a wave and headed

toward Loren's wagon while Sally approached the porch.

"I hope we ain't barging into your morning," she said. "But Jim insisted on coming over when he saw Loren go by."

Zetta smiled. "Come right on in. You know y'all are welcome any time."

As Sally climbed the few steps, Luttrell hurried out the door with his walking stick and almost bumped into her.

"I'm right sorry," he said. "I was rushing and didn't see ya."

Sally laughed. "I ain't hurt none."

But Zetta wasn't smiling as she turned to her brother. "You don't need to be working," she said. "You know what Clarie said."

"I reckon I can hold the wood in place whilst they do the nailing," he said over his shoulder as he hobbled to the barn.

Zetta huffed as she watched him go. "Well, I know he's getting better since he can't tolerate being still. But I'm sorry he almost run you down."

"If he'd throwed me in the dirt, I woulda just enjoyed the nap," Sally said. "Poor Jim ain't sleeping, so I ain't neither. But at least now he's doing something other than pacing."

"How'd he take it when he heard about Calvin?" Zetta said.

"You know I dreaded telling him," Sally said as she entered the kitchen. "But I rightly figured he was aiming to go to the jail when the burying was done. After I told him, he started pacing again. And he didn't sleep a wink. He just paced the porch all night, listening to the tree frogs and the crickets. And thinking festering thoughts."

"Oh, Sally," Zetta said.

"And then this morning when Abigail was feeding little Adah, he stormed out to the garden and started hoeing like a mad man," Sally said. "We're all worried about him. Albert even hesitated about going to the station."

As Rachel and Micah ran into the kitchen then, Sally opened her arms.

"Now these sweet little faces is what I need to see," she said.

"Me and the youngins are fixing to go to the store directly," Zetta said. "You're welcome to go with us. We won't be gone long. I mostly just need to mail a letter and get a couple things."

Sally looked toward the barn where the men were unloading the lumber.

"I'd like that," she said. "Since Jim's with your brothers, I won't worry as much. Besides, I need some baking powder for what I'm taking for the wedding food."

"I'm glad y'all are going," Zetta said. "I kindly figured ya wouldn't because of what Preacher Collins said about Norrie."

"Oh, Jim won't be at regular church," Sally said. "Just the wedding. And only because it's Loren's. But he's gonna have a hard time hearing a bride promise to obey the husband."

"I know I musta said that when me and Asa got married," Zetta said. "And I never thought a thing about it. But Asa sure wudn't a Calvin."

Sally looked out the window toward her husband. "Neither is my Jim," she said. "And if I had to say those same words today, I'd say 'em in a heartbeat."

* * * * *

Luttrell insisted on harnessing old Jack as Zetta placed Isaac in the boxed off corner of the cart and held out her hands to Rachel and Micah. Sally followed, holding a small basket.

"We washed the eggs then forgot 'em on the table," she said.

Zetta smiled. "Thank you. I'd forget my head if it wudn't attached to my neck."

"I sure know that feeling," Sally said. "Whilst you're getting the youngins settled, I'll make sure Jim don't mind me going. I don't want to add anything else for him to worry about."

As Zetta secured the egg basket and directed Rachel and Micah to sit close to the front of the cart, she watched Sally gently put her hand on Jim's shoulder.

That's what I used to do to get Asa's attention, she thought as she took a jagged breath. But never again. Never.

As Sally returned to the cart, Zetta fought tears and asked, "Jim okay with you going?"

"That sweet man said he's glad I'm doing something other than watch him," Sally said. "The way he was pacing all night, I didn't figure he even knew I was there. Well, I ain't ready to quit worrying about him, but I am ready to go to the store."

* * * * *

As Zetta guided the cart slowly onto the lane, she took a deep breath as she saw the pale green of new leaves on the old trees. On the hillsides, white dogwood blossoms and purple redbud blooms shimmered in the morning sun.

"Brother and Sister, are y'all looking at how pretty the trees are today?" she said.

"Yes, Mama," they chimed in unison.

"Well, ya better be looking good," Zetta said. "Remembering pretty days like this helps when we get stormy ones."

Zetta turned to Sally. "They don't know how right I'm being, do they?"

"No. Just like I reckon we didn't know when our folks tried to tell us things," Sally said. "But for right now, you and me can see this pretty day."

As Zetta nodded, the cart approached the chestnut trees lining the lane. No blossoms were present. And the few leaves were small and misshapen. Zetta pulled the reins to halt Jack.

"When I was taking us to church Sunday, me and Clarie was so busy bragging on Preacher Howard when he used to be at the camp, I didn't study them trees right close," Zetta said. "But look."

"I know," Sally said. "Last week, Jim walked all over our acreage and counted our trees. He said every one of 'em has the orange canker mark. You and me talked before 'bout no blooms for the bees, no food for the pigs. And no sales for cash money."

"Every time I start thinking good things are ahead, something happens to prove otherwise," Zetta said.

Sally merely nodded. And they rode the rest of the way to the store in silence.

* * * * *

A farmer and his young son carrying seed sacks to their wagon nodded to Zetta as she guided Jack into the shade at the store's side. Micah started to stand as soon as the cart stopped, but Zetta put her hand out.

"You wait right there, Brother," she said. "I don't want you getting ahead of me. And I want you and Sister to mind your manners. Y'all hear me?"

Both children nodded eagerly but wiggled in excitement. Only after their mother picked up Isaac, and Sally grabbed the egg basket, were they allowed to get out of the cart.

As they climbed the two steps into the store, Zetta looked into the narrow room and thought of the camp store. This place is so much smaller, she thought. But at least here they know who I am. And how to spell my name.

Ben turned from stacking cloth sacks of sugar on a shelf. "Hidy, ladies. And little 'uns."

He turned to Sally. "Jim done a fine job burying his sister yesterday," he said. "June wanted to be there, too, but her mother started acting worse. June's back there with her now."

"I'll tell him," Sally said. "I know he'll appreciate you saying that."

But Ben appeared not to hear her comment as he turned to Zetta.

"I'm sure glad to see you," he said. "Me and my nephew Silas been writing back and forth. I know ya recollect he's the one Loren badmouthed at the plowing."

Zetta opened her mouth to defend her brother, but Ben continued. "I been bragging on you to him," he said. "Told him how pretty you are, how well behaved your youngins are, how many acres you got on your farm. That kind of thing."

"Oh!" was all Zetta managed before Ben nodded.

"Yes, ma'am," he said as he turned back to the sugar sacks. "Let me finish stacking these and I'll take care of why y'all come in," he said. "But I reckon I done a pretty good job telling Silas about you 'cause he's coming out here the end of next week. Soon as he gets his tobacca crop in."

In the same moment Zetta and Sally turned to each other and shook their heads.

Being a widow marks me like the cankers on them chestnut trees, she thought. How can the day start so pretty and then throw this at me again?

Chapter 22

As Zetta started toward the barn the next morning, Loren unexpectedly arrived.

"Morning, Sis," he said as he guided his wagon toward the new pig pen. "Paw sent a load of old hay for the pigs after he had me and our little brothers clean out the barn yesterday."

"I know you're calling Hobie and Frankie that now just to aggravate me," Zetta said as she smiled. "And it looks like you got more than hay in there."

"Yep. I cleaned out the root cellar, too," Loren said. "All our pigs are gonna gorge on them mushy cushaws. Paw's determined to get the last bit of work out of me before the wedding."

"I appreciate the feed," Zetta said as she approached. "You gonna stay for breakfast?"

"Sure enough," he said. "Nobody makes biscuits good as you."

"Goodness! Don't never say things like that to Sarah," Zetta said. "If you do, you'll wind up making your own biscuits. Or doing without."

"You know that ain't gonna happen."

Zetta shook her head. "Don't be too sure," she said.

"Marriage is gonna hand you more surprises than you reckon."

Loren jumped down from the wagon and grabbed the pitchfork. "I don't want to hear that—unless they're good 'uns," he said. "We've all had enough of the other kind."

* * * * *

Loren reached for a biscuit as soon as Luttrell said *Amen* after the breakfast blessing.

"How 'bout passing the jelly this way?" he said as he pulled the butter dish closer.

"Hey, guess who I just thought of," Loren said. "The bald feller that worked our shift."

"What about him?" Luttrell said as he placed the jelly jar near his brother's plate.

"Remember how he'd talk about the widow woman he married with the three youngins? And how he let them know from day one who was boss?"

"Yeah?"

Loren turned to Zetta as she spooned gravy over the eggs on Rachel's and Micah's plates.

"Sis, you gotta hear this," he said. "That feller had youngins of his own, too, but when they all set down for breakfast, he never allowed her youngins to put both butter and jelly on their biscuits. They could have only one or the other. But his own youngins could have both."

Zetta's eyes widened. "And she put up with that?"

"Reckon so," Loren said as he smeared jelly onto his heavily buttered biscuit. "She hadn't run him off by the time we left the camp."

"She shoulda run him off before she married him," Zetta said.

Loren grinned. "I knowed you'd say that," he said. "But she didn't have folks who looked out for her. Her man got kilt, and she had no choice but to marry the bald feller."

Zetta shook her head. "I don't know about that."

"That's cuz you got us," Loren said. And he held out his empty cup for her to fill.

* * * * *

The next three mornings, Loren arrived shortly after dawn. Each time his excuse was to repair Zetta's fence or rehinge the outhouse door, but she was pleased to see how many biscuits he ate at breakfast. And always with both butter and jelly.

As Luttrell finished a second cup of coffee Saturday morning, he pushed back his chair.

"Sis, that was another mighty fine breakfast," he said. "Now me and Loren is gonna hoe out the corn. And I hope you won't fuss at me."

Zetta looked up from washing Rachel's and Micah's hands. "And I hope you know I'm gonna do exactly that," she said. "It ain't been even two weeks since you was at death's door."

"I know. Believe me," Luttrell said. "But I been getting stronger every day. And I quit using the walking stick last evening. So I'm hoeing corn today. It's about time I was some use around here."

Before Zetta could answer, Jim and Sally appeared at the open kitchen door. Jim took off his hat as Zetta turned to them.

"Morning, Zetta. I don't mean to be interrupting your morning," he said. "But I seen Loren come by. I figured I'd help out with whatever he's doing. If I ain't in the way."

"Come in. Come in," Zetta said. "Set down. The coffee's still good and hot."

"I appreciate that, but I'm ready to work," he said. "Me and Sally was at the store already. She's got a letter for you."

Loren grabbed his hat and stepped onto the porch. "Let's get going then."

Luttrell touched Zetta's shoulder as he stepped around

her. "I'll be fine," he said. Then he nodded to Sally. "Morning, Miz Reed."

Zetta watched the men cross the yard, relieved Luttrell had only a slight limp.

"I was fixing to come over and check on y'all," Zetta said. "So I'm glad to see ya both out and about. Is Jim sleeping?"

"As I matter of fact he is. But first let me give these sweet little youngins a hug," Sally said as she stepped inside and drew Rachel and Micah close. "Where's Isaac?"

"Sound asleep after his breakfast," Zetta said. "I reckon he'll be teething early like Brother and Sister did, so I'm appreciating this time now."

She turned to Rachel and Micah. "Y'all can get your play purties," she said. "Just don't wake your brother up."

The women watched the children run into the front room. Then Zetta gestured toward the closest chair. "Tell me about Jim," she said.

"Remember when Clarie give poor little Norrie the sleeping tea?" Sally said as she sat down. "Well, she left extra just in case. But Norrie never needed more. So I give the last of it to Jim two evenings ago. He slept all that night and half of the next day."

"How'd ya get it in him?" Zetta said. "Slip it in his coffee?"

"No. I told him straight up what it was and that it was from Clarie and would help him sleep. At first, he said he didn't need it and he wudn't gonna drink it."

"That's what I figured," Zetta said.

"Me, too. So I put my foot down and said he was heading to get sick," Sally said. "I told him we love him and need him. Then I said if he got bad off then he was gonna miss being at Calvin's trial, whenever it is. You know that got his attention."

"And he drunk the tea?"

"Every bit and headed right to bed," Sally said. "The

only problem now is he's bound and determined to be strong and alert so he can kill Calvin soon as they bring him in the courtroom. I'm praying about that every minute."

Sally rubbed her forehead. "For right now, I'm just glad he's finally sleeping," she said. "Know what he said yesterday? He said if Thorn hadn't been at church Sunday, Calvin woulda been taken care of right then. The men was all ready to hang him right then and there."

"I been pondering about Thorn happening to show up," Zetta said. "Maybe him being there when he don't normally go was God's doing. Maybe that saved Jim somehow."

"I ain't so sure," Sally said. "If the men hada hung Calvin, it wudn't been on Jim. Now he's planning to shoot Calvin first chance he gets. No matter what. And I can't get it through his head that him going to jail, or worse yet getting hisself hung for cold blooded murder, is gonna throw the rest of us into a bad time."

"Oh, Sally. This ain't the Jim I know," Zetta said.

"Ain't that the truth?" Sally said. "Well, me wallowing in worry ain't helping none. So here's that letter from Clarie. If you don't mind reading it out loud, maybe it'll take my mind off worrying for a while."

Zetta sat across from Sally and torn open the envelope.

"'Dear Zetta,'" she began. "'I sure hope this quick letter finds you doing good—and that Luttrell is doing good and on his way to being his strong self again. I hope this arrives before Loren and Sarah's wedding so you can tell them I sure am thinking about them and praying for them and their sweet baby.'"

Zetta stopped. "Oh, I shouldna read that part to you."

Sally smiled. "Us women already know," she said. "Go on."

Zetta turned back to the letter. "'I wanted to write you soon as I got home, but every minute I been helping the women pack their goods and listening to worries about what everybody's going to do. Then when I go to bed I ponder what I'm going to do. House by house is getting empty and most folks will be gone by Sunday. Mr. Gray is still here and walking around slump shouldered. But I give him credit for saying goodbye to every miner.'"

Zetta stopped again. "Mr. Gray was the camp supervisor I told you about."

"I remember," Sally said. "He's the one that's kindly decent, but his wife was uppity. His little girl, too."

Zetta nodded and continued reading. "'Know who usually is standing right by him shaking hands and wishing miners good luck? Perton himself. I was surprised he showed up after he lit out when the baby died. Last night he stopped by to ask me what I done with Polly. I told him she was safe and to leave her be for now. He didn't argue.'"

"He's the shift boss you said was always getting drunk, right?" Sally said.

"Yes. And he was mean to Polly, too," Zetta said. "Even threatened to hit her in front of all of us at the sweets party. I hope he gets straightened out now."

She turned the page over. "'Like I told you, I'm thinking I best leave here like the rest. You remember I got a cousin over at the Hindman School that helped Dosha and Jack get on there. I reckon it's time I wrote her and asked if maybe there's something for me to do to help. I'll let you know soon as I know. I best close for now. But I'm sending hugs and more prayers across the miles. Love, Clarie.'"

Zetta sighed as she put the letter on the table and slowly ran her hand over the paper.

"Clarie made being in that camp tolerable," she said. "And now Asa's gone. And the camp's gone. And she's gone."

Sally reached for her friend's hand. "I'm sorry. And I can't do a thing about any of that," she said. "But I can churn butter for ya."

And she pointed to the empty butter dish still on the table.

* * * * *

Sally scraped the last of the fresh butter from the churn paddle just as the men approached the back steps.

"Don't tell me y'all are finished hoeing already," Zetta said after she pulled a skillet of cornbread from the oven.

"Sure enough," Loren said. "Luttrell here was showing off, so me and Jim had to work twice as fast to keep up."

"I got soap and water waiting on the bench there," Zetta said. "Give me a minute and I'll have food ready. Jim, you and Sally is more than welcome to eat with us."

Jim shook his head. "Thank you, but we best get on home."

As Sally joined her husband in the yard, he thrust his hand toward Loren. "I appreciate being able to help," he said. "I'll see you tomorrow. Your big day's finally gonna be here."

Zetta nodded as the two men shook hands. Thank you, Lord, for mending the bad blood Loren's been keeping between them before, Zetta thought.

Then she watched Luttrell walk up the steps as quickly as he had before the snake bite.

"Thank you, Lord," she whispered. "May only good things be ahead now."

But as her stomach tightened, she added, "Please, Lord."

*****

After Luttrell asked a blessing over the food, Zetta set a bowl of steaming soup beans in front of her brothers. Loren pulled the bowl closer.

"When I put the hoes back in the barn, I saw your big cat chase off another 'un that was hanging around," he said. "I bet it was a tom. You gotta watch out for them, especially if there's kittens around. They don't like competition."

"You're right about new kittens," Zetta said. "Five of 'em. I hope they're all right."

"The mother cat done a good job yowling and trying to take the tom's ears off," Loren said. "So I'm sure they're okay."

"I hope so," Zetta said. "But I'll watch. You staying around this afternoon?"

"Nah, I've got to take my part of the pig feed up to our cabin and get the wagon all cleaned up for tomorrow," Loren said as he spooned beans onto his plate. "But I'll be back in time for supper if Paw don't have a bunch of last minute things he wants done. And I'll tote the water for the baths. In fact, I'd like to take my bath here, too. And even stay the night since Clarie's bed is still set up in the front room."

"I'd like that," Zetta said. "Especially since you won't be around much after tomorrow."

"Nah, I'll show up now and again for your biscuits," Loren said. "Just don't tell Sarah."

Zetta tried to frown but smiled instead. "You'll always be welcome," she said. "And no matter how old you get you'll always be my little brother."

* * * * *

Loren didn't return in time for supper. Even as Zetta washed the dishes, she kept waiting to hear his wagon roll into the side yard.

Luttrell was in the front room with the children, and Zetta wondered if he was listening for Loren, too.

Finally she pulled the water bucket from under the bench.

"Hey, Sis, I'll tote the water," Luttrell said as he came into the kitchen. "If I could chop weeds this morning on the hill, I reckon I can carry a bucket or two of water a few feet."

"I know it's useless to argue," Zetta said. "Besides, I'm worried Loren ain't showed up."

"He said he'd be back if Paw didn't have chores for him," Luttrell said. "He'll be here. Probably as soon as we get the water toted."

But even after Luttrell had carried three buckets of water to be heated on the stove, and the baths were over, Loren still hadn't arrived.

"Now, Sis, don't worry so," Luttrell said as he emptied the galvanized tub. "He just got busy, that's all. But if he don't show up tonight, we'll see him first thing at church."

"I know," Zetta said. "But that's not like him to go back on his word."

"He ain't going back on his word," Luttrell said. "He warned us about Paw. Now you and the youngins go on and get a good night's sleep. Tomorrow you'll see that everything's all right."

Zetta nodded and took the children to the bedroom. But her stomach tightened more with each step.

CHAPTER 23

To Zetta's disappointment, Loren was not sprawled in the front room the next morning.

I figured he'd slip in whilst we was asleep, Zetta thought. But maybe when we get to church, he'll be standing there grinning and wondering what kept *us*.

That hope lingered as Zetta fixed breakfast, and Luttrell took care of the barn animals. Only after the children and food baskets were safely tucked into the corners of the pony cart, and she had given her usual warning about being good to Rachel and Micah, did Zetta allow worry to creep into her thoughts again.

Luttrell held out his hand to help his sister into the cart seat then gently slapped the reins across the mule's back. "This feels good to be behind old Jack again," he said.

"So you're okay driving a pony cart?" Zetta said.

"Sure enough," Luttrell said. "Loren's gonna be busy, so he ain't gonna say a word."

As Zetta nodded, she turned toward the chestnut trees. Immediately, she looked away.

I ain't gonna worry about them right now, she thought. I'm just gonna think on this happy day. I wonder if Sarah is gonna wear that pretty blue dress with the tiny rosebuds. I hope it still fits her.

She turned to her brother. "Reckon Sarah will show up for the church service first?"

"Why wouldn't she?"

"I was just remembering a city cousin of a girl in school that come to visit," Zetta said. "She was kindly uppity and telling us about her sister's wedding. And she said the groom couldn't see her sister on that day 'til the actual wedding."

"Ya don't say."

Zetta smiled. "You don't care, but I'm gonna tell you anyway," she said.

"Fire away," Luttrell said.

"She said her sister wore a fancy white dress and had her face covered with a flimsy veil," Zetta said. "And she carried a big bouquet of fancy flowers, like white lilies and such. Our brides around here carry whatever blossom is at hand. Or none at all if it's winter. When me and Asa got married that June I carried pink wild roses from up behind Paw's smokehouse."

"I remember them," Luttrell said. "'Cause you give me a nickel to pull the thorns off."

"I plumb forgot that," Zetta said. "I hope I thanked you. Wild roses have bad thorns!"

"They do at that," Luttrell said. "But you thanked me. You always do. What else did the city girl say?"

"She said folks sent fancy presents wrapped in pretty paper to the bride's house before the wedding to be displayed. Here, we bring things to the actual wedding. Things they can use all the time. I'm giving 'em a egg basket and some pillowcases I fancied up with embroidery."

Zetta continued as Luttrell nodded. "And at the end of the ceremony, the city preacher said the groom could kiss his bride," she said. "And he lifted her veil and kissed her right there in front of everybody! That's something private that ought to stay private."

She smoothed the skirt of her dark green dress. "Well, I'm talking like my tongue is hinged in the middle," she said.

"I guess I'm just nervous about Loren. Besides, it's silly to ponder what city folks do."

"Pondering their ways don't hurt none," Luttrell said. "The trouble comes when we start wanting their ways. Worse yet, thinking their ways is better."

"Thank you," Zetta said. "I'll hush now. Especially since we're 'bout at church."

And she sighed.

* * * * *

As they pulled near the blooming dogwood trees, Zetta had hoped to see Loren waiting by the church door. But only Preacher Collins was there, nodding as families arrived.

She and Luttrell exchanged worried glances.

"He wouldn't get cold feet at this late date, would he?" Zetta whispered.

"Nope, not him," Luttrell said. "But now I'm about as worried as you."

As she and Luttrell lifted the children from the cart, the Reed family arrived. Jim pulled their wagon alongside the cart, quickly set the brake and helped Sally down with Baby Adah.

Deborah and her brothers jumped down, but Abigail shyly smiled at Luttrell. He quickly stepped forward and put out his hand to help her.

As Zetta and Sally exchanged happy glances at Luttrell's action, Mable Collins suddenly rushed forward.

"There you are with your poor little motherless baby," Mable said. "And it was just about this time last week when this child's mother was murdered right in front of all of us."

Sally managed only a feeble, "Well, yes," before Mable turned to Zetta.

"And here's this dear mother and her three little fatherless youngins," she said.

Zetta merely nodded as Paw and Becky's wagon pulled

into the yard, drawing Mable's attention away. Then Zetta smiled as Luttrell and Abigail took Rachel and Micah inside the church.

But she pulled Isaac close as she saw Jim approach Preacher Collins and put his hand out.

"I thought Jim was coming just to the wedding," Zetta whispered to Sally.

"That's what he told me," Sally said as she gently rubbed little Adah's back. "Then this morning, he declared he'd better get things straightened out in case he needs a preacher later on. I know he's pondering what's gonna happen after he kills Calvin."

"Oh, Sally."

"I know. My every breath is a prayer for the good Lord to stop this." Sally puffed out her cheeks. "Well, I better go join him. Whilst I can."

Before Zetta could follow, her father motioned for her. As she approached the wagon, Becky and Mable merely nodded as they passed her.

"Hidy, Paw," Zetta said. "Thank you for the pigs you sent over. You coming in?"

"Nah. You know I ain't interested in being singled out for finally showing up," he said. "I'm here for the wedding. That's what counts."

"Well, I'm glad you come," Zetta said. "Loren ain't here just yet, but Luttrell is doing real good."

"That's what Loren was telling me yesterday," her father said. "Did he tell you I'm gonna take your cow over to the new bull Green Wilson's brother's just bought?"

Zetta pulled in her breath slowly before she replied. "Yes, he did," she said. "I appreciate your offer, but I'm not ready for us to be that long without milk. I'd druther wait 'til this fall."

"No, this is gonna happen now whilst the cost is just a couple of dollars," he said. "Once other folks get wind of how fine this bull is, the price is gonna go up."

Zetta tried to form her next comment, but her father

shook his head. "No use in arguing," he said. "I give you and Asa that cow when you got married. So I'll see you in a day or two."

Then he pushed his hat down over his face and leaned back against the wagon seat.

"Don't you ever be like that when you grow up," she whispered into Isaac's ear as she turned toward the church.

*****

Sarah and her parents arrived as Zetta eased into the pew next to Abigail and the children. Sarah, wearing a pale green dress with a stylish loose waist and clutching a bouquet of freshly cut dogwood blooms, sat with her mother in front of Zetta and watched her father join the men on the other side of the church. Then she turned to Zetta and opened her hands in a questioning gesture.

Zetta shook her head and mouthed, *Not yet*.

Why ain't Loren here now? Zetta thought.

Her thoughts turned into prayers as she looked out the window toward the road.

Lord, I need to see Loren coming down that way right quick, she silently prayed. You know where he is. And you know why he ain't here. Please get him here. And forgive me for thinking this, but he better have a good excuse for worrying us so.

Preacher Collins interrupted Zetta's heavenly pleas as he stepped forward.

"Morning, y'all," he said. "I'm glad to see so many out, especially after them awful doings last Sunday when we had to call off church."

He paused, and Zetta waited for him to comment specifically on Norrie's murder. Instead, he nodded at Sarah and her mother.

"This is a glorious day that we get to share with Sister Sarah and Brother Loren," he said. "I see Brother Loren ain't here just yet, but more than likely he got caught up in preparations for his bride. Just like Jesus when he said he would go and prepare a place for us."

Loren better be doing something that good, Zetta thought.

"Well, let's start with singing," Preacher Collins said. "How about that old hymn 'At Calvary'? Somebody lead us off."

As one of the men started with the opening phrase, Zetta, along with the others, sang the familiar words. But she stared out the window, willing Loren to appear.

Soon she realized the preacher was watching the road, too. Normally, on wedding Sundays they sang no more than two songs, but they were well into the fifth song before Preacher Collins opened his Bible. He looked out the window again, took a deep breath and launched into the meaning behind one of Paul's letters. Zetta listened just long enough to make sure he wasn't preaching about women needing to submit no matter what.

She was vaguely aware of the preacher saying, "And that's why we always gotta be listening to the Lord," just as she finally saw Loren hurrying his mule toward the church. He was nudging the mule's sides with his heels, and his elbows were flapping as though that action would increase the animal's speed.

"Thank you, Lord," Zetta whispered as she leaned forward to touch Sarah's shoulder. The bride lifted her head and gasped when she saw her groom.

Sarah's gasp caused Preacher Collins to look out the window as Loren tossed the mule's reins over a low branch. Only then did Zetta realize the sheriff, Thorn, was following slowly on his stallion.

As Loren rushed into the church and sat in the back pew next to Luttrell, Zetta saw that his hair was slicked down, and his face was washed. But he was wearing the same clothes he worked in yesterday. What happened? Zetta wondered.

Sarah turned to Loren and mouthed, *Where you been?*

Loren shook his head and mouthed in return, *Later.*

Preacher Collins quickly recovered from the interruption. "Well, now that Brother Loren is here, we can have us a wedding," he said as he looked at them both. "Would you and the folks standing with you join me here?"

Zetta quickly handed Isaac to Abigail as agreed and followed Sarah to stand to her left at the front of the church. Luttrell stood next to Loren.

"This is a happy event," Preacher Collins began. "But it's also solemn. So whilst we ponder God's good plan, I'll ask the couple to join hands."

Sarah handed the dogwood bouquet to Zetta, her eyes full of love and happiness. Then she turned back to Loren. From that moment, Zetta didn't listen to their wedding ceremony. She was too busy remembering her own.

That wasn't even five years ago, she thought. *We started with such high hopes about our long life together. And now here I am, alone and trying to raise our youngins all by myself. Mable is right. Three little fatherless youngins.*

As Zetta blinked rapidly, determined not to cry, Preacher Collins raised his right hand. "Let's pray, now," he said and waited until everyone, Zetta included, bowed their heads. "Lord, thank you this young couple has promised before you and all these folks to help each other through the good and bad times of life. Help them keep them bright promises even when the days are dark. And help them never forget what you done for us when you sent your son to die for us. Bless their journey ahead and bless our time of fellowship with them now. And bless the food we are about to receive. In your son's name. Amen."

As soon as he ended the prayer, he gestured for Loren and Sarah to face the church members. "Now I'd like to introduce the new Mr. and Mrs. Loren Davis to y'all."

Greetings of "God bless you" and "Welcome to married life" rang out.

As Zetta hugged Sarah and returned the dogwood bouquet to her, Preacher Collins spoke.

"I seen plenty of baskets in y'all's wagons, so we'll let the men set up the sawhorses and boards waiting by the side of the church so's the women can get the food spread out on the tables. Then we'll all find a good spot under the shade trees and enjoy the Lord's bounty."

Sarah's parents, Paw Davis and various friends clustered around the young couple to wish them well. Zetta took Isaac from Abigail as the young woman joined her family. Then she smiled at Rachel and Micah.

"You two was real good," she said. "And now Miz Sarah is your Aunt Sarah."

"She's pretty," Rachel said.

"But not as pretty as your mama," a man said.

Zetta turned to face Jesse Allen.

"Whata ya doing here?" she said.

"You ain't trying to keep me away from church, are you?"

"Not if that was your regular habit," Zetta said. "What ya want now?"

"Just wanted to say you looked real pretty next to Sarah," Jesse said. "And I bet when you was standing there, you was remembering when you and Asa got married."

"That's none of your business," she said.

"And I told you before, everything you do is my business," Jesse said. "So I'll tell you this. Whilst you was remembering that, I was thinking about when you and me gets married."

Zetta glared at him. "You got no call to say that."

He shrugged. "How 'bout this then? I know you was standing up there with Sarah because Loren run her cousin off after Luttrell got snake bit."

"You're telling me what I already know," Zetta said.

"Okay, here's some news you don't know," Jesse said. "Calvin's trial is set for this coming Saturday at one o'clock. Plenty of folks will be in town then. You can tell the Reeds."

"Telling is Thorn's job," Zetta said.

"You're about to find out he's kindly busy today," Jesse

said. "Anyway, he's got a friend who's warden of a city prison. That's where Calvin is for right now. The warden says Calvin acts all high and mighty all the time. Even says he had every right to kill his woman."

"Oh, my goodness!"

"His cocky ways ain't winning him any friends. Not even with the other prisoners," Jesse said. "It won't take a jury long to convict him, so Jim's gonna get to see a hanging right quick."

Jesse glanced at his brother who was watching Loren and Sarah from the back corner.

"You take care, pretty lady," he said as he turned to go. "And keep pondering weddings."

Calvin ain't the only one with cocky ways, Zetta thought. But as she reached for the children to take them to meet their new aunt, Luttrell and Abigail quickly were at her side.

"Sis, we'll take care of the youngins," Luttrell said as Abigail reached for Isaac. "But you need to hear Loren's news. It ain't good."

Zetta turned to where the new couple had been greeting well-wishers just moments before. Now they sat in the front pew. Loren had his arms around Sarah as she sobbed against his shoulder. Her mother stood nearby with her hand over her mouth. Sarah's father was frowning, and his hands were shoved into his pockets.

"Loren, what happened?" Zetta couldn't get the words out fast enough.

He took a deep breath. "I didn't get to your place last night because I spent the night in jail," he said. "And I gotta go back in a few minutes. That's why Thorn is watching."

"Jail? Whata ya do?"

"I was passing by the store, and June run out saying her mother was awful bad off. And she begged for some moonshine to calm her down."

"Oh, Loren."

"Yep. So I give her my pint jar. Right then Thorn

stepped out. June said she was sorry, but Ben made her do that. He's still carrying a grudge about me joking over his nephew."

Sarah's father stepped forward, his fist clinched. "You could of told our girl this before y'all got married today."

Loren shook his head. "You know we needed to get this done now," he said. "Besides, I'll be out tomorrow morning."

"But tonight's our wedding night," Sarah wailed. "You can't be in jail tonight."

Zetta saw Thorn smirk as he took a step forward. That's the same look he'd give when we was in school and him and Jesse would run Asa down, she thought.

Sarah's father wasn't finished. "Wedding night? I reckon y'all done had your wedding night. Come on, girl. We're taking you home."

"No! I'm a married woman now," Sarah managed. "I'm not going back there."

"Well, you sure ain't staying by yourself up in that cabin," her father said. "So let's go."

Zetta looked at Sarah's father. "How about she stay with me and the youngins tonight? When Loren gets out tomorrow, he can get her then."

Sarah managed to say "Thank you" before her wails intensified as Thorn gestured for Loren to follow him.

Zetta wrapped her arms around the young bride. She could do nothing but cry with her.

Chapter 24

At home, Luttrell moved the bed Clarie had used back into Zetta's room while Sarah sobbed in the kitchen.

Rachel and Micah huddled together near the door as their mother clutched Isaac in one arm and held a dipper of spring water toward their new aunt.

"Drink this, honey," Zetta said. "All this crying is gonna dry you out and make you sick."

Sarah shook her head and waved her hand, knocking the dipper to the floor as she cried all the louder.

Zetta threw a towel onto the puddle and stomped on it to soak up the wasted water.

She stood quietly for a moment, holding her baby in one hand and the wet towel in the other. But as she looked at Rachel's and Micah's frightened faces, she tossed the towel into the dishpan and sat across from her new sister-in-law.

"Sarah, I'm sorry this happened," she said. "And I'm sorry you didn't get the wedding dinner and the wedding night you wanted. But your man is still alive. And he is coming to get you tomorrow. You promised for better or for worse, and a little bit of life's worse showed up sooner than you figured. Here's my handkerchief. Blow your nose and go lay down in my room for a while."

Sarah accepted the handkerchief without looking up.

"How can I face all the folks that seen Thorn taking Loren off like that?" she said. "You know they's having a big time talking about us now."

"They probably are," Zetta said. "Just like you'd be doing if it was somebody else. But everybody gets talked about sooner or later. So you're gonna hold your head up high and pay them no mind."

"Are you mad at me for crying?" Sarah managed as she looked up.

"No, this is a big disappointment for you," Zetta said. "But I don't want you thinking it's the end of the world, neither. So go lay down and rest whilst I unpack our food basket."

"Everybody brung all that good food, and we didn't get one bite of it," Sarah wailed as her tears started again.

Zetta sighed. "That's right. You didn't," she said. "But keep remembering you and Loren will have plenty of other good meals to enjoy together."

And still holding Isaac, she reached for the food basket.

* * * * *

Luttrell stepped into the kitchen as soon as Sarah headed to the bedroom.

"This sure ain't the way we thought this day would go," he said.

"Seems like a lot of that going around lately," Zetta said. "Too bad it didn't end with your snake bite."

Luttrell nodded and gestured toward the window. "We got company."

Zetta turned to see Jim, Sally and Abigail approaching the back steps.

"Come on in and eat with us," Zetta said. "I was about to set out the food I took for the wedding."

"We was hoping you'd say that," Sally said as she stepped into the kitchen and placed her own basket on the table. "Since none of us ett there, we figured we'd invite ourselves here. The boys are at the station, and Deborah is staying with little Adah. Where's Sarah?"

"I sent her to bed a minute ago," Zetta said. "She's plumb wore out from crying. But she'll be all right."

Zetta saw Abigail shyly smile at Luttrell as she hugged Rachel and Micah, who had rushed to her. Then the young woman reached for Isaac.

"I'll tend to the youngins whilst y'all set the food out," Abigail said as she gently motioned for the toddlers to sit at the table. Luttrell and Jim stood awkwardly by as Zetta and Sally pulled plates and utensils from the baskets.

"Me and Luttrell was just saying, today sure took a different turn," Zetta said.

Sally nodded. "You probably already figured folks didn't stay long after y'all left. In fact, Sarah's folks hightailed it out soon as everybody put the wedding presents in their wagon."

Zetta uncovered the cornbread and set a bowl of beans next to it before reaching into the basket for her applesauce cake.

"I'm glad for y'all's company," she said. "And I got news about Calvin's trial. I been so busy with poor little Sarah, I couldn't tell you that Jesse Allen said it's set for this coming Saturday at one o'clock."

Sally slapped her hand to her mouth and turned to her husband.

Jim's eyes narrowed as he nodded. "Good," he said. "The sooner the better. Might as well get this over with."

"Oh, Jim!" was all Sally could say as she fought tears.

"Don't you worry," Jim said. "You know I'm ready for whatever the good Lord allows."

The good Lord surely ain't gonna allow cold blooded murder, Zetta thought. But she knew it would be useless to comment as she watched Sally slowly pull bowls of sweet potatoes and fried polk from her basket.

Abigail turned to Zetta, breaking the awkward silence. "If you want to go with my folks to the trial, I'll stay with the youngins," she said. "I'll just bring little Adah over here."

"Thank you," Zetta said.

Abigail gently kissed Isaac's forehead then spoke again. "Deborah and Bernard will go, but Albert will be needed at the station since Saturday is always busy there."

My lands, Zetta thought. This girl has everything all figured out.

"What about you, Luttrell?" Jim said. "You know you're more than welcome to go with us, too."

But Luttrell turned to Abigail as he quietly answered. "Yes, I'll go," he said. "It wouldn't be fitting for me to stay and help with all the youngins without somebody else here."

Zetta smiled as the young couple both blushed.

* * * * *

Sarah slept most of the afternoon, so Zetta didn't expect her to sleep well that night. But exhaustion overtook the bride again even though she often cried out from a disturbing dream.

At sunrise the next morning, Sarah greeted the day eagerly and accepted Zetta's offer of a hairbrush as she sat on the front porch waiting for Loren.

In the kitchen, Zetta was grateful Luttrell took care of the outside chores as she prepared breakfast. She had hoped Loren would arrive in time to enjoy biscuits, but breakfast was over and the kitchen floor swept before his wagon turned into the lane.

As Loren pulled into the side yard, Sarah ran to hug him. Zetta and Luttrell followed.

"I was hoping you'd be here soon as I woke up," Sarah said. "That was mean of Thorn to keep you all morning."

Loren shook his head. "Wudn't all Thorn's fault. Look at what I'm driving. I took my mule up to our place and got the wagon."

He pointed toward the back. "And I stopped at your folk's place to get the presents for you," he said. "Believe me, that took some doing since I had to do a heap of groveling."

"Groveling? Why?" Sarah said.

"They wanted to tell me what I already know," Loren said. "How all this was my fault. How they shoulda been eating that good food and talking with folks. How I shamed them, so they collected the presents and left right soon. They ain't never gonna let me live this down."

"Well, then, I'm glad you faced my folks already," Sarah said. "You and me now just need to stay out of everybody's sight for a while. And when we do see 'em, we're gonna hold our heads up high and pay 'em no mind."

She actually listened to some of what I said yesterday, Zetta thought.

"We will at that," Loren said as he turned to Zetta and Luttrell.

"I appreciate y'all's help," he said. "We won't be off the mountain for a while, though."

Zetta hugged both newlyweds. "Y'all just take care."

Luttrell shook his brother's hand. "I'll go over to Paw's and let him know you been by to get Sarah," he said. "Today is a new day, and we all can get back to regular business now."

I don't know what regular business is anymore, Zetta thought. But she smiled and nodded.

* * * * *

With Isaac asleep, and Rachel folding and unfolding the little quilt around her rag doll and Micah stacking and restacking his blocks, Zetta grabbed the broom to sweep the back steps.

As she went outside, she heard yowling in the barn. Then a large and unfamiliar cat darted into the woods. The mother cat was close behind but couldn't catch the intruder.

The mother cat turned back to the barn, mewing pitifully. And looking at Zetta.

That must have been the tom Loren told me about, Zetta thought. She ran to the barn, dreading what she would find.

Inside, she waited for her eyes to adjust to the darkness as the mother cat continued her sorrowful meows. Finally, she followed the grieving cat and saw a dead mouse several feet from the nest. Spilled around the nest were the lifeless bodies of the five kittens.

Zetta looked at the dead mouse again. Then turned to the cat.

"Oh, little mother. You were away from your babies for just a few minutes to get the mouse. And that old tom did this whilst you were gone."

She gently put her hand toward the cat, but it darted away.

"I didn't mean to scare you," Zetta said as she watched the cat disappear. "I just wanted to pat your head and let you know I'm sorry."

Zetta picked up the old shovel that once had shielded the little family and began to dig a hole to bury the kittens in the barn's dirt floor.

That poor little mother, she thought as tears dripped down her face.

* * * * *

The distress of the mother cat lingered in Zetta's thoughts all that afternoon. Even as she took the children outside to play, she pondered the scene. Sitting on the porch with Isaac on her lap, she watched Rachel and Micah. Then she saw someone approaching on a white mule.

The rider stopped at her gate and took off his hat. "Hidy, Zetta. Is it okay I call you that even though we ain't met?"

"Depends on who you are," Zetta said and gestured for Rachel and Micah to come to her.

"I'm Silas, Ben's nephew," the man said. "I heard about him being the cause of your brother going to jail for his wedding night, so I wudn't sure today was the best day to stop by."

"That was good thinking," Zetta said, wishing Luttrell still was there.

"Well, I'm not one to beat around the bush," he said. "Mind me sitting with you up on the porch?"

"I don't beat around the bush, neither," Zetta said. "You're fine right where you are whilst you state your business."

Silas put his hat back on. "All right. I plan to court you down the road."

"That so?" Zetta said calmly. I gotta watch my mouth, she thought. Ben's already caused this family enough trouble because of this feller.

"Yes, indeed," Silas said. "I aim to be married before the year is out, and you're as pretty as I been told."

"And the fact that I already got a farm helps, I suppose," Zetta said.

"It does," Silas said. "And sooner or later you're gonna need a man to help you run it."

"I got my brothers."

"No, you got just one brother," he said. "The other 'un's got a wife to take care of now."

Zetta waited as Silas pushed his hat back further. "Pretty soon other suitors will be coming around," he said. "Right now they's getting crops in. But when the crops is laid by, they'll be showing up to court a new widow."

Widow, Zetta thought. There's that name again. A mark as clear as the one on the trees.

She pulled Isaac closer and turned to Rachel and Micah who huddled next to her. Then with the tom cat's morning destruction swamping her thoughts, Zetta gestured toward her children.

"I told you I don't beat around the bush, neither," she said. "So I'll tell you what means the most to me. They're right here on this porch. My youngins. If I was to let you come calling, I'm gonna watch how you treat them."

"And I been thinking about that already myself," Silas said. "In fact, I hear tell Lexington has a real good orphanage that takes in youngins like yours 'til they's grown. You wouldn't have to give 'em up forever."

Zetta immediately stood up, forgetting her plan to appease Ben.

"Well, Silas. You ain't welcome here. Not now and not in the future," she said. "My youngins will always come first. You can think on that as you leave right now."

"My uncle ain't gonna like this when I tell him."

"Then I reckon you better not tell him," Zetta said. "Ben's a good man, and he's not gonna be happy to hear he's got a foolhardy nephew."

Silas immediately turned his mule toward the road.

Lord, forgive me for lying about Ben being good, Zetta thought as she watched Silas leave. But I'm tired of trouble. Plumb tired.

* * * * *

Zetta had just poured cornbread batter into the skillet when she saw Luttrell appear in the side yard. But her smile quickly disappeared when she saw his unhappy expression. Close behind him was their father on his own mule.

She stepped onto the back porch to greet them.

Luttrell held his hands in front of him in a hopeless gesture.

Zetta didn't have to wait long for an explanation.

"I come for your cow," Paw Davis said as he dismounted. "Green Wilson's brother's waiting for me to bring her over tonight. I'll get her back in a day or two after she's been serviced."

"Paw, like I told you yesterday, I appreciate your offer," Zetta said. "But I don't want her taken over there now."

Her father continued toward the barn and acknowledged her comment with a mere wave of his hand.

"I'm sorry, Sis," Luttrell said. "I tried to talk to him, but you see how far I got. The only help I can offer now is to do the evening milking for you."

Tears filled Zetta's eyes as she watched her brother join their father.

How can I have a backbone when it comes to talking to men like Silas? she wondered. But I'm downright mealy-mouthed when it comes to my own paw.

Then to keep from seeing Brownie led away, Zetta went back into her kitchen and put the cornbread into the oven.

Chapter 25

The next morning, Zetta dreaded seeing Brownie's empty stall and hearing the mournful cries of the mother cat. Thus, she was grateful Luttrell took care of the barn chores and gathered the eggs while she fed Isaac and fixed breakfast.

As she offered a second cup of coffee to her brother, he shook his head. "I appreciate that, but I thought I'd get an early start on watering the garden," he said. "We sure need rain. Especially since the tree fellers is burning more chestnuts over the ridge. We can't have fire getting out of hand."

"I keep hearing they do burnings to keep the blight from spreading," Zetta said. "But Clarie says they's doing that over her way, and she don't see it making any difference."

"It's a shame all that good lumber is wasted. And I don't know if we're ever gonna get over losing all them good trees," Luttrell said as he stood up. "But me setting here and complaining ain't gonna change things. At least I can water the garden."

But before Luttrell could finish filling even one bucket at the pump, Zetta saw their father pull into the side yard. She stepped onto the porch to greet him, but he jumped down from the wagon and strode directly to Luttrell. Zetta couldn't hear what they were saying, but she saw Luttrell frown and turn toward the house as Paw walked to the smokehouse.

Luttrell's steps were slow as he approached his sister.

"I'm dreading telling you this the worst in the world," he said. "But that new bull broke Brownie's back during the servicing. Green Wilson's brother had to shoot her."

Zetta slammed her hand across her mouth to keep from crying out.

"Paw's gonna build up the fire in the smokehouse, and then we're gonna go finish butchering her out. We'll bring the meat back here directly."

Zetta shook her head. "I ain't eating that meat!"

"That's what I told Paw, but you can't let it go to waste, neither," Luttrell said. "I'm sorry, Sis. I truly am."

And he turned to go.

* * * * *

Zetta was numb as she washed the breakfast dishes. But gradually angry tears appeared.

Poor little Brownie, she thought. I told Paw I didn't want him to take her over there. But talking to him is like talking to a rock sometimes.

As she hung the dishpan on the wall, the unwelcome call of "Hello in the cabin" came from the front yard.

Jesse Allen.

She motioned for Rachel and Micah to stay with their toys before she jerked open the front door.

"I'm in no mood to talk," she said as she stood in the doorway. "Whata you want?"

"Can't a feller stop by with some news about the trial?" Jesse said as he patted his stallion's neck. "You going?"

"Not that it's any of your business, but yes."

Jesse pushed his hat from his forehead.

"That's what I figured," he said. "So you might wanna tell Jim Reed not to bother bringing his pistol. Thorn's planning to collect guns before anybody goes in the courthouse."

"What makes you think Jim's got anything planned?" Zetta said.

"Come on, we both know the answer to that," Jesse said. "But I got another reason I come by. You owe me thanks for being the feller that got Loren out of jail for his wedding. Carrying moonshine usually means four or five nights in jail. Sometimes more."

"So?"

"I was hoping for more appreciation than that."

"Keep hoping," Zetta said. "I got work to do."

"I guess your ornery mood explains what I heard at the store about you."

"So?"

"So? Is that all you got to say?" Jesse said. "Okay, I'll tell you anyway. Ben's nephew Silas said he stopped by, but you run him off."

"So?"

"Another so. Anyway, I'm glad you run him off," Jesse said. "I sure don't want another feller beating my time when it comes to you."

"I ain't interested in courting anybody right now, least of all you," Zetta said. "But I wonder how come you're all the time showing up here? Don't your farm need tending? Or is your land magic and works itself?"

Jesse smirked. "First of all, I'm glad to hear you say you ain't interested in courting *right now*. That's a good answer because a woman in these hills needs a man. And you don't have to worry about my farm. I got a couple of fellers who work when I want help. To answer your other question, I like showing up now and again to remind you I'm serious."

"The only thing you're serious about is checking up on me," Zetta said.

"Is that so bad?" Jesse said. "Now tell me why you run Silas off."

"Didn't he say?"

"Not exactly," Jesse said. "He just said something about you not being ready to court."

Good for Silas for not telling, Zetta thought. I sure didn't want to have to deal with Ben's anger again.

"Not that it's any of your business, but I told him that I think all the time about my youngins," Zetta said as she pulled in a deep breath. "And if I do ever marry again it'll be to somebody that treats 'em good."

"And?"

"*And* when I told Silas that, he said he'd already been thinking about them, too," Zetta said. "Know what he'd decided?"

Jesse shrugged.

"He come right out and said he was gonna put them in some orphanage!" Zetta said as she fought to control her voice. "There's no way that's gonna happen! You keep claiming we're gonna be married one of these days. So where do my youngins fit in *your* plans?"

Jesse rubbed his chin. "Now Zetta. There's some things you just gotta trust me on."

"Trust? Let me remind you of a time when you wanted Asa to trust you," Zetta said. "Do you recollect when you chased him down to the creek at school? And just as you caught up with him, you stumbled on a tree root and hit the ground pretty hard."

"He told you about that, huh?"

"That's not all he told me," Zetta said. "You claimed you hurt your leg bad."

"Yep. I did say that."

"Then you told Asa you was sorry and asked him to carry you to school. He carried you on his back all the way up the hill."

Jesse grinned. "So?"

Zetta pointed her finger at him. "*So* when he set you down real gentle like, you hopped up and said, 'thanks for the ride, Asa.'"

Jesse slapped his thigh in satisfaction. "I did get him pretty good that time, didn't I?"

"That wudn't funny then, and it ain't funny now," Zetta said.

"Ah, come on," Jesse said. "We was just kids. Can't you let bygones be bygones?"

"Not when it comes to you!"

And she stepped back into the cabin and closed the door.

* * * * *

Zetta was returning from the root cellar with last year's potatoes when Sally waved.

"I been to the store," she said as she approached. "I hope you don't mind that they give me your mail again."

"No, that's good," Zetta said. "I hope it's from Clarie."

"It is at that," Sally said. "I didn't open it, but you know I looked to see who sent it."

Zetta smiled. "I need some cheering up today," she said. "But I bet she's writing to tell me she's at the Hindman school now."

Sally looked at the envelope again as they hurried up the kitchen steps.

"It don't say. The only thing she wrote in the corner says *from Clarie.*"

As Zetta set the potatoes on the sideboard, Rachel and Micah ran to greet Sally.

"Y'all are getting bigger by the minute," she said as she hugged them. "Your mommy is gonna read a letter from Miz Clarie now. Wanna stay and hear it?"

Rachel immediately sat at the table, but Micah shook his head and ran back to his blocks.

"Let's see what news Miz Clarie has for us," Zetta said as she opened the envelope.

She read aloud as she sat down. "'Dear Zetta and sweet family, this won't be a long letter, but I wanted to let you know I'm at Hindman now. But we both knew I would be.'"

Zetta looked up. "We did talk about it plenty," she said. "But worrying about something bad ain't the same as finding out it actually happened."

Sally nodded. "I sure know that," she said. "Go on with the letter."

Zetta took a moment to find her place on the page, then started again. " 'When I wrote my cousin to see if there was anything I could do here, she said they could use somebody to be in charge of their new infirmary. I hope I spelled that right. So here I am with two big rooms upstairs to call my own. And I can look out the big window down toward the creek. I don't have a kitchen, but I don't need one since I eat with the students.' "

"Oh, my goodness," Zetta said. "I can't even think about not having my own kitchen."

She returned to the letter. " 'The best part about being here is seeing Dosha and Jack all the time and eating her good food. The students sure enjoy her cooking. Jack's foot is healed, but he will always limp. And I'm glad to see Polly doing better as she decides what to do about Perton. Well, I told you this would be a short letter. But I wanted to let you know where I am. Of course, I miss my little cabin. And I miss the life I had at the mine. But there comes a time in every life when we have to stop crying over what we lost and be grateful to the Lord for what we got left.' "

Zetta stopped again. "She's always saying things like that," she said. "One of these days I want to have some of her wisdom."

"You're closer to that than you think," Sally said. "What else does she say?"

Zetta turned the page over. " 'I hope you can write back soon. I'm looking forward to hearing about Loren and Sarah's wedding. I know they had a big time. Kiss your sweet babies for me. And tell Sally and her family hello. You and your babies come visit when you can. I got room for sleeping. I'm sending hugs and prayers across the miles. Love, Clarie.' "

Zetta folded the paper slowly. "She's right about her and me knowing she'd wind up at the school. But I still keep picturing her in that sweet cabin at the camp."

"Maybe you ought to go visit her soon," Sally said. "That

way you can see for yourself where she is now and that she's happy."

"I sure would like to," Zetta said. "But first I reckon we gotta get through Calvin's trial. How's Jim doing?"

Sally frowned. "Pondering what he's gonna do," she said. "And working extra hard to get everything caught up. He says now that he's sleeping again he's got more energy. But I know he's trying to get things done so the boys can handle the farm after he kills Calvin."

"Oh, Sally. I'm sorry. But that reminds me. Jesse Allen stopped by earlier," Zetta said. "He was talking a bunch of nonsense, so I put this out of my mind 'til now. But he said Thorn's gonna make all the men give up their guns before they go in the courthouse."

"Well, that news is kinda a relief," Sally said. "But when I tell Jim, he's just gonna start thinking how else he can kill Calvin. I don't know how the Lord is gonna keep another murder from happening, but I'm sure begging him to step in. And I'm glad you and Luttrell are gonna be there to help me through whatever happens."

"I'm praying it don't come to that," Zetta said as tears filled her eyes.

And she and Sally both cried as Rachel watched in amazement.

* * * * *

Sally had been gone less than twenty minutes before Zetta heard her father's wagon rumble into the side yard and continue to the smokehouse.

From the back porch, Zetta watched her father and brother carry chunks of meat and sacks of heavy curing salt into the little building.

When they were finished, Luttrell thrust his hands under the water at the pump. But Paw Davis turned toward the wagon without acknowledging his daughter.

"Ain't you even gonna say hidy?" Zetta said.

"Okay. Hidy," he said.

"I wish you'd listened when I said I didn't want you taking Brownie," Zetta said.

"This ain't gonna hurt you none," her father said as he climbed into his wagon. "Green Wilson's brother felt bad, so he's giving you one of his cows. Soon as she weans her calf."

"That ain't gonna make up for Brownie."

"Now look. He don't have to give you nothing," her father said. "After all, things like this happen. But since the bull is new, he felt responsible. You ought to be grateful."

"Grateful is the last thing I'm feeling right now," Zetta said. "How am I supposed to eat that sweet cow's meat?"

"That's all it is. Meat," he said. "You had plenty of hickory wood left in there. And we salted the meat down pretty good. The hot weather ain't hit yet, so the meat will cure all right."

Then he slapped the reins across the backs of his mules and turned the wagon toward the lane.

Chapter 26

For the next several mornings, Zetta and Luttrell divided the chores without discussion. Zetta cooked, took care of the house and children while her brother handled outdoor work and watered the garden. And when she asked, he assured her the mother cat was no longer around.

Zetta especially was grateful to be spared from having to see the constant lazy smoke from the smokehouse as Brownie's meat cured.

Friday, Zetta had just finished washing the breakfast dishes when Sally Reed visited.

"Jim was at the store bright and early, and they give him your mail," she said as she hugged Rachel and Micah. "He was getting cornmeal and lard and such."

Zetta studied her friend's face. "That's good, ain't it?"

Sally frowned. "He said he was getting ahead of the folks who'll be crowding the store when they come to town tomorrow for the trial," she said. "But that's just more of him getting supplies in and trying to take care of us for when he's not here. Jim's never lied to me the whole time we been together. But now this. What's wrong with him?"

Zetta sat at the table and gestured for Sally to join her. "Grief, I reckon," she said. "All I know to do is pray for the Lord's help. Just like you're doing."

"I appreciate them prayers," Sally said as she sat. "And I reckon we'll know where we stand come tomorrow. But for right now, here's your letter."

"It's from Dosha, over at Hindman," Zetta said. "Want to hear her news?"

"You know I was hoping you'd say that," Sally said.

Zetta smiled and began to read as Rachel leaned against her. "'Dear Zetta. I'm writing before I go cook noon dinner for everybody. I got your letter about all that's been going on there. I'm sorry we can't talk face to face like we done at the camp. But I'm glad Luttrell is doing better now. Me and Jack was real worried when we heard about the copperhead. Them things is mean. I'm sorry to hear about your neighbor's sister. I just stopped here and prayed for everybody there again.'"

Zetta looked up. "She's praying for y'all even without knowing about the trial tomorrow."

Sally nodded. "We need every prayer we can get," she said. "What'd she say next?"

Zetta read again. "'Clarie told me she wrote you to say she's here now. I'm glad you already heard. I know the news was a shock to you just like it was to me and Jack. It's hard to think the mine is closed and everybody is gone. But Clarie keeps saying the good Lord don't get surprised by what happens to us in life, so we shouldn't be neither. But that's not easy to do. Well, I better get to the kitchen. The head cook is a nice lady as long as I'm not late. Then her frown beats any storm coming in over the mountains. Come visit us real soon. And bring your three babies. I miss seeing them. Jack says hello. Love, Dosha Conley.'"

Sally leaned forward. "Thank you for reading that. When you first read Clarie's letter, I said I hoped to meet her soon. And then it happened because Luttrell tangled with the snake and she come to help. So I ain't gonna say I'm hoping to meet Dosha. I'll just say she sounds sweet."

"She is," Zetta said. "And I still can't get over how much she liked being at the camp. I wanted out of there every minute, but she was always grateful Jack had a good job and they could be together. Did I tell you Jack plays the hog fiddle? And he sings the best in the world."

"I thought you said he stutters," Sally said.

"And real bad," Zetta said. "But when he sings, you'd never know he's ever stumbled over a word."

"That beats all," Sally said. Then she looked around the kitchen. "What would you think if I was to go home and get one of the girls to come back with me?" she said. "We'll help you do a wash. I know it's bad of me, but I can't be watching Jim working up a storm getting ready for what happens tomorrow. Especially since he won't let me help."

"You know you're always welcome," Zetta said. "Even if you ain't working."

"Helping you do a wash will keep me from being so nervous," Sally said as she stood. "Reckon Luttrell will mind getting the kettles ready?"

"He won't mind at all if he knows that will give him a chance to see Abigail," Zetta said.

And both women smiled.

* * * * *

Zetta was disappointed Abigail and Luttrell exchanged nothing more than shy smiles as the young woman helped with the washing Friday afternoon. And those same shy smiles were all that passed between them when Abigail arrived with Adah just after Saturday's noon dinner.

Rachel and Micah had nodded obediently as their mother insisted they be on their best behavior with Miz Abigail and help her with the babies. But as Luttrell helped his sister into Reed's wagon, she looked at her youngsters waving to her from the porch.

"I ain't never left them since the day Asa got hurt," Zetta said. "Maybe I ought not go."

Luttrell smiled as he sat next to Zetta. "They'll be all right with Miz Abigail."

And then he whispered, "Nobody's finer than her."

* * * * *

The ride into Salyersville was quiet as each person seemed lost in their own wonderings about what the day would bring. When Jim directed the wagon to the side of the courthouse, several wagons already were there.

As Jesse Allen had warned, Thorn stood by a table near the door and demanded every man empty his pockets of pistols and knives. As Zetta and Luttrell stood in line behind the Reeds, they watched men shrug as they placed items on the table. But two brothers from near Jackson Fork refused.

"Now listen, Sheriff," the tallest one said. "I ain't planning to use my pistol today. But I ain't never surrendered it neither. And I ain't about to start now."

Thorn slowly rested his hand on his own holstered pistol. "Well, there's a first time for everything, I reckon," he said. "If you fellers is gonna go inside, your weapons is gonna stay right here."

Without another word, the brothers turned and left.

Thorn watched them go before gesturing for the Reed group to step forward.

Luttrell and Bernard, having been forewarned, showed their empty pockets. But Jim faced him defiantly.

"Why you here, Thorn?" he said. "I figured you'd be bringing Calvin to the courthouse. Or is he already in there acting all high and mighty?"

Thorn scowled. "The deputies from the other jail are bringing him over directly in their new motorcar," he said. "And it's closed, not like a wagon. So don't get no ideas."

"I ain't got no ideas," Jim said. "I'm just here to see justice done."

"You got your pistol on ya today?" Thorn said.

"You know I ain't got no reason to be toting such to the courthouse."

"Empty your pockets then."

"Sure," Jim said. "I ain't got nothing but the knife I been carrying since I was a boy."

"Open it," Thorn said. "Let me see the blade."

"Sure," Jim said as he pulled the blade from the side of the knife. "But about all it's good for is cutting a string off my overalls or peeling apples."

Thorn took the knife, turned it over a couple of times, then pushed the blade back into the handle and held it out to Jim.

Jim murmured a quiet *hmm* before accepting the knife.

As Thorn gestured for the group to enter the courthouse, Zetta and Sally looked at each other in bewilderment. Thorn knows better than to return a knife any way other than how it was handed over, Zetta thought. He's got no call to act like that.

But Zetta forgot Thorn's insult as she stepped inside the courthouse for the first time. She stared at the polished high desk in the front of the room and the oak railings across the row of benches. Still marveling at the shiny wood, she turned to Sally to comment. But her friend was watching Jim study the room.

Is Jim looking for something he can use to kill Calvin? Zetta wondered. What if he tries to tear into him with his bare hands? Oh, Lord. We sure need your help.

As they settled into an empty bench near the back, Zetta looked around. The other attendees were mostly men. But some women from church were with their husbands who had been ready to hang Calvin that awful day.

As Zetta noted the time of twelve-forty on the wall clock behind the judge's desk, her father tapped her on the shoulder.

"I figured you'd both be here," he said as he nodded to Luttrell. "And look at us all gussied up. Anybody can tell we took our Saturday night baths last night."

He turned to Jim. "I hope this goes the way you want," he said.

Lands, Zetta thought as Jim nodded his thanks. That's the nicest Paw's ever been to him.

Her father then spoke to Zetta. "Me and your little

brothers is over there," he said. "I figured they needed to see what all's involved with trials. But Becky ain't interested."

Zetta smiled at Hobie and Frankie, fighting the urge to scold her father's refusal to use their actual names.

"Looks like they ain't little no more, Paw," she said.

"Yep. And about the time they get big enough to be any real use, they'll leave," he said. "Just like y'all done."

He looked at the wall clock. "I hope this starts on time," he said. "I got things to do."

As he turned to go, he almost bumped into Jesse Allen.

"Hidy, John," Jesse said. "Good to see you today. You doing all right?"

Why's Jesse calling Paw by his given name? Zetta wondered as her father nodded and returned to his young sons. *Both them Allen boys is outdoing themselves in being rude today.*

Zetta sighed as Deborah giggled at Jesse's appearance. Then to Zetta's relief, he merely nodded and looked at Jim. "I figured you might be interested in knowing Thorn offered to have the preacher here," he said. "But Calvin just laughed and said he's getting a city lawyer, and that would be a whole lot better than some preacher."

"Appreciate knowing that," Jim muttered.

Jesse waited, perhaps expecting Jim to say more. But when no further comments came, he quickly turned to find a seat.

Jim watched Jesse go. "You'd think a man facing hanging might think about his soul," he said to Sally. "And the only lawyer who'd take Calvin on is some shyster."

"I know," Sally said quietly. Then she looked out the window.

Zetta glanced at the clock again. Two minutes to one. And still no sign of Calvin.

I hope the youngins are all right, she thought. *Abigail's got her hands full watching all four of 'em. Please, Lord, let this be over with soon.*

As the clock struck one, a stout gray-haired man stepped behind the tall desk.

"I'm Judge Montgomery," he said. "We'll get started soon as the prisoner arrives."

He gestured toward the open window as he sat down. In unison, everyone turned to look out the window and toward the empty road.

Zetta continued to watch the clock and worry about the children. Finally, at one-twenty, a black motorcar exited the dirt road and pulled next to the building. Everyone turned, expecting to see the prisoner, wearing handcuffs, pulled from the back of the vehicle. But only the driver, a deputy, exited. A few minutes later, he and Thorn entered the courtroom together and walked directly to the judge.

Zetta held her hands in a questioning gesture and looked at Luttrell. But he shrugged.

She, along with everyone else, watched the deputy talk to Thorn and the judge. As the deputy turned to leave, his shiny black boots struck the wooden floor with unnecessary stomps.

Thorn hooked his thumb over his belt and stepped to the judge's side, waiting.

"There ain't gonna be a trial," Judge Montgomery said. "I just got word that Calvin Risner died today. So y'all go home now, and don't be asking questions. This case is closed."

And he brought his gavel down loudly on the desk top.

At first, everyone exchanged bewildered looks. Then exclamations of "How'd he die?" and "Reckon he tried to escape, and they shot him?" filled the room.

As someone yelled, "I hope they got him right between the eyes," Thorn stepped forward.

"Y'all can do your talking outside," he said. "And right now."

Zetta and the others on that bench stood up, but Thorn motioned for them to wait.

Sally gripped Jim's hand and whispered, "It's over."

But Jim merely frowned.

Thorn watched the last person leave before he approached.

"Well, Jim, since Norrie was your sister, I figured you'd want to know how Calvin died," he said. "You want to hear by yourself or in front of everybody else?"

"They might as well hear the story same time I do," Jim said. "That'll save me from telling them later."

"And this news probably saved you from killing Calvin," Thorn said.

Jim frowned. "Don't be blaming me for what I ain't done."

Thorn hooked his thumb over his belt again. "All right. Calvin choked on a piece of tough bread at the new jail," he said. "Nobody helped, not even to thump his back. They just stood around and watched him choke. Finally, one of the guards noticed the commotion."

No one spoke for several moments. Then Jim stood and thrust his hand toward Thorn.

"I appreciate you telling me, Sheriff," he said. "We won't be butting heads again."

"Glad to hear it," Thorn said as he shook Jim's hand. "And the news is yours to tell."

All of them watched Thorn stride away. Then Sally stood and put her hands on each side of her husband's face.

"Jim, honey, it's over."

But he shook his head. "No, it ain't. Norrie's still dead."

"Well, maybe you can rest easy now," she said.

"Maybe *you* can," he said as he gently pulled her hands down. "But I ain't never gonna rest easy knowing I didn't save my little sister."

"You know my heart hurts for you," Sally said. "And you know I been praying for you all the time. Them prayers is gonna continue."

Jim leaned into Sally's face. "Are you saying God killed Calvin, so I wouldn't have to?" he said quietly. "And if your prayers kept me from killing that man, why didn't my prayers keep him from killing Norrie?"

    Sally took a sharp breath. "I don't know," she said. "All I know is you're still gonna be with us. Let's go home."

    Zetta rubbed her forehead as the Reeds filed out of the bench. Luttrell turned to her.

    "You okay, Sis?"

    Zetta nodded. "I reckon," she said. "It's just that Jim asked a good question, and now I'm pondering how all this fits together."

    "Yep," Luttrell said as he stepped away from the bench.

    "You know if it wudn't for my sweet youngins, I'd wish we could go back to the day when I paid you a nickel to fix my wedding bouquet of wild roses," Zetta said.

    "I know, Sis," Luttrell said. "But now it's time we went home."

    "Believe me, I'm happy we can," Zetta said.

    And she took his offered arm.

Chapter 27

In the churchyard the next morning, both Zetta and Sally had to endure the usual pitying comments about fatherless and motherless children from Mable Collins. But before Mable could finish a sentence, the other women swarmed around Sally, demanding to know what Sheriff Thorn had said to Jim at the courthouse. As Sally clutched Baby Adah and reported Calvin's choking, Zetta glanced toward the men clustered around Jim at his wagon as he offered the same account.

Jim's question yesterday sure got me wondering, Zetta thought. Did God answer me and Sally's prayers by killing Calvin outright? If God did answer that way, why didn't he answer Jim's prayers for Norrie? And why didn't he protect Asa in the mine when I was praying?

Zetta switched Isaac to her other arm and rubbed her forehead. "Father God, I can't figure this out," she prayed to herself. "All I know to do is ask you to help us through bad times."

As the listeners in both groups asked questions and insisted on more details, Loren and Sarah arrived. Loren guided the wagon under a dogwood tree dropping the last of its blossoms. Loren smiled as he looked from group to group. No one seemed to notice their arrival.

Zetta nudged Rachel and Micah.

"When the wagon stops, run and hug your Uncle Loren and Aunt Sarah," Zetta said.

Loren helped Sarah from the wagon, and they both embraced the children. A few men raised their hands in greeting to Loren, but quickly turned back to Jim. Zetta walked toward the young couple.

"I was wondering if y'all would show up," she said.

"I figured we might as well quit dragging our feet," Loren said. "Then yesterday evening I was at the store and heard about Calvin. So I figured folks would have more interesting things to talk about today than just us."

"You figured right on both counts," Zetta said. "Now I hope y'all will eat with us. It's just beans and cornbread and such, but I've got plenty."

"We'd like that," Sarah said as she turned to Loren. "Is that okay, honey?"

"But we can't stay long," Loren said. "I gotta water our pitiful little garden again since everything's so dry. But don't tell Paw I was working on a Sunday. Beats me how he won't go to church, but at the same time he don't like us working on Sunday beyond caring for the critters or getting a meal on the table."

Zetta nodded. "Sometimes I wonder if he'll ever see us as adults."

Loren chuckled. "You let me know when that happens, Sis."

* * * * *

During church, Zetta was disappointed Preacher Collins ignored Calvin's death, which was on everyone's mind. Nor did his sermon provide insight about prayer. Instead, he preached about Jesus calming the storm on the lake and scolding the disciples for their fear.

"Lord, I sure need some calming of my own," Zetta silently prayed as she tried to listen. "And I reckon I'm gonna be tangling with fear 'til my dying day. You already know that.

But you also know I'm trying to hang onto you with every breath."

Noon dinner was another disappointment for Zetta as Loren and Sarah ate quickly and left instead of lingering to visit.

Zetta had insisted Sarah not help with the dishes even though she had hoped to hear details of Sarah's week of being in charge of her own little home. Zetta was sorry to see them leave. Even with the children and Luttrell still there, the house seemed lonesome without Loren's boisterous teasing.

Isaac cried for his own meal just as his mother tossed the dishwater onto the patch of weeds and wild flowers near the kitchen door. Zetta hurried to tend to him and smiled as she passed Rachel and Micah playing quietly near Luttrell, who was sitting on his bed.

Zetta settled into the bedroom chair to feed Isaac, but he was fussy and wiggly. When she finally succeeded in pulling him close, he took only a few gulps of milk before he bit her.

"Oh! Don't tell me you're teething already," she said. "I sure wish Clarie was still here. All I know to rub on your little gums is clove oil."

Zetta buttoned her dress again and started to the kitchen with Isaac. Luttrell stood as she entered the front room.

"Sis, I'm gonna walk to the cemetery," he said. "Reckon it's okay if I was to take Sister and Brother with me?"

Rachel grabbed her rag doll and rushed to her uncle's side. "Say yes, Mama. Me and Brother will be good."

Zetta chuckled at the child's insistence. "All right. But you better stay close and mind your uncle."

Rachel hopped from foot to foot and smiled while Luttrell nodded his thanks and cleared his throat. He started to speak, but closed his mouth again.

"Why you hemming and hawing?" Zetta asked.

"Well, I was wondering if you reckon it'd be all right if I was to stop by the Reeds and see if maybe Miz Abigail would like to walk with us," he said.

"Yes, do that," Zetta said. "But leave the youngins here.

They don't need to be interfering with your courting."

Luttrell's face flushed. "I don't figure a walk is courting exactly," he said. "But if it is, I'd druther the youngins was with us. I don't know if I'm ready to have folks see just me and Miz Abigail together."

"Then you and the youngins go have a good time with Abigail," Zetta said. "And don't worry one bit about other folks."

Luttrell nodded and held out his hands to the children.

* * * * *

The oil from the crushed clove buds soothed Isaac's sore gums long enough for him to get his tummy filled.

With Isaac asleep, and Luttrell and the children gone, the cabin was eerily quiet. Zetta rubbed her hands against her sides.

Might as well answer Clarie's and Dosha's letters, she thought.

But the call of "Hello in the cabin" came from the front yard and interrupted her plans.

Jesse Allen.

I've got half a mind to ignore him, Zetta thought. But if he saw Luttrell and the youngins leave, he knows I'm still here.

Finally, she jerked open the door. Jesse remained seated on his stallion and did not take off his hat.

"Howdy, pretty lady," he said.

"Why you out bothering folks on a Sunday?" Zetta said. "I've got things to do and listening to you ain't one of 'em."

Jesse pushed back his hat. "Well, there you go again, acting all high and mighty," he said. "I just come by to tell you why me and Thorn wudn't in church this morning."

"I hope you ain't thinking I even noticed," Zetta said.

"But I bet you did," Jesse said. "Because you know I ain't about to give up easy. In fact, now that the Calvin business is all settled, I'm aiming to step up my courting. And right soon at that."

"You call bothering me courting?" Zetta said.

"Think of it as me making sure I'm staying in your thoughts," he said. "But back to the reason why me and Thorn wudn't in church. Remember Thorn told Jim the Calvin news was his to tell. And he didn't want to be pulled into giving more details when there ain't none to tell."

Zetta crossed her arms. "You said what you come to say, so it's about time you went on about your business."

"I'm tired of telling you that you are my business," he said. "And to prove that, I'm gonna show up even more. I'm tired of waiting. And one of these days, you're even gonna invite me inside instead of making me stay outside like some vagrant."

And without tipping his hat, Jesse abruptly turned his stallion and rode out of the yard.

"Father God, every time he shows up, he scares me more," Zetta whispered as she stepped back inside. "Please help me. Please protect me and the youngins."

And she pulled in a ragged breath as she leaned against the door.

* * * * *

Zetta watched Isaac's little chest move with restful breaths before going to the kitchen. But as she reached for the writing paper, she saw Sally Reed approaching the back steps.

"Come on in," Zetta said as she opened the door. "It's good to have proper company."

Sally nodded. "That's what I figured when I saw Jesse Allen leaving," she said. "So I meandered over to make sure you're doing all right. And to tell you that Luttrell and the youngins stopped by to ask Abigail to walk with them. But first he asked Jim if that was okay."

"That's a mighty big step for him," Zetta said as she motioned toward a chair.

"It is at that," Sally said as she sat. "But I was plumb aggravated at Deborah for giggling the whole time he was there."

Zetta bit her lower lip as she sat, hesitating to comment about Deborah's earlier reaction to Jesse. Finally, she spoke.

"You know Jesse Allen's been pestering me," Zetta said. "He all the time shows up and says we're gonna get married. But then he acts all smiley around other women, including your Deborah. I even saw him wink at her after Norrie's burying."

Sally leaned back, frowning.

"I probably got no business saying that," Zetta said. "But I don't trust Jesse."

"We don't neither," Sally said finally. "I was just pondering when Jim hisself saw Jesse wink at Deborah at the store."

"Oh!"

"Soon as they was on their way home, Jim told her about the time a widow woman dropped her coin purse in the store," Sally said. "Nickels and dimes rolled all over, and folks was helping pick them up for her. But a half dollar rolled at Jesse, and he put his boot on top of it. And kept it there."

"Kept it there?"

"Yep. He aimed to keep that poor old widow woman's money even though I hear tell he's got plenty of his own," Sally said. "But Jim, polite as could be, told Jesse he was standing on the half dollar and would he mind lifting his foot."

"What did Jesse do?"

"First, he glared at Jim," Sally said. "Then he acted all surprised about standing on that much money. So Jim told Deborah she better watch herself when Jesse's around."

"I'm glad I ain't the only one knowing the truth about that feller," Zetta said.

"So what you gonna do?"

"Keep praying and trying to stay out of his way, I reckon," Zetta said. "Maybe me and the youngins ought to visit Clarie over at Hindman for a while."

"You should," Sally said. "Luttrell's here to tend the farm, and we're handy if he needs us. Maybe that'll cool Jesse down. It's about time you done for yourself."

* * * * *

The next morning, Luttrell was watering the garden and Zetta had just finished sweeping the kitchen floor when she heard a wagon rumble into the side yard.

She glanced out the open door just as her father waved to Luttrell and jumped onto the ground.

"Morning, Paw," she said. "You're out awful early. Come on in. The coffee's still hot."

"I'll take ya up on the coffee," he said as he climbed the steps. "I just been to the store. And I got something to tell ya."

I don't like the sound of that, Zetta thought as she reached for a cup. But she waited for her father to sit at the table.

"What happened at the store?" she said as she poured the coffee.

"I went about as soon as it was open since I needed lead rope for the plow," her father said. "Jesse Allen already was there picking up his mail, and he hung around whilst I told Ben I needed twenty-six feet."

"Oh?" Zetta said as she tried to steady her hand at the mention of Jesse.

"Ben cut what I needed, and I told him to put the charge on his book and I'd pay later," Paw said. "But Jesse stepped right up, dug in his pocket and said, 'Let me get that for you, John.' Ain't that something?"

"He paid cash money right then and there?" Zetta said.

"Sure did," Paw said. "All twenty-six cents. I told him I'd pay him back soon as I sell the first of the crop, but he just grinned and kidded that he'll take it out of my hide later."

Or out of *my* hide, Zetta thought.

"That got me to thinking," Paw said. "Pretty soon you're

gonna need your own man to help you run this place. And Jesse is your best bet."

Zetta quickly put the coffee pot back onto the stove. Jesse said he was gonna step up his plans, she thought. But I sure didn't think he'd start so soon.

"Well?" Paw said as he swallowed the hot coffee.

Zetta eased into the chair across from her father, determined not to lose her temper.

"Paw, I know you worry about me and the youngins, but I can't be thinking about marrying again just yet," she said. "And I sure don't wanna move too fast and wind up jumping from the frying pan into the fire."

Zetta rubbed her hand across the table's smooth wood, trying to calm her pounding heart. "I'm thinking the youngins and me need to go to Hindman for a while and visit Clarie."

"No, you ain't gonna do that."

"Well, I am," Zetta said as she put her clutched hands into her lap. "Jesse ain't showed you his true colors yet. But they ain't pretty. And I'm needing to see Clarie."

"Why you wanting to traipse off to a stranger?" Paw said.

"I told you before that she ain't no stranger," Zetta said quietly. "She's a friend who lets me talk. And she listens instead of telling me what to do."

Her father leaned back in the chair and hooked his thumb over his belt.

"No need to get your back up," Paw said. "All right. Maybe by going you'll see things better and come back ready to settle down."

"But when I come back, it won't be to marry Jesse Allen," Zetta said. "I want to get that straight right now."

"We'll see," Paw said. "But I got a question. If you was to get over there and decide that your so-called friend is more important than family here, what ya gonna do about this place?"

"I'm only going for a visit, Paw," Zetta said. "But I reckon if I ever did leave here, I'd probably rent it out and get a little income that way. Asa paid for this place with his life. So I can't just sell it outright."

"All right, then," Paw said. "But you keep thinking about what I said about Jesse."

Zetta nodded. She knew she would, indeed, think about her father's plan. And sadly.

* * * * *

The next morning, Loren and Sarah arrived as Zetta pulled the skillet of biscuits from the oven. Their wagon was filled with household goods, a crate of chickens and two small pigs.

Zetta rushed outside to greet them as Luttrell came from the barn.

"Y'all okay?" she asked. "What happened?"

Loren helped Sarah from the wagon then pointed toward their mountain ridge.

"There's too much smoke from the trees being burned," he said. "Nobody can breathe good with all that going on."

Zetta held out her arms to Sarah, "Especially one carrying a baby," she said.

Loren nodded. "Yep. And if the fire gets outta hand, our cabin's right in the way. So we brung what all we could get in the wagon easy like."

Sarah leaned against Zetta. "We ain't got much in the way of furniture yet other than the big old bed we can't move," she said. "But we did get my quilts and the wedding presents."

"Sis, I'm sorry we had to show up here," Loren said. "But neither of us wanted to go stay with Sarah's parents or Paw and Becky. So here we are. And we're happy to sleep in the barn."

"You ain't sleeping out there," Zetta said. "Y'all are family and will stay right here. Besides, me and the youngins is gonna take tomorrow's train to visit Clarie."

Zetta nodded toward Luttrell. "I was gonna tell you at

breakfast," she said, trying to sound as though she hadn't just thought of this.

"You sure, Sis?" Luttrell said. "I can move back with Paw and Becky."

"Nobody wants you doing that," Zetta said. "So here's what we're gonna do. Loren, you and Sarah are gonna sleep in my room. Luttrell, after Isaac's awake, you and Loren will move the children's bed to the front room for me. And move the crib in there, too. The youngins can sleep on a pallet on the floor. We'll be in there with you for this one night."

"That's so good of you," Sarah said as she pulled away. "Thank you."

"Y'all go in and make yourself at home," Zetta said. "Me and the youngins are gonna go to the Reeds and get Bernard to send a telegram for Clarie to expect us. I just took the biscuits out of the oven."

At the mention of biscuits, Loren grinned. "You got this all figured out, huh, Sis?"

"I'm thinking the good Lord is who done that," Zetta said. "But this is gonna work out just fine. And I'm glad y'all are here."

As she started for the porch where Rachel and Micah waited, Zetta looked around her.

"Lord, you was already preparing me to leave here," she silently prayed. "I still don't know everything about prayer, but I'm glad I can talk to you about all my troubles."

She looked toward the chestnut trees along her lane. "I don't know why the blight had to hit," she added. "I just know I'm tired of feeling marked like them trees. So please help me and my youngins in the days ahead."

She reached for her children's hands. And stepped toward a bright future.

* * * * *

MORE THOUGHTS ABOUT
ZETTA'S MARK

I hope you enjoyed spending time with the characters in *Zetta's Mark,* which is the sequel to *Zetta's Dream: An Appalachian Coal Camp Novel* (available via http://bit.ly/Zettas-Dream).

But please remember this is only a story. The last names I used are common in Eastern Kentucky, and are not to be interpreted as representation of any particular family. As I said earlier on the copyright page, any resemblance to persons living or dead is purely coincidental. Well, except for Zetta's father's insistence that she marry Jesse Allen. In real life, my paternal grandmother did marry the man who paid for her father's twenty-six feet of lead rope. I've heard that my great-grandfather was much nicer than Zetta's father, but I still carried a grudge about the family story for years. However, writing this book has given me a deeper understanding of the limited and sad choices women had in the 1923 hills of Southeastern Kentucky.

Another sad truth is the American Chestnut Tree blight of the early 20th century, which resulted in the loss of four *billion* majestic trees from 1905 to 1940. In fact, one out of every four hardwood trees in Appalachia at that time was chestnut. Thus, losing those trees brought extreme economic hardship to folks depending on the spring blossoms for honey, on the abundant nuts in the autumn for saleable crops and food for their hogs. Additionally, since many of the trees were burned in a feeble attempt to stop the blight, valuable straight-grained timber was lost.

Those trees at maturity were splendid. Imagine a tree that grew straight and branch-free for about 50 feet. From there, wide branches grew for the next 50 or so feet until the tree reached a height of 100 feet. The diameter of the trunk easily was 14 or 15 feet. Many of us remember the opening line "Under the spreading chestnut tree" from Henry

Wadsworth Longfellow's 1840 poem "The Village Blacksmith." Truly, the blight stole a great treasure.

I appreciate information from Sara Fitzsimmons, Director of Restoration for The American Chestnut Foundation (TACF). In our phone conversation, she graciously answered my questions about the economic devastation of the blight and confirmed what I had learned about the failed control methods. She also suggested that anyone interested in a more scientific description of the blight should read the lengthy papers of the 1911–1913/14 Pennsylvania Blight Commission—available via the Internet.

While the American Chestnut tree no longer is in my beloved Appalachian Mountains, the copperhead snake is. And that reptile continues to be an aggressive threat.

Kay Hulen, RN, helped me with the medical treatment for Luttrell's snake bite, including the importance of keeping his head higher than the bite. That position kept the blood from rapidly flowing to the heart. I wrote the snake bite scene with my feet up. Even now I shiver.

Those of you who read *Zetta's Dream* know I loosely based that novel on my paternal grandparents' time at a Kentucky coal mine. When I wanted to research what the local paper had reported about the March 4, 1923, accident that killed Grandpa Ted, I contacted the archive department at the University of Kentucky. Shell Dunn, Senior Image Management Specialist at the Special Collection Research Center at UK spent countless hours helping.

Nicole Miller, the creative designer for the cover of *Zetta's Dream*, designed this cover as well. I appreciate her skill and willingness to work with me again.

But back to Zetta and some of the other characters:

Zetta and her children enjoyed a lengthy and restorative visit with friends at Hindman Settlement School.

Zetta had been widowed a month after her twenty-third birthday, so she eventually did remarry. But, thankfully, not to Jesse Allen.

Of course, Luttrell and Abigail married. And they raised five children together.

Deborah outgrew giggling and became a school teacher at the Benham coal camp.

Loren and Sarah's nine-pound son arrived in November. He was perfect, except for a red capillary hemangioma birthmark on the left side of his chest. To her dying day at 87, Sarah believed he had been marked by her having witnessed Norrie's murder.

Poor Norrie. As the author, I wrote numerous scenes trying to prevent her death. But nothing worked. I shared my frustration with friend and fellow author Cheri Gillard, who sympathized but insisted Norrie displayed the greatest maternal love by using her last breath to hand her baby to Sally Reed. Dare I confess I had tears in my eyes as I finally wrote that scene?

The other characters who peopled these pages now belong to the imagination. Thus, I hope you enjoy pondering what happened to them.

Recipes for Zetta's cornbread and Sally's fried polk follow. Twenty-nine authentic recipes are in *Zetta's Coal Camp Recipes,* available via Amazon.

The glossary of commonly used Appalachian words and phrases follows the two recipes.

Finally, after the glossary are the first three short chapters of *Embracing Eden: Zetta's Granddaughter Returns Home,* which is scheduled to be available via Amazon soon. These pages feature Zetta's granddaughter, Drucilla Jean Mills, whose family moved to Michigan because of the lack of jobs in Kentucky. Bill Colby is the trooper and recovering alcoholic who welcomed her with a speeding ticket. And Levi Stahl is the widowed Amish farmer who is guilt-ridden because of the accident that killed his pregnant wife.

Thank you for caring about dear Zetta and her family.

ZETTA'S CORNBREAD

1 egg
1 cup of buttermilk (or add a dash of vinegar to regular milk)
½ teaspoon baking soda
½ teaspoon salt (or less if watching sodium intake)
1 teaspoon baking powder
2 Tablespoons cooking oil (Zetta and her friends would have used lard)
1 cup flour
1 cup yellow cornmeal
Mix ingredients. Pour into a hot cast-iron skillet that has been greased and sprinkled with cornmeal. Bake at 450 degrees for about 15–20 minutes until golden brown.

SALLY'S FRIED POKE

(If you aren't familiar with poke—the shortened name for pokeweed—imagine tall asparagus-type stalks with leaves.)

Remove leaves. Wash the stalks, cut into two-inch lengths.
Put the cut poke into boiling water just until the pieces are wilted (softened). Remove.
Dip pieces in a mixture of beaten egg and milk. Roll in yellow cornmeal.
Fry in lard covering the bottom of a cast-iron skillet. (Modern cooks may prefer olive oil to lard.)
Cook until browned on side. Turn pieces and allow to brown on other side.
Best if served hot, but can be served at room temperature if browned and crunchy.

GLOSSARY OF APPALACHIAN TERMS

NOTE: Several of these words originally appeared in *Zetta's Dream: An Appalachian Coal Camp Novel* by Sandra P. Aldrich, available on Amazon or via www.amzn.to/2m6CWED. Additional terms have been added from this present text of *Zetta's Mark: An Appalachian Widow's Victorious Journey*.

A mess: When used to describe food—plentiful or a large portion, as in a mess of poke.

A sight: Surprising event.

Addlebrained: Unintelligent, dim-witted.

Aggravate: To annoy unnecessarily.

Ails: Troubling or bothersome.

Ain't got no quarrel: Not disagreeing with a situation or a decision by another person. Yes, the author realizes this is a double negative. But double negatives are common even in present non-Appalachian speech.

All barbed wire and gristle: Strong to the point of being unfeeling and tough.

All by my lonesome: Alone.

All fired up: Eager, often to the point of being angry.

All gussied up: Dressed in one's finest.

All high and mighty: Arrogant.

Around the bend: In the future.

Zetta's Mark Glossary

At the get-go: At the beginning.

Back bone: Emotional strength, courage.

Bad blood: Intense dislike, animosity on the part of one or both in a long disagreement.

Bad off: Physically not well.

Badmouthing: To criticize or belittle.

Bandana: A large red handkerchief with white designs. During Zetta's time, these would be carried by men.

Bank the fire: Rake the coals together. In the morning, the coals are raked apart to expose the innermost red ones to be used as the base for the new fire.

Beat around the bush: Delay telling the truth.

Beats me: Action by another (or oneself) that causes bewilderment or confusion.

Beating my time: Usually used in the romantic sense of one man getting ahead of another in a relationship with a specific woman.

Beholding: Obligated.

Being ugly: Rude or disrespectful.

Bernard: The younger son of Jim and Sally Reed. His name is pronounced "Burn-erd" and not "Ber-nard."

Big eye: Insomnia.

Boiling around his heart: Emotional turmoil that is building.

Book learning: Formal education.

Bound and determined: Adamant, refusing to change one's mind.

Broody boxes: In the spring, chickens such as Zetta's were allowed to eat bugs and new grass throughout the day and return to the coop at night. Hens hiding their nests outside the coop until they hatched baby chicks were "broody hens." But nests outside the coop often made the hen and her eggs targets for predators. Thus, to keep broody hens within the safety of the coop, special nests called "broody boxes" were provided along one wall.

Burying (the): The funeral.

Bygones: The past. When Jesse wants Zetta to "let bygones be bygones," he wants her to forget his meanness toward Asa.

Butting heads: Constant disagreement. The phrase comes from animals who fight by hitting their heads together.

Cain: In the Genesis 4 biblical account, Cain is the jealous son of Adam and Eve who killed his brother, Abel.

Can't get it through his (her) head: Unable to convince another person of a better choice.

Clambering: To climb in or out of something, such as a wagon, in an awkward way.

Cash crop: The usual farm acre crops, such as hay and corn, provided food for the livestock and the family. However, an acre or two planted with tobacco would provide cash needed for items the soil could not produce.

Cash money: Actual money—as opposed to payment in goods or work.

Catch more flies with honey than with vinegar: Sweet or kind words get better results than harsh words.

Conundrum: A confusing or difficult dilemma.

Cotton batting: Soft cotton fibers formed into layers to add warmth to clothing or quilts.

Crops laid by: The weeds have been conquered for the rest of the growing season, but the harvest isn't ready.

Cold feet: Change one's mind about a previous decision.

Coldcock: An unexpected and powerful punch to the jaw, usually causing unconsciousness.

Conjure: To create as if by magic.

Contraption: An elaborate device or piece of equipment.

Cooking pot calling the kettle black: This old saying is used when one person is guilty of the same thing about which he or she accuses another.

Copperhead: A notoriously dangerous and often aggressive Appalachian snake.

Correct way to return pocket knife to owner: If the owner offers the knife with the blade open, that's the way it is to be returned. If the knife is offered closed, then the knife is to be returned in the same way. To return the knife otherwise is a statement of distrust and, thus, an insult.

Curing insect bites with the combined juice of three different leaves: In 1994, the author personally experienced this bizarre cure at a molasses stir-off in Wolfe County, Kentucky. The fragrance of the boiling molasses had attracted bees and wasps, resulting in several people being stung. The author watched victims rubbing weeds on the stings, but wasn't sure what they were doing. Then she was stung. An older woman nearby instructed her to pluck a leaf from three different weeds, rub them together and put the juice on the sting. Immediate and miraculous relief!

Curing meat: In a small building (smokehouse), meat would be preserved first with heavy salting to draw out moisture. Then it was hung over a fire of smoke but no flame.

Cushaw: A large crookneck squash, usually green and white striped. More popular than pumpkins in Appalachian gardens.

Dancing man: A popular Appalachian toy featuring a wooden male figure about 10 inches long with moveable arms and legs. The figure was attached to a wooden stick about 10 or 11 inches long, which would be held by the child and used to bounce the standing figure against a hard surface. This bouncing caused the arms and legs of the figure to swing.

Dinner on the ground: An older version of the modern potluck. Under shady trees, long board tables would be set up and filled with the finest in country cooking. Each family provided their own plates and utensils. Notice the correct long-time phrase is "dinner on the *ground*" and not grounds. The participants sat on the ground as they ate.

Directly: An unspecified amount of time, but soon.

Don't amount to a hill of beans: Of no value.

Down the road: In the future.

Dragging (our) feet: Moving slowly toward an unpleasant chore or responsibility.

Drove his ducks to a bad market: Made a bad choice.

Druther: Rather—as in "I'd druther go fishing today."

Duds: Clothing.

Egg gravy: Milk gravy to which sliced boiled eggs have been added. Especially useful for transportation of the dish to another household.

Feedsack: Before the age of plastic, animal feed was sold in cloth sacks. These sacks were repurposed in countless ways, including as tote bags and material for various items of clothing.

Feeding bottles: Modern term is baby bottles. However, farmers used them to feed orphaned or rejected young livestock before bottle feeding became popular for human babies.

Feller: Fellow, a human male.

Fending off: Defending self from.

Fester, Festering: Growing worse and becoming infected, as in a physical wound. An emotional festering means someone is dwelling on a wrong and pondering revenge.

Figured: Reasoned, thought.

Fire away: Go ahead and say whatever is on your mind.

Fit as a fiddle: Healthy and energetic.

Flabbergasted: Greatly surprised, astonished.

Flat out: Immediately.

Fodder: Hay, or similar food, for animals.

Food paper: Wax paper. Name of the actual inventor is greatly in dispute. Some sources cite Thomas Edison; others, his assistant Thomas Conners. Still other sources name Gustave LeGray for inventing it in 1851 for use first in photography.

Foolhardy: Rash, prone to thoughtless actions.

Free rein: Total freedom—as in loose reins for horses or free will for humans.

Fried corn: Fresh corn kernels cut from the cob, seasoned with lard and cooked in an iron skillet. Not at all like the modern-day corn on the cob that is battered and deep fried in hot oil.

Gall: Highly irritating, exasperation.

Get wind of: Hear about.

Getting out of hand: Not capable of control.

Get your back up: Unable to discuss a concern without being angry and argumentative. Comes from the position of an animal that is cornered and ready to fight.

Go between (the): One put in the often uncomfortable position of delivering news from one person to another.

Go that route: Make a particular decision.

Gom: To make a mess.

Gonna look a sight: Calling undue attention to oneself.

Gorge: To eat without restraint.

Got half a mind to: Thinking about following a particular action.

Got no call to: Have no right to say or do.

Got your head set on: Determined.

Got your heart set on: Longing for something.

Granny woman: An older woman of the community who was skilled in knowledge of herbs, country medicine and childbirth.

Gray graniteware: Metal cookware covered in heavy gray paint. Contained lead.

Grinning from ear to ear: Smiling joyfully.

Green lumber: Fresh-cut lumber that has not been allowed to dry properly. The resulting warping leaves cracks between the boards.

Gritted bread: Field corn or other overripe corn would be scraped against a board into which several small nails had been driven. This would make a coarse cornmeal, which would make a heavier cornbread batter.

Grovel: To emotionally crawl, as in self-abasement.

Grub: Food. A modest cook, such as Clarie, often would disparage her abilities by assigning this term to the results of her culinary skills.

Had a falling out: An unsettled argument.

Haints: Ghosts.

Hanker after or hankering: Have a strong longing for.

Hardtack: A hard, unsalted cracker. This was carried by the soldiers during the War Between Brothers (aka: the Civil War) and was often infested by weevils.

Heard tell: Heard.

Hemming and hawing: Hesitation. Not getting directly to the point of what one is trying to say.

Hidy: A common greeting that is a blend between "Hi" and "Howdy."

Highfalutin: Unreasonable, pretentious.

Hightail: Move quickly—much like an animal who raises its tail as it runs away.

Hillbilly: First found in 17th century documents to describe supporters of English Protestant King William III who were called "Billy Boys." Most of the early American colonists were from Great Britain, and some scholars believe the British soldiers of the 1770s applied the term to immigrants in the Appalachian Mountains/hills. The term became derogatory after a 1900 *New York Journal* article gave an unflattering definition that became the basis for modern stereotypes.

His'in: His.

Hobble: To walk awkwardly, usually due to an injury.

Hoe cakes: Griddle cakes usually made with cornmeal. So named because they could be baked on the blade of a garden hoe when one was working in the fields.

Hog wild: Unrestrained.

Hope chest: The collection of quilts, linens and household goods in preparation of a young girl's future marriage. The items usually are stored in a cedar chest for protection from insects and rodents, but the term can be applied to the collection even if not stored in an official chest.

Hot-footing: Going someplace in an extreme hurry.

Hunker down: To crouch or squat.

I'd give a pretty: (pronounced "purty") Willing to trade something of value.

If it'd been a snake, it wuda bit me: Said when someone is looking for an item that is close at hand but overlooked at first.

In a heartbeat: Immediately, without hesitation.

"In my father's house are many mansions": Statement by Jesus to his disciples in the Book of John, chapter 14, verse 2. Here's the entire verse: "In my father's house are many mansions: if it were not so, I would have told you. I go to prepare a place for you."

Irish potatoes: White potatoes. Zetta and her neighbors pronounced "Irish" as "Arsh."

Jesus claiming the storm: This is the sermon Preacher Collins gave that caused Zetta to ponder another layer of prayer. The three books of the Bible reporting the calming of the sea are Luke 8:22–25, Matthew 8:23–27 and Mark 4:36–41.

Job saying what he feared: Clarie knew the coal camp's future was in jeopardy, but hadn't expected the sudden closing. Thus, when she received the confirmation, she recalled part of Job's statement from the Book of Job, chapter 3, verse 25: "For the thing I greatly feared is come upon me, and that which I was afraid of is come unto me."

Jump from the frying pan into the fire: Going from a bad situation to an even worse one.

Ivy Point: Several skirmishes during 1863 and 1864, including the one on November 30, 1863, were fought to gain control of the small town of Salyersville. The name of this battle originated from Ivy Point, the small hill where the Federal army camped above the town.

Laying out: The dead body washed and dressed for viewing before the funeral.

Lazy man's load: Carrying several heavy objects all at once rather than dividing the load and making two or more trips.

Left-handed compliment: A statement presented as a compliment but actually is an insult. Example: Loren's statement that he would marry Clarie if she were forty years younger emphasizes her advanced age.

Left in another man's dust: Missing an opportunity that, in turn, went to another man because of one's slow action.

Lit out: A rapid departure.

Lollygagging: To waste time on unimportant activities or chatter.

Lye soap: A strong soap made from homemade lye and animal grease. To make lye, water is added to clean wood ashes and boiled in a kettle. To test the strength of this lye, a chicken feather is dipped into the liquid. When the soft part of the feather dissolved, lean kitchen grease collected from cooked meats can be added.

Make over me: Pay too much attention to—as when Zetta was reluctant to face the folks at church after not seeing them since Asa's funeral.

Making a mountain out of a molehill: A molehill is a little ridge of earth pushed up by a mole, which is an underground animal. Thus, this saying suggests turning a small challenge into a greater problem.

Man (or woman) of his (her) word: Doing what one has promised to do.

Mantrip: The railed vehicle taking the miners to their work stations. The engine or "air donkey" pulled several open cars and would be stopped by throwing it into reverse.

Marble stone: A large, hard stone in which several small round holes had been drilled. A creek pebble would be placed in each hole, and the stone would be placed under the gentle part of a waterfall. The constant bouncing of the pebbles against the stone eventually would produce round pebbles used as marbles.

Marking a baby: The belief that if a pregnant women witnesses trauma—such as murder or fire—her baby will be born with a deformity such as a birthmark or misshapen limb.

Malarkey: Foolish talk.

Mealymouthed: Timid, unable to be straightforward.

Mess: A large amount, as in a mess of poke stalks.

Mine face: The area of unmined coal where the miners will work on any given day.

More than likely: Without a doubt.

More than one way to skin a cat: With apologies to cat owners, this old expression merely means there's more than one solution to every dilemma.

Newfangled: The latest fad or fashion not appreciated by the speaker.

No account: Useless.

None the worse for wear: Not harmed.

Noon dinner: The meal commonly called lunch today. During Zetta's era, the three daily meals were breakfast, dinner and supper.

Not exactly partial: Understatement about not liking something or someone.

Obliged: Obligated.

Ornery: Bad tempered and ready for an argument.

Outdoing themselves: Going beyond expected or accepted behavior.

Ought to suit: A favorable action.

Out of earshot: Away from being able to hear a conversation.

Out of hand: Out of control.

Out of the woods: In a good condition.

Pallet: A makeshift bed of several quilts placed on the floor or in the back of a wagon.

Pay them no mind: Not worry about the opinion of others.

Perryville: In October 1862, Union and Confederate forces fought in what is reported to be the largest battle on Kentucky soil during the War Between the States. The Confederates had hoped to win and, thus, draw the Commonwealth officially into the Confederate side. They were not successful. During this campaign, Central Kentucky was suffering from a severe drought. Both sides encountered dried up rivers, streams and creeks. Forced to drink stagnant, smelly water from farm ponds, countless soldiers on both sides died of dysentery and typhoid. That number was in addition to the nearly 8,000 men who were killed or severely wounded during this battle.

Peter out: To diminish in size, strength or amount.

Play like: Pretend, make believe.

Play pretties: Toys.

Planting by the signs: Belief that the moon phases and the stars control success or failure of crops, depending on the time of planting. Genesis 1:14 often was quoted as biblical source for belief.

Plumb worried: Extremely concerned. Putting the word "plumb" before any condition (such as tired or angry, for example) stresses the severity.

Preaching (someone) into hell: If an old-time preacher wasn't sure of a deceased person's salvation—or even if the person hadn't been a member of that particular church—the preacher would describe in vivid detail the eternal torment the soul now was experiencing. Supposedly, the goal was to make other unchurched folks change their wicked ways. But such declarations were agony for the mourners.

Poke: Short for pokeweed, a wild growing green single stalk used as a spring tonic. The large leaves growing on the stalk are toxic and should be discarded. Some Appalachians cook the small leaves, rinse them several times in clear water, and serve them with cornbread. Zetta and her neighbor, Sally Reed, cooked only the stalks, which they dipped in a mixture of egg and milk, rolled in cornmeal and fried.

Ponder: To dwell on or consider a situation at length.

Pony cart: A small three- or four-sided cart meant to be pulled by a pony. But the harness could be adjusted for a larger animal, such as a mule.

Poultice: A heated mixture of medicinal salves and/or herbs spread on a clean cloth and placed over a wound or on a congested chest.

Zetta's Mark Glossary

Puny: Sickly, not feeling well, but not to the point of death.

Purple fever: Childbirth fever. Medical term "puerperal fever," which developed from a piece of the afterbirth remaining in the uterus, causing an often fatal infection.

Purty: Pretty.

Put it on the books: Provide credit for regular customers.

Put my foot down: Demanding one's own way.

Quare: Different, strange.

Ought to suit: Supply a person's need.

Ragtag: Misfits.

Reckon: Guess or think.

Recollect: Remember.

Riffraff: Undesirable people.

Rigamarole (also spelled rigmarole): A long complicated or unnecessary speech or event.

Right then and there: Immediately.

Riled up: Upset, raising one's voice.

Roasting ears: Corn on the cob.

Ruckus: Disturbance or commotion.

Run that by me again: Repeat that.

Running things by me: Seeking approval first.

Sashay: To walk/strut in a prideful or flirty way.

Sallet: Various greens mixed together for salad. Good as a spring tonic after a long winter.

Sawhorses: A sturdy wooden V-frame, about waist high, on which lumber would be placed for hand sawing. Larger boards could be placed across facing sawhorses to form a makeshift table.

See eye to eye: To be in total agreement.

Serviced: A bull mating with a cow. The resulting gestation period would be 39 weeks.

Shenanigans: Rude or questionable conduct.

Shortsighted: Lacking foresight about the future.

Shyster: Someone, usually a lawyer, who uses dishonest methods to win.

Sideboard: Kitchen furniture with a flat top and drawers or shelves beneath. Used to stores dishes and various linens.

Skulking: Hiding with sinister intent.

Smokehouse: A small out building where meat is cured via dense smoke. Most of the smokehouses in Zetta's community contained pork.

Snake won't die until sundown: The commonly held Appalachian belief during this time was that a snake wouldn't die until sundown even if the head was totally severed from the body. Perhaps there is truth to that belief based on the August 9, 2017, media report of a Chinese chef who was preparing a cobra dish, and the snake's severed head bit him. The chef died!

Snit: Aggravation caused by disappointment in an event or dislike of another person.

Sore eyes: Medically known as trachoma, this highly contagious infection of the inner eyelid and front of the eyeball caused blindness if untreated.

Sorry or sorry-looking: When used as an adjective, as in a sorry-looking mule, it means of no account, useless.

Soup beans: Dried beans soaked overnight and simmered for several hours the next day. Flavor often provided by adding a fatty piece of pork or lower portion of a pig's leg called a ham hock.

Speak (speaking) of the devil: Mentioning someone's name just as he or she appears.

Spoilt: Spoiled, damaged or pampered to the point of harm.

Springhouse: A small building placed over a freshwater spring and used for cool storage of milk, butter and other items needing temporary lower temperatures.

Squared away: Completed, taken care of.

Standing up for: Taking a person's side of an issue. Defending another even to the point of risking personal reputation.

Standoffish: A distant or cold manner.

Starts showing and **starting to show:** When changes in the woman's body makes it obvious she is pregnant.

Stir things up: Make a situation more difficult.

Straight from the horse's mouth: The truth from the original source.

Stout: Overweight but strong looking.

Sugar tit: A small piece of cotton material, shaped like a cone and filled with sugar. Given to babies shortly after birth to help with their sucking reflex.

Take it out of (your/my) hide: A not-so-innocent joke meaning that the debtor will have to repay the debt in a way other than monetarily.

Taters: Potatoes.

Thick as thieves: Close but questionable association.

Tight as a tick: Extremely full.

Time and time again: Repeatedly.

Tobacca: Tobacco. The main cash crop for Kentuckians during the first half of the 1900s.

"Today shalt thou be with me in paradise": The promise of Jesus to the repentant thief as they were being crucified. This is from the Book of Luke, chapter 23, verse 43: "And Jesus said unto him, Verily I say unto thee, Today shalt thou be with me in paradise."

Told (him/her) straight up: Giving straightforward accounts or insisting on a particular action.

Zetta's Mark Glossary

Tongue is hinged in the middle: Talking rapidly and without interruption, as though the tongue had double its normal ability.

Tote/Toting: To carry.

Took a shine to: Appreciated, liked, usually in a romantic way.

Traipse off: Walk away from a situation.

True colors: The truth about a person's character.

Unthoughted: Thoughtless.

Uppity: Arrogant, convinced he/she is better than others.

Vagrant: A person, often unwanted, who doesn't have a settled home. A wanderer.

Vittles: Food items.

Wallowing: The act of animals rolling in mud or a shallow stream to cool off. But in the human emotional sense, this is to continually dwell on unfortunate present or potential events.

War Between Brothers: The Civil War, or more rightly, the War Between the States. Since the loyalties of Kentucky inhabitants were split between the Union and the Confederacy, members of the same family often were on different sides.

What all: Giving details of an action.

Whilst: While.

Widow's weeds: Simple black clothing traditionally worn by widows.

Widow woman: Widow.

Will wonders never cease?: An expression of amazement.

Wolf in sheep's clothing: Someone who pretends to be harmless while holding less than honorable intentions. This idiom originates from a warning Jesus gave in the Book of Matthew, chapter 7, verse 15: "Beware of false prophets, which come to you in sheep's clothing, but inwardly they are ravening wolves."

Woman submitting to the man: Preacher Collins is reluctant to conduct a proper funeral for Jim Reed's murdered sister, Norrie, because she had not obeyed her cruel husband. To support his reasoning, the preacher leans on the first part of Ephesians 5:22 (from the *King James Version*) without naming the source: "Wives, submit unto your own husbands...." Jim responds with the previous verse and wonders why that Scripture isn't quoted: "Submitting yourselves one to another in the fear of God."

Won't think twice: Won't give the situation a second thought.

Wore out: As in "plumb wore out"—exhausted.

Wore out my welcome: No longer welcome to stay.

Worrisome: Cause for concern.

Wouldn't be fitting: Action not considered proper or moral, especially in the case of a young couple alone without a chaperone.

Wuda: Would have.

Wudn't: Would not.

About The Author

SANDRA P. ALDRICH, a Harlan County, Kentucky native, is an international speaker and author or co-author of 24 books. Known for her Kentucky story-telling style of speaking and writing, Sandra loves the Lord, family and all things Appalachian. Eastern Michigan University granted her a Master of Arts degree, but she says life granted her a Ph.D. from the School of Hard Knocks. Currently, she resides in Colorado Springs, Colorado because of its lack of copperhead snakes. Well, that and the fact that her two grandsons, Luke and Noah, are also there. Learn more at www.sandraaldrich.com and www.facebook.com/sandra.aldrich.

Keep reading to enjoy the first three chapters of

EMBRACING EDEN: ZETTA'S GRANDDAUGHTER RETURNS HOME

DEDICATION

To all those who, like me, have searched for their own Garden of Eden.

Chapter 1: Dru Mills

Dru Mills cranked up the car radio as "Foggy Mountain Breakdown" came on.

"Yessir! What a great song to welcome me!" she shouted as she sped toward her new life and past flowering dogwood, redbud and sarvis trees sprinkled across the gentle hills of Eden County, Kentucky.

Next stop, Garden Grove, she thought.

The radio's blaring banjo chords kept her from hearing the siren, but the flashing red and blue lights behind her grabbed her attention.

"Shoot!" she groaned as she eased to the side. A police cruiser pulled up behind her.

"Some welcome, all right," she murmured as she snapped off the radio and put both hands to the top of the steering wheel as she often had seen her father do.

When the tall officer leaned toward her, Dru could smell his cinnamon gum. She wondered if he was curious about the contents of the jam-packed back seat.

Finally, he spoke. "Well, Miss. How are you this fine Saturday?"

What a stupid question, she thought. But she turned toward him.

"I think that's about to depend on you, officer."

She saw him press his lips together while his brown eyes betrayed his amusement.

He moved the gum to the other side of his mouth.

"Do you have any idea how fast you were going?"

Dru shrugged and tried her father's usual answer.

"No, sir. I was just moving with the traffic."

The officer shook his head. "You weren't *moving* with it; you were *passing* it. May I see your driver's license and registration, please?"

Dru clinched her teeth as she pulled the items from her wallet and handed them over. As the officer took them, Dru noticed the name Colby on the identification badge above his shirt pocket stuffed with packs of Big Red gum.

"Stay here, please."

She huffed. "I'm not planning to race a police car in a second-hand Ford."

He turned quickly. Through the rear-view mirror, Dru watched him enter his vehicle and lean to the right of the steering wheel.

Yeah, check all my information, she thought. Make sure I'm not some Michigan ax murderer.

She drew a deep breath as the cars she'd passed earlier now passed her. Peter would love seeing this.

Shortly, Officer Colby was back at her window. He began to read from her driver's license.

"Well, Miss Drucilla Jean Mills…."

"Dru. I go by Dru—not Drucilla."

Her voice was harsh. She was in no mood for pleasantries.

"Okay, Miss *Dru* Jean Mills, you were going fourteen miles over the speed limit, but you're not in our system, so I've lowered your ticket to *seven* miles over as a welcome to our fair state."

"This isn't a state," Dru snapped. "It's a commonwealth. One of the U.S. four."

Officer Colby moved the cinnamon gum around again.

"Well, now. Most folks I give tickets to aren't interested in that fact."

He handed the driver's license and registration back to Dru, then tore the top paper from his ticket pad.

"You can pay your fine by mail at the address listed," he said. "But slow down for the remainder of your visit to our fair *commonwealth*."

Dru forced herself not to snatch the ticket from his hand.

"I'm not visiting," she said. "I'm moving here."

"I hope you've got a job already," he said. "This area isn't as prosperous as Michigan was years ago."

"Yes, I do have a job," Dru said. "In the new computer department at the Garden Grove Hospital."

Shut up, Dru. Shut up, she thought. Peter always said you talk too much.

"Best cheeseburgers in town at the hospital grill," Officer Colby said. "Well, good luck. And slow down."

Dru waited for him to walk back to his vehicle before she started her car. She was tempted to peel out to show him just what she thought, but she took a deep breath instead as she pulled behind a passing 18-wheeler. She glanced in the rearview mirror to make sure Officer Colby wasn't behind her. He wasn't.

She reached for the radio knob but changed her mind. Instead, with her eyes on the truck ahead, she fumbled for the notepaper on the seat beside her and pulled it to where she could read the next item in her aunt's string of directions: *Leave highway at Garden Grove exit, turn right.*

I'll worry about that stupid ticket later, Dru thought. Aunt Wilma said she'd have supper waiting. I bet Mom's called her a million times by now.

After cautiously exiting the highway and turning right at the bottom of the ramp, Dru drove for less than a mile and turned left onto a two-lane paved road. For the next several miles, she glanced at the directions clutched in her hand and was relieved when she saw the red brick church ahead. The building hadn't changed in the past two decades. The brick still was faded and the five concrete steps leading to the porch still were cracked.

I wonder if Miss Mable still teaches the second-grade girls, she thought as she read the next instruction: *Turn right at the first road past Garden Grove Community Church. Go past three stop signs.*

Dru turned right, smiling as she remembered her long-ago Sunday school teacher's welcoming hugs each Sunday morning. As she approached the first stop sign, a black Amish buggy rounded the curve on her right, the horse trotting smartly. The bearded driver pulled on the reins, slowing the buggy and watching the car as though to make sure the vehicle stopped fully. Then with a light slap of the reins, he gave the horse permission to resume its gait. His passenger, a younger man, never looked her way.

Dru watched, fascinated. Aunt Wilma said the Amish are buying farms around here, she thought. I hope an Amish family bought our old place. I hope they've got a little girl and a big tree swing. And a puppy named Rusty! And she eased her car forward.

Chapter 2: Bill Colby

Officer Bill Colby leaned against the hood of his squad car as he watched Dru's blue 1981 Ford Fairmont pull in behind a passing 18-wheeler.

Well, Miss Dru Jean of Ypsilanti, Michigan, height: five feet, six inches, hair brown, eyes hazel, he mentally repeated from her driver's license. If you're working at the hospital, I'm gonna see you again real soon. And ya gotta be impressed I can pronounce Ypsilanti. Got an uncle who moved there for a job years ago. Now you're moving here for one.

He grinned, remembering her comment about racing him in her used car.

I like your feisty style, he thought. I almost busted out laughing when you said that, and it's been a long time since a woman made me laugh.

Suddenly, he shook his head and looked down at his polished black shoes.

"Who ya tryin' to kid, Bill?" he whispered. "A woman like her would never be interested in somebody like you."

He walked beyond the pavement shoulder and spat his gum far into the tall weeds. As he unwrapped two new sticks of Big Red, he had one thought: I want a cigarette.

He shoved the fresh gum into his mouth and looked over the guard rail to the old road below. An Amish buggy came into view.

Might be Levi Stahl taking his little boy home after therapy, Bill thought. No. That department's not open on Saturdays.

He half-heartedly raised his hand in greeting even though the buggy was far below. Then his stomach tightened as he pondered the accident last fall: the tourist slumped over the steering wheel of the car, the horse on its side with his entrails spilling out as he kicked at the overturned buggy, Levi frantically trying to pull his pregnant wife and little boy out from under the buggy's wheel.

Bill had just started his shift and was on the old road headed for the main highway when he came upon the scene. He drew his pistol as he ran toward the buggy, knowing the horse had to be killed—not only to put it out of its misery but to stop the destruction the thrashing hooves were causing. The crack of the single shot brought the driver of the car out of his stupor, and he emerged from his vehicle still holding his camera and babbling repeated apologies. Bill had shouted and ordered him back to his car, then turned to help the Amish father pull his wife and son from beneath the buggy.

When Bill's hands had gripped the young wife's shoulders, her eyes fluttered open, and she murmured, "Oh, my poor baby," as she put her hands over her bloodied belly. And then her eyes had closed for the last time. Levi had cradled her head in his lap while his tears and blood from the cut above his eye flowed into his beard. Bill had pulled the little boy free and carried him to the police car. There he quickly radioed for an ambulance as he held compresses on the unconscious child's mangled leg.

At his meeting that autumn night, all Bill could say was, "Today was tough. I saw a bad accident that took innocent lives."

Now from his position above the old road, Bill lowered

his hand but continued to watch the black buggy until it disappeared behind a grove of white flowering dogwood trees.

He rubbed the back of his neck. Easy now. Dwelling on the accident won't undo it.

He glanced at his watch. Two more hours 'til my shift's up, he thought. With any luck, maybe I'll get to tonight's meeting on time.

Chapter 3: Levi Stahl

Levi Stahl watched the blue car on his left come to a complete stop before he lightly slapped the reins and allowed the horse to regain her gait.

His younger brother, James, was seated beside him. "This road has the right-of-way," James said. "But I guess it'll take you a while to get over what happened."

"I don't plan to ever get *over* it," Levi said as he tried to keep his voice calm. "Some things a man doesn't get *over*."

James shifted his weight. "I wasn't being unfeeling, Levi. Hannah was a good woman, and I'm sorry she died. But I watch you, and it's as though you died, too."

Levi released a slow breath. "What would you have me do?" he said. "Forget that my life—and my son's—changed forever that day? One minute Hannah was smiling at Nathan, and a minute later…."

"I'm not asking you to forget," James said. "I just want my brother back."

Suddenly he leaned forward and gestured toward the lane meandering through a grove of flowering dogwood trees.

"Ah, the church wagon just turned in," James said. "We're right on time to get everything unloaded for tomorrow. And Martin's wife always serves pie when we're finished."

Levi caught the eagerness in his brother's voice—as though he was happy to change the subject. He forced himself to smile as he glanced at James.

"Somehow I think you are more interested in Martin's sweet *daughter* than his wife's sweet *pie*," Levi said.

James returned the smile as he ran his knuckles across his clean shaven chin.

"I won't deny that," he said. "Don't tell the bishop, but knowing I'll see Mary is the best part of church for me."

Levi nodded, remembering how he used to wish church was every week—like the English—so he could see Hannah more often.

As he tugged gently on the right-hand rein to direct his horse onto Martin's property, he turned toward James and started to tell him how he used to sit on a back bench with the other young unmarried men at the worship services and hope for an unobstructed view of Hannah as she sat between her mother and grandmother. And how at the youth sings he listened for the sound of Hannah's voice. But his brother's eyes were on the men carrying benches and hymnals from the church wagon into the house. As Levi slowed the buggy, James jumped down and raised his hand in greeting to the others.

Levi directed the buggy to the hitching post at the side of Martin's barn, but was slow in climbing out. He adjusted his straw hat over his light brown hair, dreading the pitying looks that would be tossed his way before the men welcomed him. He especially dreaded seeing the bishop who would ask yet again how he was coming along on his forgiveness journey. "Forgiving the tourist who was taking pictures of the autumn leaves while he drove is getting easier because of thoughtful effort and prayer," was the answer Levi always gave.

But *how can I tell the bishop I'll forgive that stupid English driver long before I forgive myself?* Levi thought as he slowly looped the reins over the wooden post. *I had turned to* smile at Hannah as she told Nathan what a good big brother he would be. If I had been watchful of the side road, Hannah and the baby would be here. And Nathan wouldn't be walking with a limp.

He turned toward the church wagon. No, forgiving myself is something I'll never be able to do.

Made in the USA
Coppell, TX
04 January 2020